2

Stephanie
and
Josephine

Stephanie and Josephine

The Time of Their Lives

June Barraclough

ROBERT HALE · LONDON

© June Barraclough 2001
First published in Great Britain 2001

ISBN 0 7090 6835 2

Robert Hale Limited
Clerkenwell House
Clerkenwell Green
London EC1R 0HT

The right of June Barraclough to be identified as
author of this work has been asserted by her
in accordance with the Copyright, Designs and
Patents Act 1988.

2 4 6 8 10 9 7 5 3 1

Typeset by
Derek Doyle & Associates, Liverpool.
Printed in Great Britain by
St Edmundsbury Press Ltd, Bury St Edmunds, Suffolk.
Bound by Woolnough Bookbinding Limited.

'Our deeds determine us, as much as we determine our deeds.'
George Eliot: ADAM BEDE

'I often feel, and ever more deeply realise,
that fate and character are the same conception.'
NOVALIS

INTRODUCTION

1996

NEWS OF OLD STUDENTS

... BJ Ross (née Hill) is writing on young women in the 1950s, with special reference to the lives and careers of women arts graduates ... for example, how many of them carried on with their careers after having children? ...

The question that Jo really wanted to address was whether their lives had been influenced above all by their emotional attachments. Had women always been their own worst enemies? You could understand people's lives only through examining individual cases. Even then, you were often left with more questions.

How else could the past be recaptured, except through words? Photographs perhaps? She began to sketch out some ideas. Maybe people's memories might one day be transferred from private mind to computer screen and shared by others. She did not believe that, distrusting 'technology'. How could she obtain a 'representative sample'? Better to rely on her own knowledge and memories.

She began:

In the 1950s women graduates often married pretty well straight after university, or continued their careers or jobs for a few years before they settled down, found a man and had a baby ...

She remembered herself and her friends beginning to recover after a year or so from their collective depression over leaving university, never having enough – or any – money, and working at jobs they often did not find very congenial.

There were no women high-fliers in the City then, nor many women solicitors, never mind barristers. There were however journalists, and novelists, and artists. But most arts graduates of that generation were some sort of secretary, or teacher, or slaved in some remote government department, never seeing the whole picture.

The way young women led their lives, their expectations, and their plans, in spite of certain similarities, varied according to temperament, gifts and luck. Those who got married – very few in those days 'lived in sin' – mostly went to live in London suburbs or the provinces. Some went to live abroad, following husbands' careers. But after marriage their old friends remained friends.

By thirty-five *some* graduates had secured wonderful careers that took them all over the world, but these great success stories belonged mostly to men.

There are now far more examples of women in academia, in politics, making scientific discoveries or a lot of money in the City, becoming barristers, solicitors, accountants, explorers, inventors, but they are still the exceptions. Like their mothers, some of the daughters have adapted, managed careers as well as babies; others have declared they do not intend to have children. Some marriages have already failed; a few women have 'come out' as lesbians....

Now and again old friends would meet in London, go to an exhibition or a matinée, or just have lunch together and talk. Those of them lucky enough to continue working – especially if they could work at home – were still busy. Those who earned no money from their efforts were kept busy with grandchildren, gardening, the Church, voluntary work, and a lot of travelling to far-flung places....

'How It Really Was' is one definition of history, but if anyone writes about lives and times she can have only a partial vision. No one person can see everything that happened; the great tides of history are not easily discerned in the middle of active life. If people cannot see the past through anyone's eyes but their own, there are still certain elements of it they all shared, just as there are things their children's generation share, and their children's children, some of whom are even now starting on their adult lives.

Most women who grew up in the 1950s were fairly romantic, or at least started off that way. The ideal of marriage had been held up before them all ever since they were little girls. Some of them succeeded in approximating to this ideal and are still married to men they met at university. Others have made the best of impossible husbands and put their eggs in the basket of 'family'. There are still a few who belong to the very last generation of women to be called spinsters, though their lives may not have been very spinsterlike. Just a few have gone it alone, followed wherever life led them, had lives like male adventurers.

Most of the present generation are very much better off materially than they were all those years ago, but have not yet come to the conclusion that when things go awry it might occasionally be their own fault, not the world's. For older women it is often a world they don't much like, or don't want any more to keep up with – which just shows that they are getting old. Each older woman may begin to feel she is part of an old world that is disappearing. There was once a long-running show in London called *Stop the World, I Want to Get Off*, and even then some young people felt sympathy for this cry from the heart.

People under thirty may sometimes appear to older generations as more or less mad. The old still shudder with embarrassment when they remember the idiotic things *they* did. Why can't all

9

human beings have a rehearsal, a trial run? They get only one chance, and by the time they have, hopefully, improved it is usually too late. If they all had a second chance would they be different, act differently? Perhaps, but it's no good thinking about it. They can never fulfil their longing to go back in time, to repair and improve upon their experiences. Only after a certain age do people begin to see they are not immortal, and glimpse the next generation waiting in the wings. To the young their feelings are sacred; even more so now than forty or fifty years ago when young people were not listened to very much. There still existed at that time a reverence for the old, for experience, and the young were brought up to behave politely and respectfully towards their elders.

These women graduates had a certain education in common, and certain presuppositions they didn't even know they possessed. Chatting now to someone of their own generation who picks up all their references is refreshing. The women are just too old to have been influenced overmuch by the 1960s, that supposedly revolutionary decade, which many of them spent washing nappies.

The previous decade, the 1950s, the Time of their Lives, is a period now seen by many younger folk as a dead, paltry, post-war time, boring and goody-goody.

It was not boring, even if they were still rationed for various items until 1954, and never had much money. And many of them were not paragons of virtue....

For years after the end of the war most goods were for quite a long time in short supply, or non-existent, or as elusive as female sexual pleasure was supposed to be. Items made in the new material, plastic, had arrived, however and so had biros. But wine was much dearer then; holidays far shorter.

As early as 1947 she was given a pair of American nylons from one of her ex-classmates, who was doing his National Service in Egypt where such things could be acquired....

As there were few cars on the road, if a family possessed one motoring was a pleasure. There were not so many places where you could eat out; most hotel and restaurant food was pretty appalling, and fresh coffee was terrible, if it existed at all. Yet it was this decade that saw the last of the London smog; it was during these years that public opinion decided that suicide was not a crime; it was the time when some people were agitating for reform of the abortion laws, others for homosexual reform, others for less complicated divorce. One or two friends were very active in some of those campaigns. The results arrived in the following decade, and everything was changed. Some people eventually decided that certain of these reforms had not in fact helped women. But the pendulum never stops in the middle; young people are still reacting against the first half of the century, which was a totally different world.

For those who were in their twenties in the 1950s those were the days. They were *young*. Whatever else these women had in those days, they had their unmistakable youth. Not one of them realized, as far as men were concerned, what an advantage this was. They did not know that after the age of fifty or so, every woman becomes invisible; they had, like every generation, to discover it for themselves. For the time being they had good health, though many of them smoked. The way they lived, the assumptions they all had, arose from being young at a certain time in a certain place, and the longer they live the more some of them become nostalgic for that older, solider, dirtier London.

The new young seem to think that things don't change quickly enough. Grandchildren don't even realize that less than fifteen years ago there were no mobile phones, no Internet, and most people did not possess computers. However did their parents manage? As for their grandparents, they lived in the Dark Ages....

People say that human nature doesn't fundamentally change, yet all young women starting work now expect more from life. For one thing, apart from the higher standard of living, they are all

11

consumers, bombarded with hundreds of choices: of food, clothes, newspapers almost as heavy as encyclopaedias. Choice is a life style now; hardly anyone bothers with party politics, though they are attached to good causes....

She stopped typing and allowed herself to ponder further those 'dear dead days beyond recall'....

PART ONE

Josephine and Adam

1952–1957

ONE

The monarch who had been placed on the throne during the childhood of Stephanie Fischer and Josephine Hill was George VI. He was not very old but he died of lung cancer on a cold February day in 1952 whilst the young women were still undergraduates. The coronation of his daughter Elizabeth would take place the following year. Jo refused to take an interest, fancying herself a republican, but most people were wildly excited, and crowded into the homes of all those who had a television set.

On an afternoon of late July that same year several young women left the University of Oxford to begin their working lives. London had always beckoned the most enterprising or ambitious graduates, for reasons quite apart from any work they might find there. Before them now was the land of promise, and it began on Oxford station.

The women were Jo Hill and two of her friends, Stephanie Fischer and Susie Swift. At Oxford station they lugged their cases on to the Paddington train.

A letter from a man called Adam Angelwine was in the pocket of Jo's mackintosh. She was thinking that her real new life might begin the day she replied to this letter.

She had not yet done so.

Their examinations, Final Schools, were thankfully over. Even their vivas, which Jo had rather enjoyed, were now past history. None of them knew what degree they would be awarded though Stephanie had been viva'd for a first. Never having worked for a first, Jo hoped she had done enough work for a good second. She was pretty sure that her best grades would be for what she was naturally good at – writing about novels and poetry – and her worst for philology, whose details she found tedious, and had therefore toiled over most – but, alas, too late.

After three years Jo was sad to leave Oxford, though London did beckon seductively. The year before, she had made an attempt to acquaint herself with London's vastness during the Easter vacation, but had not been able to find the paid work she needed and had been reduced to warming up tinned spaghetti on the gas-ring of a cheap hotel room. Stephanie, whose parents lived in north London, had been brought up with the attractions of the metropolis on her doorstep and thought her friend overrated its charms. She suspected Jo had gone there in search of some masculine will-o'-the-wisp, rather than to confront the capital.

At this time a young woman's career was still marriage. Indeed, some people were so old-fashioned that a woman who had not gone down from university with a fiancé was regarded as having missed the boat. There were even loud lamentations at being left on the shelf at twenty-four. Many women undergraduates did get married a year or two after going down, some even the minute they finished their Schools examinations. Jo had always despised such people until she fell in love with Will Morgan.

She had met him in the February of this last Oxford year, and weeks of ecstatic romance had followed. They had stayed up together for a week or two during the Easter vacation, ostensibly to catch up with work and revise. At least, that had been the idea, but they spent most of their time together talking and kissing and confecting fantasies, becoming almost inseparable. Before Will, Jo had been in love with men met abroad, and had been out with

16

countless young men in Oxford, but she had never met anyone as sweet and amusing as Will.

By the beginning of the Trinity term she was already imagining they might share a future. She had no burning desire to marry, just wanted Will to love her as much as she felt she adored him. He was a volatile, effervescent, imaginative young man with a lack of belief in himself combined with enormous ambition and spasmodic energy.

Seeing him every day, Jo became fascinated by him and fond of his physical presence. They had talked and laughed and kissed for hours in his room in New College Lane, and done the same over wine at the Trout Inn, but at the end of May, in a letter, Will told her that he could not match her 'spiritual ardour'. For how long had he been contemplating this lack in himself?

He did not flag in his devotion – they still spent a lot of time together – but in his attitude towards himself. He had little confidence in his work, and however much confidence he had in her, he must have begun to realize he was not ready to put her first. Over a drink at the Trout on a lovely summer evening he told her once again that he could not live up 'spiritually' to her intensities and ardours.

Jo was upset but not really surprised, for this was not the first time a man had intimated something similar to her. She had been in love so many times, and so far her feelings had never been entirely reciprocated. On the other hand she had been pursued by men who found her attractive but were not the kind of men she could ever fall in love with. Was that why? Could you ever love only the impossible ones? Yet Will had reciprocated at first and she did not know what had gone wrong, suspected it was not really to do with anything she had said or done but rather with his own difficulties.

He had invited her to spend a few days with his widowed mother who was staying with his married sister near Thame, and the invitation still stood even after his letter and his declared inadequacies. Jo supposed that if she wanted to go on seeing him it would have to be on his terms.

It was at this stage of her relationship with Will that the man called Adam Angelwine, on his way back from Paris, suddenly arrived in Oxford to see Jo. He was Professor of Political Science at a university in the English midlands. Jo had met him for the first time four years previously when she was seventeen, youth-hostelling in the Yorkshire dales, accompanied by her sister Annette and a French friend. The man was with his young daughter. They all talked, over the hostel's home-made tomato soup. The child seemed a bright little girl.

Jo also remembered a long walk in the moonlight, and more conversation. Among other things, she told him she was hoping to go to Oxford.

After she returned home Professor Angelwine wrote regularly to her, about literature and poetry rather than economics, and sent her books. Jo thought nothing of it until in her first year he visited his old college and took her out for lunch.

Since then he had visited her only once more but had continued to write to her, evincing, if Jo had only realized, the very intensity which she longed for with the much younger Will.

'I shall come to see you next when your last term is over,' he had said. And he had been true to his word.

Jo had come to believe that Adam was chiefly interested in her mind; she certainly had no designs on him. She had wilfully disregarded any liking he might have for other parts of her being.

This time, in June, just before her final examinations, Adam took her out to lunch to a slightly grander place than her younger men friends could have afforded, though he said there was nowhere decent to eat in Oxford.

'The George used to be good – but that all went with the war,' he said.

This time Jo did not commit the solecism of offering to pay her share, which was what you did with a young man, even if he refused. Why a young man, who only had a similar grant to her own, should be expected to pay for a girl as well, offended her feminism. Adam Angelwine was not the sort of man who would ever expect a woman to pay. During the meal, which she enjoyed, he said: 'Your mouth is awful.'

She was hurt.

He added: 'I meant – too nice.'

Her astonishment was genuine. Other remarks followed that at first puzzled her before she realized he was in earnest.

It seemed that he had thought a lot about her, and she began to be a little worried. It had never been her idea of herself to be the object of middle-aged passion. She had enjoyed writing to him, and he obviously liked writing to her. He was apparently married, as he must already have been when they first met, and his intentions might all be in her imagination, for she could not understand what such a man over twenty years older than herself, could see in her. But she could not deny that she was flattered to be admired, if that was what it was. He was clever, and could tell her about things most young men knew nothing about.

When he arrived, she was still feeling unsettled over Will Morgan, whom Adam said he would like to meet, Jo having injudiciously mentioned his name in a letter when she was at the stage of taking pleasure in writing the name of the beloved.

She and Adam and Will had therefore imbibed a rather awkward few drinks at the Union, of which Will was a member. Then Adam walked her back to college. They stayed chatting on a bench before he went off to his room at the Randolph. She had noticed him looking very intently at Will as though he wanted to ascertain how the land lay.

Adam now hinted that he would like to see her in London. What with the 'awful' mouth and this idea of meeting in London, and the intent gaze that was now fixed on herself, she felt she must find out a little more about his feelings.

Next morning, when she saw him off at the railway station, she said on an impulse, 'Will you write to me?' It would be best to have it in writing since she was not quite sure what his intentions were. He had always behaved impeccably, and in his letters had appeared to take an interest in her as a person. He promised to write.

Jo retailed to Stephanie over lunch some of what Adam had said to her and ended up giggling.

Stephanie looked more serious. 'He is certainly persistent,' she said.

'Yes – he's kept in touch now for about four years but he's never said that sort of thing before.'

Will came to her room for tea that day. Having done no work whatsoever, he was desperate about his forthcoming finals. Jo tried to cheer him up, but could not resist telling him a little bit about Adam Angelwine in a light-hearted way. Will agreed that she must have made a conquest.

She wished it worried him more.

After their exams and before the delights of the commemoration ball which Jo and Will were to attend at Will's college, she went on the promised visit to his family for a few days in Thame, a beautiful little place. They were only renting a house there, for Will's sister and brother-in-law worked abroad and his widowed mother lived in Belgium. She thought perhaps he would have changed his mind and thought better of the invitation, but no, it apparently still stood. But why did he want to introduce her to his mother when he had no wish to make their relationship more formal?

Nothing startling happened. They walked over to Long Crendon, spent long hours talking to each other, and embracing. They did not share a bed though Jo felt quite dizzy with lust. Will was possibly exhausted by his examinations; he was now dreading the results.

After returning from Mrs Morgan's rented cottage, Jo had her viva and then had to pack her things before giving up her room in college. There was still the ball to look forward to. For this you had to stay on in the town, so Jo splashed out on a few day's rent for a pleasant sunny basement room in a house in Beaumont Street.

She felt happy in one part of herself, sad in the part that had recently been filled by thoughts of Will. She still felt frustrated over his elusiveness, knowing that many people had assumed they would get engaged before they left Oxford. She still thought a lot about him as she lay on the comfortable bed in the sunshiny basement. He seemed to move through his life half-awake. It must have been unusual for him to get to the point of writing her that letter in May about his feelings. Quite different from Adam Angelwine whose letter she had just found in her pigeon-hole at college. She had collected it with a few others, already feeling that she no longer belonged in Oxford, which was depressing. It had been a nice surprise to find letters still arriving there.

She suspected Adam had enjoyed writing his letter because he enjoyed writing, but it had set her heart beating irregularly. She would try not to think about it until she left Oxford.

She was sad that her romance with Will, never technically an 'affair', seemed fated to follow the course of her other great loves, young men encountered mostly away from England, and she hoped she would be able to survive without missing him too much. She ought to be used to it by now, she thought. Will was about to go abroad for work, but said he wanted to continue to see her. Their love – his at least – was on the wane but Jo did not want to cut herself off from such a nice man. Perhaps one day he might known his own mind better.

At the house in Beaumont Street she could not help noticing the free and lively manners of the family whose home it was. . . . This is the sort of place where I'd like to live, and how I'd like to be, she thought. Might she still have a future?

Jo enjoyed the commem ball. Although apparently exhausted, Will also appeared to enjoy it, before he departed to London to pack up the rest of his affairs. Soon she would follow, rather than returning to her parents' home before she started work in November. Parents clipped your wings, and to return home before she had sorted out her life would be a mistake. Neither did she want to ask them for money. But she was weary over the endless arrangements: a place to live, money, possessions to settle.

She would still see all her friends in London; they had known each other for three years. Clever, artistic Susie Swift was a person she certainly wanted to get to know better, but she was closest to Stephanie Fischer, with whom she had been invited to stay for a few days before settling on a place to rent. Stephanie intrigued her; she still felt she was a mystery. Clare Jackson, who was not a mystery, was another good friend, already armed with a lowly job on an unknown but worthy political publication. Jo felt sure she would soon be its editor.

Many other friendships had been embarked upon during the years they were all thrown together. Jo always made friends easily and had many acquaintances, onlookers standing on the margins of her life. Who knew but that some of them might one day come to mean more, away from the artificiality of undergraduate existence? In the last three years they had all met so many people. When they all arrived in London they would already have a wide circle of friends and friends of friends, and would make new friends when they began work.

She often thought about all the people as yet unknown who might be waiting to get to know her in London. There were so many interesting human beings. She already had an introduction to a woman poet from one of her tutors.

On her last afternoon in Oxford she went back into college and projected her imagination into the distant future. Would she one day return to the place? Would by then the young faces of her friends have changed and grown old? She found it difficult to live in the present; part of her was always looking back to the past, whilst another part wondered about the unknown future. She certainly saw this journey to London as a voyage into the future.

*

Susie Swift settled herself into a corner seat and was already reading her book when the train left the station. Jo wanted to savour
her farewell to Oxford. Of course she would visit the place again,
but this was the *real* goodbye. She looked out of the window as the
train left, and felt nostalgic. Reflected in the window was
Stephanie, looking at her; she was sure that Stephie knew the
thoughts going through her head. Stephie was apt to call her
friend 'the last romantic'.

Stephie was looking at a young woman with thin arms and legs,
almost olive skin, dark-blue eyes and thick brown hair. She was
thinking, Jo is pretty, but not glamorous. She turned her attention
to Susie who was a year older than Jo and herself, so had been the
year above them in college. However, since she had read classics,
a four-year course, she had come down at the same time as the
other two. Susie was dark and bespectacled, not ugly, but not
pretty either. Perhaps one day she might be beautiful. Stephanie
smiled. Susie clearly didn't give any of her attention to such triv-
ial matters. She wrote poetry and painted and had a reputation for
absent-mindedness.

Her family lived in Bristol; she was always very offhand about
them. At present she was on her way to stay with an aunt and
uncle in London before going on holiday in Switzerland.

Stephanie Fischer stopped thinking about her friends and
thought about her viva instead. She was not a good extempore
speaker; it took her some time to formulate her thoughts. Jo on
the other hand was not like that. She spoke quickly and was an
ideal examination candidate. If only she had possessed an ounce
of Jo's quick wits last Thursday. But if she were any good she'd
have got an unviva'd first, and it was depressing to know she had
not.

Stephanie always set the highest possible standards for herself.
She was the opposite of Jo not only in speech but in looks and

height and temperament and personality. She was tall, even a bit gawky, but with wonderfully slim legs and a nice figure. Jo told her she was a quietly restful person. Perhaps that was why her friend intrigued her. Jo knew she always said too much and then wished she hadn't.

Stephanie had often been taxed by others, not Jo, with being an observer at life's feast. Jo had defended her friend and said this was not true. However, if it were true it would carry the advantage of not making too much of a mess of love. If you were wary of committing yourself you were less likely to come a cropper.

Jo herself was the expert on croppers. An attitude like Stephie's might make some people feel lonely and cut off, though she never felt Stephie was lonely. She was certainly self-sufficient, but this did not stop her having lots of friends, both male and female. As far as love-affairs were concerned, Stephanie never divulged anything. This had made Jo wonder about Stephanie's attitude to sex. She was such a very discreet person, usually to be found working in Bodley.

Stephie and Jo had once gone on holiday together in Austria, and shared a room, and Jo had been surprised by the contrast between her own exiguous bosom and Stephie's voluptuous one. Later, she had even said to her friend that she could be a 'sweater girl'.

'I haven't the right face for it,' said Stephie. Her face was rather long, and her light-brown hair nondescript. Her mother was always begging her to perm it, as it flew off in all directions, stuck out all over her head at different lengths, but she never would.

'Oh, you have such nice brown eyes and such a nice smile,' said Jo, who never stinted her praises as she also never stinted her angers. Some rude young woman who specialized in outrageous comments had told Stephie her face would be improved if her mouth were larger and her chin smaller. She 'ought to go to a beauty parlour for a make-over'.

Stephie had just smiled, and said in her lazy voice, 'Oh, I don't think I'll bother, but it's kind of you to take such an interest in me.'

Now, Jo felt too restless to read but opened a novel. Stephie had her eyes shut, might be asleep. *She* didn't need advice from others – *she* didn't want to conform, to fit in, to be like everyone else. When they had talked about how they wished they looked – female undergraduates did sometimes waste their time on such conversations – Stephanie would look, and be, bored. She was considered cynical or sceptical, but Jo thought she was just realistic.

'You'll always plough your own furrow,' Jo once said to her. 'I wish I were like you.'

Jo would soon have the opportunity to discover more abut her friend as she was on her way to stay with her in Edgware. At a pinch you might regard it as London, she thought. Her own ancestral home was in the north of England.

She had discovered quite a lot about Stephie's background. Her maternal grandmother, Ethel Trevaron, had been born in Cornwall in 1880 and was in service when she was officially courted by the son of the house. It wasn't a grand hall or anything, Stephanie had explained. Cornwall wasn't like that. Lionel Lorrian, the son, was only a year older than Ethel, and was the child of artists who had bought an old house near St Ives and joined a colony there to paint. He married Ethel in 1904, and the following year they had a little girl called Lamorna who eventually became Stephanie's mother.

Jo had met Lamorna Fischer, née Lorrian, when – just once – she visited her daughter in college. Her looks were a throw-back to ordinary Cornish stock, mixed with a kind of easygoing grace. She would not put herself out, but did not judge others. Stephie said she was tolerant and Jo wished her own mother were more like her. Mrs Fischer evinced an apparent indifference to her daughter's interests and life, which Jo had found refreshing, having been herself brought up by parents who showed, in her

25

opinion, far too much interest in their daughter's doings. She would soon see Stephie's mother again.

Over time she had elicited from Stephanie that her mother had married a Jewish businessman she'd met in London in the 1920s when she was working as a secretary in the City. He was ten years older than she, and Stephanie was their only child. Samuel Fischer had marketed pharmaceuticals, but was now 'diversifying'. Whilst Stephanie was up at Oxford he had set up some business connection in America.

'I think Mother sometimes wishes she were back in Cornwall. When she was a little girl she adored her father – my Grandpa Lorrian. He's a very impressive gentleman,' said Stephanie.

She'd been surprised at the interest Jo took in her family, though it was not really unusual. In their first term people had spoken at length about their families and schools. Not Stephie. Only persistent questioning had enabled Jo to establish her friend's family in her mind.

'Shall I meet Mr Lorrian when I stay with you?'

'He might come up to London to his gallery, I suppose. If he does you must certainly meet him. He loves young women. He's very tall and handsome.' Stephanie obviously adored him.

'He sounds like everyone's idea of a painter.'

'But he's not one – he's a dealer. He bought a gallery but I believe he's about to sell it, and concentrate on his own collection.'

'Is your grandmother still alive?'

'No. Mother's mother died a few years ago. Grandpa then moved to East Anglia, bought a new house – well an old one, really – and comes up to London only when he's forced.'

'It's an unusual name, Lorrian.'

'His father was French; that's why he has a foreign-sounding name. Great-grandpa belonged to a nineteenth century school of painting in Brittany, and for some reason they moved to Cornwall.'

Jo thought it all sounded very romantic. She did hope she would meet the grandfather one day. She would have loved an artist or two on her own family tree. She was a great believer in heredity, and her own family history wasn't so colourful.

Jo had always been interested in people, which was why she was also interested in herself. You had to disentangle yourself from your ancestors and your parents to become something new, jump off into your future. Her ambition was to write, but at present she wrote only poems and short stories. She was also interested in what Stephanie called a 'philosophical' outlook.

How far was the story of a life within the power of the person who owned that life? Did only blind chance decide whether you were a success or a failure? You couldn't be held responsible beyond a certain limit for your intelligence or the state of your health; your heredity had probably decided them for you long ago. The way you lived, all your puny efforts, could perhaps only remove disadvantages.

At school or in college when they discussed novels or tragedies they were always told that plot depended upon character, and that the bad things that happened to people were the result of a tragic flaw. At least that was said about some plays; there were others – Greek tragedies, and some of Hardy's novels – where Fate or the President of the Immortals, or whatever, intervened, and the poor human was powerless to avert his miserable end.

What about happy endings though? Were they Fate too?

Jo was actually thinking about this as the train puffed along. She knew she wanted to be liked, and was a mixture of the self-confident and the socially shy, endowed with much puzzled envy about the world in general, the rich and successful of the world, and successful writers – who must surely all live in London. She was horribly self-conscious, which Stephie was not, and certainly not Susie Swift.

Susie went on reading her book, and Stephie kept her eyes shut, and Jo continued to muse whilst she stared unseeingly out of the window.

Slough would be next. Their adult lives would soon begin.

They all had one enormous advantage, Jo and Stephie and Susie, and all the other women who were to arrive in London about the same time: Clare Jackson and Elinor Knight, Primrose Bowden and Flora Hargreaves; they were all very young.

When they arrived at Paddington they were met by Stephanie's father, Sam Fischer, in his smart new car. That was a relief. If there was one thing Jo had never liked it was carrying suitcases in the Underground. Their trunks were to arrive later from college, packed with everything they didn't want to leave there, or give away, or sell: books and clothes and all the detritus of three years' life. Until then, Jo would manage on a few clothes, a sponge-bag, one or two paperbacks, and a diary. There was also a coffee-table to arrive one day but as yet she had no idea where to have it sent. She must find a room to rent somewhere; she couldn't impose herself on Stephanie's family for more than a week though she was assured they would be delighted.

Since Jo had always hated change and liked to have all her possessions around her it would paradoxically help that on having to leave Oxford she would be in a strange place where she could dispense with her usual props. She had tried to keep a little money back from her grant, and had sold many textbooks back to Blackwell's in the past weeks to make a bit of extra cash, but she didn't have much of it left. She'd have to find some lowly occupation until her permanent job started in November.

Perhaps Mr and Mrs Fischer would think it odd she didn't go back to her family for three months or so before she started at the Municipal Halls? Jo knew she'd feel the trap slide over her if she ever got on that train from King's Cross and returned to her old life. Her mother might suggest that she ditched the London job and took a teaching post locally, and that would be the end of her freedom. She shuddered before the prospect. Her father would probably agree, though it was on his advice she'd applied for the administrative post. Many, many, other jobs had been applied for as well, but somehow they'd all petered out or were near misses, so Jo had been left with the one she did not want.

After Mr Fischer brought the two friends back from the station he deposited them in the hall of his house, which might have been called stockbroker Tudor if it had been larger. It was one of eight built around a small green, away from the centre of the suburb in a leafy estate called Curate's Row. Stephanie said her father thought it was the English countryside.

Mrs Fischer appeared from the kitchen. Her husband had vanished and she greeted her daughter with a slight smile but no other fuss. Jo was introduced again.

'Ah, Josephine. I remember – such a pretty name,' she said.

Jo happened to like her own second name, that of an Empress, and also of the favourite literary character of her childhood, Jo March, in *Little Women*, but she heartily disliked her first name, Betty, and had dropped it as soon as she left home. Names were important. Imagine Stephie's mother being called Lamorna!

Lamorna showed Jo the small bedroom she could use.

'There's a Bendix handy down the road,' she added, as they toiled upstairs with their cases. 'That is, if you want to wash all your stuff. Stephanie usually takes hers in on a Monday.'

Perhaps she was just making it clear that she was not going to wash her guest's clothes, but Jo thought how different Mrs Fischer was from her own mother, who would never use a launderette and would make much more fuss of her friends, partly out of nerves, partly out of kindness.

Lamorna Fischer was not unkind but she seemed somehow removed from everybody, probably thinking about something else. Mr and Mrs Fischer did not seem to pay as much attention to each other as her own parents did, and were rarely together in the same room, except at meal-times.

Stephanie said her mother enjoyed her bridge and her shopping.

She was a great one for buying clothes, now that they were off the ration.

Jo liked Curate's Row. It was pleasant, if characterless, and she strangely relished feeling herself in a kind of possession-less limbo as she waited for her degree results. Her feelings of limbo were always more pronounced when she was expecting the 'curse'. At this time, the world appeared to shimmer, and she had vague states of mind that were almost mystical. She put them down to mysterious bodily changes. Later, people would learn to ascribe these moods to hormones but Jo did not yet understand that word.

The results came on the Thursday, and Jo had the good second she had expected. She telephoned her parents, thinking this counted as an important call. Stephanie however, who had been viva'd for a first, was disappointed that in the end she ended up with the same degree as Jo – in history of course, not in French. But she had already secured a grant to do postgraduate work at London University.

Not having a job, and missing Will, depressed Jo, but at the same time she felt adventurous. She'd be ready to try something new once she had uttered the formal goodbye to Will, on his way to Germany and a job. It was no good wishing he loved her as much as she would have – indeed had – loved him. Part of her understood that young men of twenty-two were in a different position from young women of the same age. Jo knew she *ought* to believe that women should be just as keen to make careers for themselves as young men but felt an overwhelming need to settle her emotional life before she took the plunge into serious work. This was, she knew, a hopeless proposition. Part of the trouble – and yet a saving grace if you looked at it another way – was that nobody expected girls to take their careers as seriously as did young men.

'Oxford is just a marriage market,' was often said. Jo feared it was true. As she'd failed in this, perhaps she should try to remodel her ideas of love and work?

*

The letter from Adam Angelwine that had arrived in Oxford just before the commemoration ball and taken Jo's breath away was still being carried around by her. She had unfolded it many times and pored over it. How should she reply?

Dear Josie

I am taking you at your word, more than you and more than I had expected. I suppose it is having an empty carriage and my thoughts. I don't really know how or where to begin, and I expect I shall know less how or where to stop.

I don't know whether I should have kissed you, on the station or anywhere else. Of course I should have liked to. But you would not have expected me to *faire des bêtises*. (I hope.)

I think I shall one day, but it will be when you tell me to – not of course in words – and not otherwise. This has always been one of my rules. Anyhow, I love you (not passionately, thank God) and that for me means everything: one can make love without loving, and one can love without making love – but I don't really distinguish. I had of course no thought whatever of making love to you, quite apart from your own emotional entanglement, and was very happy with you so. But in the end I think the two things go together.

I shouldn't and couldn't say any of that if I didn't feel it was a beginning and not an end. Of course my instinct may be quite wrong and I have not much use for instincts – and if so for your sake I should be very happy. We don't know and we can only wait and see. I'm not really as wicked as you think – I get carried away by my own eloquence – but I certainly have no 'morals' in the sense in which one uses the word, though I hope and think I have in the real and true sense. As a result of waiting I know pretty well that I really do like you, and that it's not merely youth or face or (the worst snare of all) adolescence. Really I like you because you are one of those few women who have something there – a soul and a mystery, if that is not too portentous – and beneath all that, something that one can never quite exhaust or get to know.

Does all this sound vastly impertinent, seeing that you are, as you are, 'in love'? I was careful not to ask what your feelings for me, if any, were – knowing that the answer was bound to be one that would hurt my *amour-propre*. Still, I don't think that, having asked for a letter, you could possibly expect one in any other mood. Perhaps it's written more for me than for you. Certainly it was you who kept me awake all my last night in Oxford – much to my surprise – but not from unrequited passion. I didn't feel for one moment passionate about you – though I certainly love you no less than I thought I did – nor of course did or do I feel the slightest jealousy of your Will.

What kept me awake was some sort of curious intellectual over-excitement – I suppose what I really wanted, though I didn't think of it, was to go on talking to you far into the night. I regret the advice, if I gave any. I thought I was careful to comment and not give advice. It is of course quite useless. But you have a face as though made for suffering and I should like – if it were not impossible – to spare you some of that, and anyhow hope I shall never add any. And maybe here I am deceived by an appearance which is wrong.

Still, I don't think you are the sort, any more than I am, to be satisfied with superficialities and not to keep on searching – and that makes for unhappiness, or at any rate not for easy satisfaction. I am pretty sure I know you better than anyone else ever can or will – though of course it is only one thing of lots – and that also is one of the things which makes me feel that there is a lot ahead of us yet. Which again may be sheer imagination.

Anyhow, Jo darling, I think you know I have a genuine if unrespectable emotion for you – and not merely that I shall always help you if I can, but also that I shan't do so with ulterior motive.

32

You obviously can't reply to this – or I don't see how you can, and I don't expect you to. But I should like to hear from you some time, probably more than you would really like to hear from me. I'm sorry I have not said anything about your young man, for I'm sure that's what you really would like. And now – with the carriage loading up, I stop. I know it's not only illegible (perhaps a very good thing) but also uncoordinated and, where I wanted most to make myself clear, far from comprehensible – but if you wanted better you should have let me sleep that night and if you wanted something quite other, you should have known it was impossible. But I hope and suspect that this at any rate, more or less, was what you wanted and expected. If you are going to be in London, as you said you were, may we see each other? Do write.

With love, always, from
Adam

TWO

Whilst staying with Stephanie, knowing that Will would soon be far away, Jo had puzzled over what to say to Adam Angelwine in reply, for reply she must. The trouble was she just could not see herself doing anything very interesting in the near future, or being exceptionally good at anything and she did not want to be the sort of woman who thinks only about love. Yet think about love she did.

If she had been invited on a wonderful holiday, or if she had managed one of the more interesting jobs on her long list, she might have felt less depressed. It is impossible to put old heads on young shoulders. Adam's shoulders however were not young.

Jo was still uncertain what to do when after a week with Stephie she departed to her rented bed-sitting-room in a maisonette in Forest Top, a suburb of north London, which she had seen advertised in the *New Statesman*.

Adam's letter was still metaphorically burning a hole in her pocket, and it was in an excess of rashness that, unhappy over Will's imminent departure, and over the end of the lovely Oxford life, and even more depressed by the general ugliness of Forest Top, she decided to answer it.

She told Adam where she would be, but did not dare at first to post her letter, with the same feeling she had had earlier, that when she did the die would have been cast.

After she had been only a few days in Forest Top, however, she did finally post her answer. The first day she had spent moving in her scant possessions and arranging for a few things to be sent on from Oxford, a box of books and the little coffee-table that her Aunt Elsie had given her. Her big trunk she would ask the college authorities to send north.

She would have to follow it herself one day, for she wanted to sort all her books that were still at home. She knew her mother's proclivities for throwing things out, or rather giving things away to Oxfam or deserving children.

One evening towards the end of July, she went to Victoria Station on the Underground – miles and miles away it was – to say goodbye to Will who was departing on the first leg of his journey. He was travelling on the night train to Paris, and thence to Germany and probably central Europe.

She felt choked with misery. Will too seemed a little shame-faced, but there was no going back, so she left him there, waving to her from the platform of the night train to the Dunkirk boat. It would not be true to say she never saw him again.

In the big post box on the station near the news cinema she posted her answer to Adam Angelwine.

She did not cry then, but wept a little when she got back to Forest Top, aware that she was suffering from self-pity. She decided she must pull herself together. As usual, to help in this endeavour, she turned to a novel. It was in the dismal brown room that she read *Sapho* by Alphonse Daudet, a book about sexual love. She thought about her failure to make Will love her, and considered her general character. She would have been a good candidate for a Catholic examination of conscience since she so loved making lists.

It was no good being choked with misery; she was young, and

she had always before now bounced back from each disappointment like a rubber ball. She took up her pen and immediately felt a little better.

She wrote:

What is making me miserable:

One: I miss Will, but no more than that I hate things to come to an end.

Two: I am always oppressed by the number of practical things to be done, which hang over me in a cloud now that the easy life of the college has been taken away.

Three: I dread hurting my family, or giving them any cause for concern. But I am determined to go my own way.

Four: I want to understand other people, but all the different complicated thoughts of the people I read make me feel inadequate.

Five: I know I act one way with one person and a different way with another. I am a chameleon. How could I ever show a man like Adam what sort of person I really am? He seems to think he knows me, but how can he? Perhaps he likes me just because he doesn't know me, and so once he knows me better his feelings for me will disperse. He is a totally different kind of person from me – but so is Will.

Six: Am I just searching for a kindred spirit?

She read through her list. At least she had tried to define her problems. She made a cup of tea in the shared kitchen. The landlady was out, and that was a relief.

She christened Forest Top 'N 99'. The maisonette was on the ground and first floors of one of a long line of houses on a main road, and she had never seen such an ugly place. The slummy

36

streets of a small northern mill-town could not compare with this depersonalized, treeless, endless, hoarding-edged road that began outside a far-flung tube-station and led nowhere she had ever heard of. But strangely enough she was reminded of home by the steel fire-hydrant covers that were found on pavements all over London, all made in her home town.

Her room had the ugliest modern furniture she had ever seen or could imagine. The owner of the furniture, Kathleen Dawson, the landlady who had advertized this 'bed-sitting-room with all mod cons and share of kitchen and bathroom' in the *New Statesman* was a woman in her late thirties who walked around in the nude, told her tenants she was divorced, was a Communist, had a daughter who did not appear to live with her, and wanted her tenants to be her friends. This last piece of information meant only that she interrogated them about their lives. Jo suspected she would read their correspondence and diaries, if they were injudicious enough to leave either lying around.

Mrs Dawson made her feel quite ill, but Jo felt she should put up with the room for a time because she knew that to go home would still be an admission of defeat. She *must* be independent. Being free meant having a love-life, and she wanted a proper sex-life, something Oxford had never quite come up with. Jo still loved her northern home, and certain members of her close family, but she had been hiding her opinions from then since she was four-teen, and had already begun to conceal her real life from them. She would have liked not to feel obliged to do this. She was sure that Stephanie's mother did not bother about her daughter's morals.

How lucky her friend was! But most girls' parents worried lest their daughters might become involved in that reprehensible activity called sex, and even spied upon them to discover if this was the case. The girls were better employed helping in the home, until a nice young man, the traditional boy next door, bore them off to their marriage-bed. Housework – shopping, cooking and cleaning – would then be their allotted tasks in life. Jo's sister Annette agreed with her about all this but went her own sweet way, worrying less about disappointing her progenitors.

Here, in ugly 'N 99', Jo hoped at least to be free, especially when she could escape on the tube to central London. If her family had been different she would have gone home for a good rest, for she knew she needed one.

If she had packed up then and there and taken the train home, the whole direction of Jo's life would have been different. Certain decisions, made only after due consideration, but also out of boredom, low spirits, a longing for excitement, and a lack of money, would inevitably lead to others. Maybe she needed to suffer a little, to be thrown back on her own resources, and to cope. But in 'N 99', having recognized these low spirits in herself, she realized that the place was making them worse.

Why could she not be like Milton and believe the mind was its 'own place', to make a 'heaven of hell, a hell of heaven'?

Lack of trees, a cold wind, a sunless side of the road, horrible billboards, all made her feel worse.

She said aloud: 'Oxford is over. If you are serious about writing you must write whatever the circumstances. You have to earn your living. Will Morgan has gone away, abroad, probably for years. You must take your chance with Professor Angelwine.

Next morning she tidied her possessions and sorted the short stories and poems that she had packed with her clothes and a few books. There were so far only four stories and the beginnings of a fifth. As she reread them she realized that they were all about nostalgia, disillusion, or fear. One was a story about an apparently happy middle-aged man she had glimpsed in a train, who was certainly not happy but put on a brave front in his office where he was a clerk. She had entitled this, ironically: *A Happy Man*. Another was the beginning of what she intended to be a novella or a very long short story about a little girl called Karen. At least it was not about herself. Another was concerned with the sudden infatuation, and therefore sudden disillusion, of a fleeting summer romance. In yet another she had written of a young woman feeling a kind of nausea over the 'too-muchness' of all there was to buy in a department store. This was after visiting Harrods with Stephanie. Jo had entitled this, *Shopping in the District*.

She was now meditating a much longer story for which she had only jotted down a few notes, a fantasy with a mystic streak, about a young man called Kristin. The name had come to her suddenly a few weeks earlier. She often thought about it during the day, and in bed at night, but feared that once she put pen to paper it would appear shoddy and silly. On the other hand, she could not allow her ideas to vanish like blown bubbles: so many phrases and pictures came to her when she was half-asleep, and she must hold on to them, develop them. The best thoughts came in the dark.

She took up her diary, and wrote:

Ideas burn in the daytime like matches in the sun. At night they clarify the interior world.

She was rather pleased with that.

She got up, put all the stories into a file and decided to sort out a few clothes. Her wardrobe was not very extensive. Her best blue-cotton dress needed a wash; the one with a ruffle round a low-cut neck that she had bought at Elliston and Cavell in May for five guineas. She went into the tiny bathroom to soak it in Lux flakes.

The she sat down again to write up her diary.

I am alone now [she wrote] my life seemingly reduced to the problems of Work, Money, and Love. I need more experience of life; I want Something to Happen, and I am tired of my feelings being unrequited.

Reading this through, she thought she sounded too gloomy.

39

Why was it that she almost never wrote her diary when she was happy?

She cheered herself up with the notion that whatever happened to her, whatever awful job she had to do for cash, it could be the food for a story. There were so many interesting people on the tube, in the shops, in queues. She'd like to follow them, be an invisible visitor in their homes, make a story out of their lives. It was the same as after reading, or waking from colourful dreams; walking in London always gave her the feeling that there was too much in the world for her to grasp whilst she had to live a daily life that was far removed from her preoccupations.

Well, 'experience' might soon arrive, not as the result of one of her long romantic infatuations but from Adam Angelwine, who loved her, 'not passionately'.

Was that to make her want him to love her more? It would be her own decision to accept a civilized 'fling' with him. She wanted it to be that, for experience: the sort that Oxford undergraduates were not very good at providing. Not 'A Great Love'. No.

She had given him no encouragement whatsoever. If Will had loved her, Adam would not have got a look-in. But he had come specially to Oxford to tell her, in slightly ambiguous terms, that he loved her, had loved her for years.

She had only to let him know. He would be working at the British Museum. She had agreed to see this man who appeared to find her so attractive.

Jo had spent so much of her life up to then 'in love', and the first person to say he was 'in love' with her was married, a generation older, and in every way unsuitable, the word that was the bane of her childhood and adolescence.

Why should this have happened to her? Was there something about her that attracted an unconventional kind of love?

Would it not have been surprising if, fresh from the loss of the young man she adored, jobless, until she began her permanent 'safe career', a young woman full of insecurities, who needed above all a holiday, was not tempted by the urgent overtures of such a man as Adam?

Here for the time being she was in Forest Top; she seemed to have lived there for years though it was only ten days. On the second Friday she received another letter from Adam. He was renting a flatlet in South Kensington and would love her to come round and see him. He would telephone that afternoon. The call came about four o'clock.

'For you,' said Mrs Dawson, with a disapproving air, so the voice must be male. Jo decided to cast caution to the winds.

'Hello – how nice to hear your voice,' he said. 'Was that your landlady? She sounds as if she comes from Birmingham.'

'Yes,' Jo murmured. 'She does.'

'Look, I won't hang on, I don't like the phone. I'd love to see you. Can you have a drink with me about six and then we could go out for dinner? I'll get you back on the tube in time, I promise. Don't worry.'

'I'd love to,' she said. It seemed ages since she had heard the voice of anyone intelligent.

She went out about five o'clock, afraid of being late. All the commuters were coming back home in the opposite direction and by the time the train reached Piccadilly she thought she might be too early. But she changed trains and got on to the Circle Line – all this bustle was new to her – and alighted at Gloucester Road. He had given her detailed directions and she soon found 19 Courtfield Gardens, in a quiet backwater. It was raining as she reached the house, one of a long row of tall early Victorian houses split into flats. The house she approached had a porch with bells for numbered service flats.

She rang the bell and then pushed at the outer door, which opened. Adam's rooms were, he had told her, on the ground floor. He was standing at his door at the end of a short hall, waiting for her.

He smiled and turned and she followed him through the door into a separate hall, glimpsing a small kitchen and bathroom leading off it as Adam led the way into his sitting-room. How lucky he was, she thought. No Forest Top for him. He looked nervous.

'We shall have to get you out of that place,' he said, when she had given him a long account of how depressing her own quarters were. 'We must have a long talk.' He poured her a glass of sherry from a full bottle waiting on a side table.

His things were neatly organized in the room. There was a large window, a single bed, a wardrobe, an electric fire. His brief-case was on a chair; a pile of books on another table.

She was wearing her freshly washed and ironed blue dress. Taking her hand, he said:

'Oh, you do look appetizing!'

He began to ask her about what she had been doing since he had last seen her. She told him about staying with Stephanie but he did not seem very interested in her girl friends. She told him Will Morgan had gone away and he looked pleased. She had the impression he wanted to know if her young man was serious about her. It must be clear to him now that Will wasn't.

In her handbag she still had the letter Adam had sent her after he had stayed in Oxford, that letter which said a good deal but in such a paradoxical way that she still couldn't be quire sure what he meant, or intended.

Now, as she went on describing her thoughts and feelings about Forest Top, and her future job, and the three and a half months she had to wait until she could begin work, she found herself making excuses for not going home.

'Surely your father could send you some money to be going on with?' he said.

'I wouldn't ask them for any. If they gave me money I'd feel obliged to go home. *You* should be glad I'm alone in London!' she added, with a laugh. It *would* suit Adam, wouldn't it? As it might suit her – for the same reasons. He looked at her rather seriously.

'They would say: "why not come home until November?"' she explained.

She seemed to be in an unequal position *vis-a-vis* Adam. She didn't want to be seen to be depressed, or at a loose end, or penniless, for she was sure his idea of her, from what he had said in all his letters, was of a cheerful lively person who did not allow circumstances to get her down. On the other hand he might as well realize that she felt a bit down after Will's departure.

'As soon as I begin work I'll be all right, but before November I'll have to find a temporary job,' she said.

'I see.'

Not for the first time, and certainly not the last, she thought how they were in some ways such very different kinds of people, in others rather alike. She would never be on a level with Adam though. She wished she were older, and independent, and had some money. But then he might not like her. She feared lest she could never be entirely natural with him, already finding herself acting the part of the woman she thought he thought she was.

But after another glass of sherry Adam put his glass down and moved towards her and began to stroke her hair. They were not sexy caresses, but she felt swimmy, excited, even more peculiar when he kissed her with little tender darting kisses on the nape of her neck, and on her arms.

Then he poured another glass of sherry for each of them and pulled her gently on to his knee.

She stroked his head. It was unsettling, strange. She had been used to the thick curly dark mop of a much younger man.

Was this really Adam Angelwine who was murmuring endearments to her?

He seemed really moved – even looked at her shyly at one point.

'Will you go away to the country with me? Don't decide now – think about it. You deserve a bit of fun. Don't worry – I shan't seduce you here.'

She thought: well, yes, fun *is* what I'd like.

*

This was to be how their love-affair started. She was both flat-tered and slightly incredulous that such a man felt for her what he said he did. Apparently these feelings of his for her had been growing under his skin for years whilst she, all unknowing, had been pursuing her young life. He said that he would not have moved towards her when he did if she had showed the least disinclination, or had been happy with Will, and she believed him.

Naturally, at the time she could not imagine that what would take place over the next few weeks or months might set her life in a certain direction. She wanted an affair, fun, to be grown-up. She wanted experience. She wanted pleasure.

This particular evening everything happened so quickly that she was breathless. Quite apart from all the sherry she had drunk, which made her heart beat like a drum.

'We must go out for a meal,' he said.

They went out, even though there was thunder in the air. Earls Court in a downpour, dinner in an Italian restaurant. What were they going to talk about?

Jo was glad to be able to tell Adam that her degree was quite good – in fact what she had hoped for.

He was quiet, looked at her a good deal, seemed disturbed.

The thunder was roaring in their ears when they came out of the restaurant.

'You will come back with me to my room, won't you?' he asked her. 'Just for half an hour before you have to go?'

'Yes. But I'll have to get back to N 99.'

She sat in the armchair and he began to kiss her again. It was still strange to be so close to him. Less than a week since she said goodbye to Will.

Adam's face was serious, even agonized. They lay on the bed but he did nothing more than kiss.

It was when she was in the bathroom that she heard a ring on the door-bell. Then a woman's voice.

Good God, she thought, is it his wife? Hermione?

She waited, heard a murmur of voices but could not make out what Adam was saying. At last she heard the outer door close. She ventured to put her head round the door of the bathroom. He was sitting on the bed and looked up when he saw her.

'Come in. She's gone.'

She looked enquiringly at him.

'That was Patricia,' he said heavily. 'I told you about her.'

She remembered. In Oxford he had mentioned a Pat whom he saw occasionally in London. A married woman. She must be a sort of part-time mistress. Jo was a little shocked.

'I'd forgotten she knew I'd be here in August,' he went on.

'Off with the old, on with the new?' Jo said flippantly, not really meaning it, because what did this Patricia mean to him anyway? He had given her no details.

'You're right in a way. But I was never in love with Pat,' he said. He looked a bit ashamed, upset.

The penny dropped. 'Does your wife know about her?'

'Oh, she's probably guessed I might still see her now and then. We both knew her in the war,' he said ruefully.

She went up to him, sat down next to him and put her arms round him. He clung to her as if he were drowning.

'Forgive me,' he said. 'It really is over. I told her just now. She guessed I had someone here. *Will* you forgive me?'

She said nothing to that. Life with Adam was obviously going to be full of surprises. How did he find the energy – and the time? At his age.

She thought, he is quite old. She had the disadvantage of youth. How old was Patricia? How long had he been seeing her? What was the nature of their relationship? The words sounded pompous even in her head.

'How long have you been seeing her in London?' she asked.

He looked up. 'Oh, just off and on – since the end of the war, I suppose. Not more than a few times a year. But I did go to see her before I saw you in Oxford last month.'

'Why?'

'Because I wanted to make sure the feelings I had for you were not just sexual ones – if there was any unsatisfied desire hanging around. . . .'

You used her, she thought. She must be fond of him. 'Is she still married?'

'Yes – and I loved you even more than I had expected – it doesn't matter if I never see Mrs Harris – Pat – again.'

'Like I said: "Off with the old—".'

'You are right to be tough with me. How surprising. You make me feel wicked. But you don't seem to mind.'

'Well, I suppose it must happen a lot to you?'

'I am not a monster, Jo. I think you understand me.'

She was thinking – a fling then? That suits me fine. Then I shall learn things from him and not feel guilty if I too have others around.

'I am not going to make love to you here,' he said. '*Too* sordid. I want to take you away. To the country. Start afresh. Will you come? Next weekend? Think about it.'

She said she would think about it.

It was late when at last he saw her off on the Underground to the ugly suburb. She was missing him even as the train moved away.

When she was back in her shabby room her thoughts were once more in turmoil. She would rather he had made love to her then and there, when he told her he loved her, because that and his physical proximity had made her desire him. She would rather they just wanted each other and that he did not make her feel she was to be so . . . 'special'. But she was still incredulous. Was he mad? Was she?

Had she made up her mind to go away with him?

46

*

She slept badly, tossing and turning, her heart still beating like a drum. It must have been the big meal and the wine as well as the evening's revelations. When she did fall asleep again towards dawn she had a strange dream.

She dreamed of a young man, Dennis Swann, whom she had known in her very first Trinity term at Oxford, not a man she had ever been or could ever be in love with; more a friend. He came like herself from the north and they had met at the Hispanic Society. Dennis eventually detailed to her the overwhelming lust he felt for his landlady, and, as the term went on, it appeared that she reciprocated. Jo felt he was running a risk, for his landlady was married. He was a daredevil sort of young man, hardly more than a boy; an athlete and a good swimmer.

Towards the end of term, when she had not seen him for a week or two, she was about to open the *Oxford Mail* one lunch-time to see what was on at the local cinema when she saw on the front page the headline:

UNDERGRADUATE DROWNS IN ISIS.

There was an account saying Dennis Swann had got out of his depth in the river that flowed quite near his digs and that his landlord had tried to save him, but to no avail. Hadn't she been sure Dennis was courting danger? As far as she knew she was the only person who knew about his affair. Except for the lady, and perhaps her husband.

Jo had been deeply suspicious. Injudicious sex had led to death. But it was all so incredible. Dennis was a superb swimmer, and much younger than the man who said he had tried to save him.

What could she do? She had no proof, but she remembered thinking later that this was the first time that she had seen in real life an example of passion leading to destruction. She felt sure it had not been an accident. She realized that some kinds of sexual passion were very destructive.

Now, in her dream, she was speaking to this man's parents, still feeling a little guilty for not having gone to the inquest. She was filled with a sort of terror of sex, but when she awoke and thought of Adam, the terror was dissipated. How could there be a parallel between Dennis Swann's foolishness and her own if she accepted Adam's invitation to go away with him? She felt safe with Adam who had after all known her for some years, if not in a quotidian fashion. She wanted to be able to tick off a new experience, and then start afresh in London, forgetting all her previous botched romances.

Jo was to give Adam her answer on Thursday 7 August. If she decided to accept his invitation they would go away on the Saturday the 9th for the weekend.

It was now or never, she thought. Nobody had ever taken her away for the weekend before. Not like this: what people called a dirty week-end.

She always preferred to be positive, to say 'Yes' to people, unless she did not trust them, and she did trust Adam, though it was a bit like being propositioned by God.

Well, Will was not going to come back, was he? And Adam said he was in love with her. He would probably wait for her if that was what she wanted. Yet if anything were going to happen she would rather get it over straight away. She thought: usually when people say: *If anything happens*, they mean, *if I die*.

She needed – wanted – sexual experience; she was in limbo until her proper job began. Who could be better to give her that experience than Adam? Yet did she want to get in too deeply with him? Was he only the charming, intelligent, pleasure-seeking man she had thought him to be in Oxford? If he loved her, as he kept telling her he did, would he let her go when she had taken from him what she needed? Put like that, she was forced to see herself as a selfish, shallow person. Adam obviously didn't see her like that, and she did not like disappointing people. Some girls, she knew, would hang back to make the man even keener. But she didn't think he could be keener, and she had never been like those girls. Did he know that?

Next morning she telephoned him from the phone in the hall of the maisonette, All she said to Adam was: 'Yes, I'll come.'

He caught his breath. 'I'll book straight away. Darling.'

She left all the arrangements to him. He would be sure to find somewhere nice. She was already longing to get out of London.

On the Friday afternoon she met Adam outside the British Museum and they went to the service flat in Courtfield Gardens. They were to leave the next morning from Marylebone Station. That night he insisted that she should return to her bed-sitting-room. Was it to make her more excited? He kept saying he was not going to treat her as a casual affair. Everything had to be perfect. But perhaps he might now make love to her since she had agreed to go away for the weekend with him.

As soon as they got inside the room he said, 'Oh, I do love you so!' and kissed her tenderly.

She felt a rush of desire rather than tenderness, wanted to lie down on the narrow bed and have him make love to her then and there. She was wet with longing.

She realized how frustrated Will had made her feel. If it was off with the old and on with the new, that applied to her too. Adam must have realized that she was ripe for picking, and jumped whilst she was on the rebound.

That sounded so sordid. But then, she thought, Adam was going to come and see me anyway. It just happened that this time circumstances conspired to make this the psychological moment. Had it been inevitable? No. If Will had wanted her she would never have agreed to see Adam. But now she decided she was ready for an adventure.

Now he was kissing her slowly, but not with passion, staring at her all the time.

'Let's wait,' he said. 'Till tomorrow.'

She knew what he meant but was disappointed.

'It mustn't be sordid,' he kept saying.

She thought, but it isn't. I don't want to have a 'thing' made of it. I just want to make love, for him to take me and to get on with it. Not even with talk of 'love'. Just pleasure and closeness.

But he was determined to do it his way.

She knew he thought it was for her sake, but why should she need to go back to the dreary bed-sit and repack before the next day's journey out of London?

The parting on the tube station at South Ken was even more fraught. What if I died, she thought. Without having been made love to by him?

The next morning she was up and out of the house as quickly as possible. She went straight to Marylebone as he had asked her to do. He was already there waiting, two tickets in hand.

It was not too warm but it was sunny. At least not a rainy August day. He told her they were going to Hertfordshire, to a little town he knew quite well, to a hotel, the Rose and Crown.

'Had I better wear a wedding ring?' she asked him in the train.

'If it makes you feel better,' he said, teasing her.

'Well, it might embarrass the maids,' she said. 'I mean if I didn't.'

She thought, I am so much younger than him. I hope they won't think I'm with my father.

She was excited and also a little apprehensive. It was pleasant for once to have someone take charge, sort things out, look after you. None of the men she'd been in love with had been the sort to do this, except perhaps for Will who liked hiring cars and driving around but who was always exhausted when she suggested other things they might do. Her father hadn't been the sort to organize people either.

There was no trouble over signing the register. They only asked Adam to sign, and he put: *Mr and Mrs A. Angelwine.*

After lunch, the usual hotel fare of roast beef and apple-pie and coffee, they went for a short walk, and then back up to the bedroom overlooking the yard; they had taken what was offered since the booking had been made only two days before. But it was quite large, with a gas fire. The bed had a pink eiderdown.

She felt nervous, wished they were back in London. This seemed so ... bourgeois. She turned on the gas fire, for it was a little chilly.

'Please, let it be like yesterday,' she begged him as they sat on the bed together. She needed time to adjust. She meant, when I felt desirous – and when I wanted you.

This was like a honeymoon. Was that what he had wanted? She wanted him to make love to her soon, and quickly.

'I shall just undress you and we can talk before we change for dinner,' he said and proceeded to slip her dress over her shoulders. It was the blue-cotton dress with the wide neck-ruff and the puffed sleeves.

They lay on the bed with their arms around each other.

'Oh, you are so beautiful,' he kept saying.

She was quite sunburnt and slim, had no embarrassment over nakedness. He was not a big man but he had strong wrists. His feet were small, his torso not hairy.

She told him about her previous experiences – or experience – and about the people she had loved. It was cosy.

'They'll come in soon to turn down the beds,' he said at four o'clock.

They went down to dinner quite early. Adam ordered a bottle of wine – wine was one of his great enthusiasms. He seemed to know a lot about it but did not try to impress the waiter. She had gathered so far that he liked Pouilly Fuissé and Chablis and

Mouton Rothschild and an Alsatian wine made from the grape Traminer, which he said was not usually obtainable in England.

That evening they drank a bottle of Chablis between them, Adam drinking twice as much as she did. She listened to his accounts of France before the war and of his first love. He rarely talked about his work, yet she thought it must always be just below the surface of his mind.

The dining-room was hushed with that occasional ringing of cutlery and tinkle of glass and subdued conversation found only in England. One thing they had in common, she thought again, was love for what was not England, especially for France.

They went up to bed after a short walk in the garden of the hotel.

It was chilly. She felt like a good sleep and wished they had got over the love-making in the afternoon.

When it came it was tender. He was not a greedy lover. In fact she could not have wished for a more considerate one. Afterwards, his avowals were passionate. He was overcome. He seemed more interested in love than what people called sex. Wasn't it women who were supposed to want love more than sex?

'I thought you had more experience,' he said, 'but I am glad that you have not. Not that it makes a scrap of difference.'

The die is cast, she thought with a leap of the heart, before she fell asleep snuggled close to him, her heart still beating like a hammer from emotional excitement rather than love.

In the morning he made love to her again, explaining that she need not worry about babies. He would take care of that, until she could get herself sorted out.

They went for a longer walk in the afternoon across a field where the corn had just been stooked up. She could not believe it was an ordinary Sunday for most people, that things were going on much as usual for them. The cornfields lay burnished in the sun. Adam was a little abstracted, though always attentive, always keeping her alert in conversation and expecting, she thought, intelligent remarks from her. She could not quite put her finger on it but knew that she would not be able to go on as she had been, that loving Adam, if that was to be her fate, would not be easy. Almost it was as if she had decided to try to love him in return for his love. Love called out by love, an unusual experience for her.

How could she have said 'No' to him after he had said to her such things as: 'I've been waiting for you all my life'?

It was a wonderfully exciting experience to be loved by this particular man. Also, even at this time, perhaps especially at this time, she did not want to hurt his feelings, even if her own had been hurt hundreds of times.

He said she was tender, had no hang-ups, was easy to love physically, was 'made for loving'.

He said she was 'innocent', because she was not sexually animalistic. Yet he had said about her 'woman-like' remark concerning Mrs Harris, that she spoke like a woman who understood all. She knew that her remark had only been a sort of clever throw-off. She had not really imagined he was carrying on an affair in London.

She knew she was not 'innocent', and that her feelings for this man were more psychological than physical. But now that she had this experience, what more might she want?

In the train they were in a closed compartment, empty but for themselves and he made love to her there as the train rocked along back to Marylebone. It had never occurred to her that people did this sort of things on trains. Her first estimate of him had changed.

He was probably still charming, intelligent, pleasure-seeking, but he seemed, from what he had told her about his life, always to have had a need to be falling in love. In this, she thought, he was like her, except that she hoped that by the time she was his age – forty four – she would have calmed down.

She saw straight away that he had an enormous amount of energy. His energy was not only for loving but for talk, for food, for drink, for physical exercise, for work. He told her that if he was alone he always wrote his lectures or his reviews on long train-journeys, was never idle. Or he would write his letters there as he had done that first time on returning from Oxford.

Soon they would have to part; in two weeks he would return to his wife and children.

It was no longer experience she found herself wanting, nor even love, but more, much more. Either freedom, or a different way of life, away from London, with children.

Adam had begun to tell her the story of his life, a story he was to take up many times later. Indeed, he was to talk so much about his childhood and his family that she could have written a book about them. But what was he really like? She often felt she had to retire, baffled. She realized he was very left wing, but also that he was a snob. Would she see him differently if they were not intimate? She realized he was a very clever man, but also, she sometimes suspected, a very foolish one as he moved through his life of comparative recognition and success. He was so sure of his tastes, of his opinions, in a way she felt she would never be.

He told her that originally he had expected a passionately phys-ical fling. The kind, thought Jo, to which he was clearly accustomed, the kind she had decided she needed. But this was not to be.

If Jo had been more experienced, more sure of herself, more comfortably situated in her life; if she had even perhaps had a higher opinion of her own value, she could have avoided falling in love with him – or appearing to herself to do so. But she was an impetuous girl who liked taking emotional risks. She had not wanted to wait any longer.

Sometimes she was not even sure what she felt, was in the state of wanting to be in love, and determined to please him. But it was still strange having love called out by love; not an emotional situ-ation she was used to. It was exciting to be at last 'the beloved',

54

though she found that hard to reconcile with her true self. If she tried to explain this to Adam he would be hurt. She was aware however that she was capable of 'confecting' love, especially where sex was concerned. The odd thing was that she was not in any way frightened or in awe of Adam. She felt that in spite of the situation he was fundamentally to be trusted.

He was to go on saying it was not an 'affair'; in the end that she was the supreme love of his life. She believed him as long as she knew that he believed it to be true. In the meantime she had to take up the threads of her own ordinary existence.

If his love for her had been Agape rather than Eros, Adam might have given her affection without anguish. But he fell in love with her, and what could have been a memorable fling would turn into a serious love, a mixture of pleasure and misery, security and insecurity.

She had had no chance of escaping him, it seemed to Jo a little later, and she did not want to let him down. But often she wondered, and was to wonder even more as time went on, what could possibly be the end of it all.

THREE

When Jo first came to London even coffee-bars didn't exist, never mind wine-bars. If she met her men-friends it was either in the pub or, if a male journalist or writer-friend took her there, a seedy Soho afternoon drinking-club like the Mandrake. London pubs were mostly the domain of men too, though women were tolerated in the saloon-bars if they were accompanied by a man. Rarely did women go with female friends into pubs for a drink. More often women without men would meet in a Jo Lyons tea-shop, or go for a meal at a Corner House. Jo Lyons became an old friend for about fifteen years, for they served a good cup of tea in the tea-shops, and things like poached egg on toast – or just toast, if the budget wouldn't stretch to more that week. Jo was often to eat her East End lunch too in the district's Lyons where a plate of stew was welcome after a morning's teaching. When women invited their friends for a meal at home, the 'at home' would be digs. Occasionally, and more frequently as time went on and the circle of friends grew wider, there would be bottle-parties on Saturday nights. Wine was not cheap.

Like most young graduates, Jo would not be able to afford a flat of her own for some years. Only those with small private incomes could do this and were envied by others. Most of her friends whose parents did not live in London rented bed-sitting-rooms, but these were usually in delightful areas such as Kensington, Bayswater, Maida Vale. Nobody yet shared a flat and certainly not a mixed-sex flat.

The bed-sitters were usually cold, central heating was for the rich; most families still had coal fires, but as it was always chilly in English bedrooms, the 'digs', like the bedrooms, were heated by shilling-in-the-slot gas-meters. Clare Jackson even reported having seen a *penny*-in-the-slot meter. Fridges and freezers weren't yet owned by most families either, but as extreme heat was a rare occurrence food was usually kept fairly fresh in larders with perforated screens. London did not then reach 90°F in summer.

When Jo looked down on London from Hampstead Heath in the late 1950s, or if Clare, who was renting a flat for the time being in south London, looked at the view from the top of Crooms Hill in Blackheath, the tallest building either of them could see would be the dome of St Paul's. The Houses of Parliament were visible too in the years between the passing of the Clean Air Act and when traffic pollution conjured them away again. These two buildings, the representatives of politics and religion, stood like gigantic statues. Even by the beginning of the 1960s they were joined only by the Vickers building on Millbank.

There were no motorways until just before the end of the decade; country roads were pleasant, winding by fields full of wild flowers and birdsong. The worst crimes anyone Jo knew had ever committed in those years were riding a bike without lights, and – her crime – 'forgetting' to pay for a wireless licence in a house of multi-occupation.

The workers lived in streets of nineteenth-century terrace houses that were often without inside lavatories. These little dwellings all over London, especially in the east and south, were rented, but the architects Jo was soon to meet at work already had their eye on them. Many were to be demolished, to be replaced by great cliffs of tower blocks. The architects despised the nineteenth century for not being Georgian – or Regency – or an up to date Corbusier imitation. The town-planners amused themselves with pretty models of the new London, all planted with trees and little pools and flowers. Jo wondered how the inhabitants would feel in the cold winds that would blow down every stark facade of their flats. The gleam in the eyes of architects, who intended above all to 'improve' London's East End, seemed to want to imitate some Italian town where cold winds and constant rain never penetrated. But the poor had little say in their future domiciles.

Whenever Jo or Stephie and their friends had any money it would be solid half-crowns and florins, sixpences and shillings and threepenny bits, that they jingled in their pockets. Twelve pennies would make a shilling and twenty shillings a pound for twenty more years. The heavy pennies, embossed with the head of George VI, or that of his father, or even his grandfather, were soon to carry the likeness of his daughter. They were useful for the payment of such items as chocolate bars, stamps, and newspapers.

Jo had to stay on at Forest Top until the beginning of November. The landlady, Mrs Kathleen Dawson, had now taken it upon herself to charge her with the error of her ways. Apparently Jo had exchanged the interdictions of parents for the interference of a woman she scarcely knew. Mrs D, who wanted her tenants to call her 'Kate', must have read some of the letters Adam had written to her. One morning Jo found in her room, propped up against a pile of books, a letter addressed to her from 'Kate', in which she urged Jo to 'give him up', adding, 'He's using you like a little factory girl.'

Mrs Dawson had known about Will too, for when Jo had seen him off at Victoria that night she had mentioned it to her. Jo was the sort of young woman who told people everything about herself that they wanted to know. She was to learn more discretion as time went on.

How *dare* Mrs Dawson! As Jo had always imagined she would, the woman must also have read her diary. Jo went into the ugly bathroom, tore up the woman's missive, flushed it down the lavatory and felt sick. She had no intention of giving up a man who clearly adored her. She knew all the arguments against, and she still hoped that he would eventually become part of her 'experience', however impossible that was beginning to appear as time went on and his impassioned letters arrived daily.

It was no 'fling'. Of that she was now convinced. But she decided to tell Mrs D that her honour had not been breached. Perhaps she would then leave her alone.

Adam and Jo were walking in the parkland around the Alexandra Palace. Jo noticed a woman with a little girl, then the child's father waved to the couple across the grass and came up to them, and the woman smiled, and the baby laughed. . . . Suddenly, Jo wished she had a baby.

She would like to be welcomed by a child and a spouse, safe and happy and settled. She was ashamed of herself. Not all that 'Bohemian' then? It was Adam's wife she envied – envied her not Adam but her children, her house, her life.

What was the matter with her? Had only envy or jealousy evoked these sudden desires? She had been Adam's lover for only a few weeks and here she was already constructing a future that included marriage and children. But she might not be feeling like this if he had not already had these things – twice – with somebody else. Perhaps you wanted only what you could not have.

When she was once more alone, she would think: if I cannot have these conventional things I would rather be free to do what I want, enjoy sex with other men. I have the worse of two words now. How true clichés sometimes were.

Adam wanted to have his cake and eat it. And did.

Life in Forest Top had not consisted only of anger and unsettledness. Apart from Adam, who after all was away from London most of the time, Jo was to learn what real work was like when she signed on as counter assistant at the local Jo Lyons tea-shop.

After only one day serving behind the counter and sweeping the floor at the end of the day, her efforts the subject of much kindly hilarity from the other women, Jo was so exhausted she scarcely had the energy to crawl into bed after a bath.

The next day one of the women, an Irishwoman, said to her earnestly: 'You don't need to work here, dear, you could find work in a bank.'

Jo knew that this was the best way her fellow slave could explain that she was, in spite of all her efforts not to appear different, a white-collar type.

Another woman took her hands and turned them over, saying: 'I can see *you* haven't had to work for your living.'

They did not know that she had so recently been a student; there were not all that many women graduates who did such work then, and Jo was touched that the woman should think she ought to have a different sort of job. She had done her best not to 'talk posh'. But she was clearly a hopeless cleaner. The washer-up, an elderly lady, threw a tantrum that morning and cast all the cutlery plus the salt and pepper pots over her shoulder all over the kitchen floor, making a terrific clatter.

'She's mad,' they said. 'She can't help it – she's usually a good worker but it just takes her like that now and then.'

Jo nearly ruptured herself staggering with a tea-urn. She was ashamed of her muscular weakness. What was she good for? Adam, when consulted by letter, told her to leave the place. He could lend her enough to tide her over until her permanent job started. But she didn't want to be 'kept', and did try, without much success, to find other employment of a less physically taxing variety. Snack-bars and tea-shops appeared all she was good for, so she went on a course with Jo Lyons' management to learn how to make salads. All you needed, it appeared, was a lettuce leaf, some diced beetroot and half a tomato and so long as it was 'nicely presented' it would do very well.

*

Mrs K. Dawson had worked in the war as a secretary at the BBC and decided she would introduce Jo, along with her other two lodgers, both female, to a 'real' writer. This man, Noël Gersheim, was now in his fifties and had not written anything since before the war. Jo didn't think he would want to come to a dinner in N99, but she was wrong. There must have been some affair between him and her landlady in the war. Or perhaps he just liked to be given dinner. He was tall and cavernous-looking and his clothes smelt as if they had been shut up for too long in a damp yet dusty cupboard.

Jo had read one or two of his books and supposed Mrs Dawson wanted to show him off. He chomped steadily through the shepherd's pie and the trifle with frequent recourse to the bottle of red wine that had been supplied. Jo was chosen to walk him back to his bus stop where he gave her an unequivocal invitation to visit him in his mansion flat. She was quite aware of what this might mean and had no intention of being caught, so she thanked him politely and left her answer in the air. He did not insist, and his bus came shortly after whilst they were in the middle of a discussion about psychoanalysis.

She described this meeting to Adam who was amused, but a little wary, and even a little jealous. Not that Jo had found Mr Gersheim in any way attractive, but there he was, and there Adam was not, and that would be the situation for a long time. She had to manage as best she could whilst he was away. At this point she was still half hoping she would get away with it and not be engulfed in a tide of love-misery as she had been with Will Morgan.

The next writer she met was the result of the introduction given her by one of her Oxford tutors, Dr Schwarz. Tilly Smith was a friend of his wife and known to be helpful to young women who wanted to get into the literary world. Jo still hoped to do this one day as a writer. As she could not touch-type and had no shorthand and ought to go to a secretarial college for a rapid three-month course, but had no money to pay for it, she knew she would be useless in a publisher's office. If she went home now she could go to a course in Manchester but that in her opinion was even more out of the question.

Tilly was a tiny birdlike woman with big dark eyes who took Jo to the Strand Palace for tea where they both consumed cream cakes. She was easy to talk to and recommended that Jo learned to type and then jumped off from there. The same advice had been given to her by the many publishers to whom she had written in search or a job. She did not intend to stay too long at the Municipal Halls.

In the meantime she wrote several short pieces about 'London Life for the poor graduate' but had no success in selling any of them. She continued to write and improve her short stories.

By the time her 'real' job began Jo had left Forest Top for the more central delights of Browncliffe Square, Earls Court – South Kensington if you stretched a point. It was not really a square but an oblong bisected by a road. Not a busy road but a useful one for getting down to World's End and the river. For two guineas a week she had found a 'top floor back' bed-sitting room in the house of a Mrs O'Connor, a spry, blue-rinsed widow in her late fifties, who owned one of the tall old houses on the square. Jo's new habitation was an eyrie with a sloping ceiling and a view over trees to the Boltons. Never mind that it had only a small gas-fire and a small gas-ring, it was hers, and nobody could visit it without her invitation. No more Mrs Dawson and problems over the butter ration or her correspondence.

For many years, as a child, in bed on sunny early mornings, Jo had lain watching dramas being enacted on the ceiling. The milkman would arrive, cars set off, all in colour. At first she had not understood what she was seeing, or how it was formed, and thought it must be magic. Later, she realized that a pinhole camera had been formed from a tiny chink in the dark blue curtains of her bedroom. She hoped she might find the same magic in the eyrie, but no, the curtain she had hung over the dormer window did not fit tightly enough. There was certainly no such magic in Browncliffe Square.

On Saturdays she would lie in bed for twenty minutes savouring the fact that she need not get up to go to work. Then she would let her mind wander and it was at these times that she occasionally had ideas for writing a poem or a short story.

Six months after the end of the war she had been taken to London on a visit and remembered the whispering gallery at St Paul's, Renoir's *Les Parapluies* at the National Gallery, and the queer stuffy smell of the tube. The St Paul's effect was not so impressive a phenomenon as the old mysterious silent cinema she had watched on her bedroom ceiling. This new London now had no apparent connection with her first visit, nor with her childhood. Neither was it quite yet the London of duffel-coats, coffee bars and the Partisan café. It was still often bitterly cold, and Jo's 'room at the top' was so chilly that Adam had given her a scarlet hot-water-bottle for her birthday – in lieu of himself.

'I told the girl in the shop it was for a girl who was cold in bed alone,' he wrote. He liked making suggestive remarks to young female shop assistants.

It was the last winter of thick, yellow-grey London smog. At the beginning of December they had said it was the worst smog London had ever known, shrouding the capital in near darkness for five days. One evening, Jo had stood with a torch by the roadside, along with Mrs O'Connor's other tenant, Martha, to help guide motorists lost on the Old Brompton Road. They did not know then that once the smog had gone, and the Clean Air Act had come in, London air would be fresher, until that new menace – traffic pollution – replaced the smog.

*

Jo had not at first believed that after all she had gone through with Will Morgan she could so soon feel for any else. Yet her feelings, aroused this time by Adam's, could be strong and tender. Was there something wrong with this? She had always till this time been the prime mover in matters of love, and she knew that she was now loved in the way she herself had loved in the past. She had not expected anything like this and felt that she had been given a precious treasure, was even a little frightened that she might drop it or smash it. She did not have to yearn for his love, but began to yearn for his presence. Most of the time she was alone, and did not mind that. She had always enjoyed solitude; it was the transition between the two sorts of life that depressed her. Whenever he went away it was strange at first to be alone at night; it was anguish of a different sort from what she had suffered with Will Morgan.

She dared not think too much of the future. To live in the present was enough at first – even if she felt she could hardly bear all Adam's adoration. She was happy to be loved, for nobody had ever loved her in this way, but where would it lead? Adam, in spite of his denials, was a very romantic man and she knew that he was actually asking a good deal of her when they both knew his wife and children had to come first.

She supposed that was the bargain she had made with him. However did he manage to fit the different compartments of his life together? Were men just better at doing that? Did she truly feel that with all her soul and body she belonged to him as much as a human being ever could 'belong' to another?

She felt she needed a certain ordinariness, an assumption of equality between them, a line to the future, and these things were not possible. Her love for Adam was marked from the beginning by the pain of missing someone she had never missed before. Although she tried hard not to feel resentful, she did feel resentment, not only that he was not free, was already involved, that he could not live with her, even eventually marry her, but that he had also taken away her own freedom.

She had sensed all this from the beginning but had discounted it, thinking she would have a brief and satisfactory love-affair with an older man. It was Adam who had turned it into something else. If he loved her, and if she returned his love as he wanted her to do, she would not be able to help wanting more. He said that since their first love-making she had changed him, that he could not believe how much she had made him feel. Sometimes he felt the situation to be impossible. Wasn't she too in an impossible position?

Adam wrote her many letters on the trains that took him back home after each visit to London, a visit he contrived to manage every two or three weeks. They were long letters, passionate, occasionally written in French. He said the effort to write in French calmed him down. Only by trying to express himself could he give back a little to her of what she had given him. His mistakes in French would make her smile, he said, but he liked to think of her smiling.

He made it clear in the midst of his avowals of love that he still loved his wife and that each woman had her place in his heart. They were both 'natural' yet both 'fatal' loves. Comparisons were odious; both his loves were complete in themselves. There would be crises but they would distrust them. They must hold fast to what was valuable and above all have trust in love. He said he was not a bad man; he wanted her to be happy, and her happiness was his. He needed her in order to be happy himself. Making love to her was valuable only because he wanted to make her happy. Truth resided in Josephine, he said – and reality. A deep truth, a delicate truth, which he could catch only in her, from her eyes and her feminine mouth. She was, he said again, 'innocent', and innocent most of all when she gave herself to him. . . . There was much more, and she was touched, but still always a little incredulous.

In the tube on their journey to Euston, the very first time Adam had been obliged to return home, a man had come up to them both. To Adam he said, 'I envy you your girl. You have made her very happy – everyone can see.'

It was an unusual incident. She must look transfigured. Adam himself had a yearning look she had never seen before on a man's face.

In another letter he went on to say that they would not be able to continue always 'on the heights'. Love must make them both bold, enable them to see a little further than each could alone. He wanted her to do great things; they must not lose themselves in love but find themselves through it. Everything was different since he had made love to her – the trees, the shadows, the sun – all were elemental things and she had brought them to him, enabled him to see them in a new light. He was not a man with much poetry, he said, but there was poetry in everything if you had poetry in your heart.

She thought, he is sincere in his sentimentality.

'I know no philosophy to which you do not hold the key,' he wrote the following week. He would adore her for ever.

From September until Christmas Adam wrote to her every day they could not be together. The first meeting after the weekend away and his subsequent return home had been in a small hotel on Bloomsbury Square. Adam had to attend a committee meeting for some academic body, and Jo stayed alone reading whilst he got on with his work. She wished she had something important to be getting on with; she did not like to see herself as a woman await-ing a man's return. But what could she do? Being with Adam was not conducive to writing. For that she needed quiet and solitude and time. Until November she was in a work limbo. If Adam had not been part of her life she would already have been continuing to work in some provisional job until then. As it was she would soon in any case have to find another.

'I heard you talking to me,' he said when he returned. 'All the time I was supposed to be giving them my opinions I was hearing your voice.'

'It's because we had been together talking for ten hours,' she said, for he looked genuinely frightened. She thought: he does keep his work and his love-life quite separate. That's why he was disturbed that I entered the other compartment of his life.

She still saw herself as uncertain, unworldly, quite intelligent, if not as intelligent as he was.

'Oh, you have a beta-plus brain,' he had said. Apparently her looks were alpha, and 'this was just as it should be with a young woman'.

She did not resent this, not having a very high opinion of her purely intellectual powers.

They stayed the next time in Chelsea, near the river, in a tall house that was not like a hotel, and had polished floors and flowers in vases and a general air of *fin de siècle* bohemianism. Adam said Jo was a bit of a Bohemian. Well, what was wrong with that? If she were not, she would not be here with him.

Christmas came, with only Thursday and Friday off, and the weekend, but it was her first visit home for many months, a journey that would take four or even five hours. King's Cross was crowded with people returning north. The big engines kept releasing their steam and there was a general air of excitement. Eventually she was pushed on to the train and had to stand in the corridor. A man came out of a first-class compartment and offered her an empty seat next to him. He was a businessman from Sheffield and said he enjoyed a chat. Jo obliged, and was offered a drink. Why was it that when one man found you attractive, all the others did? He got out at Doncaster, and Jo half an hour later at the terminus, still clutching the great bunch of mimosa she had bought in London.

Her mother and father were obviously pleased to see her, her mother quite nervous with apprehension, a great high tea drawn up on a trolley. Jo was terrified of saying Adam's name out loud, but controlled herself.

Christmas was as it always was. Relatives arrived to see her, and Jo would have liked to have had a little longer rest, but she had to return to work. London called, and Adam would soon be there in the New Year. Since childhood it had never been in Jo's character to seek sanctuary with her parents, where there was in any case no sanctuary, and where a private life was impossible, but she was tempted by the comfort, the big open fires, the food, and the genuine affection of Aunt Elsie and Grandma who came over on Christmas Day. But to enjoy all this she would have to become a child again.

'You like London then?' her father asked. Without thinking she replied, 'Oh yes!' and told him about Noël Gersheim and Tilly Smith.

She thought, Father thinks: 'London Fair' and all the world before me! The reality was already a little different.

In her eyrie Jo had her little Bush radio that had been given her the previous year for her twenty-first birthday. She wrote her diary every day with the Parker Duofold that had served her so well at Oxford. She missed Oxford and still wished she might study further, though what, exactly, she was not sure. Anything would be better than the work she now found herself doing at the Municipal Halls. It paid a bit more than Jo Lyons and you did not quite rupture yourself carrying files and forms, but it held no interest for her.

'Why can't you take an interest in it?' asked Adam on one of his visits.

'I can't. I'm thinking about you and that you're going away tonight.'

Her life was marked now by his departures and his absences, and by being without him for most of the rest of the time. He still wrote long letters to her almost every day and she replied. It was something they were both good at.

Every three weeks or so he would come down from Birmingham to see her, combining his visits with work. They always stayed in hotels, and Jo was now a hotel connoisseur; there was the Mount Royal, blissfully impersonal, where one could hide from the world. She thought he must have taken other women there. There was the pleasant old hotel in Bloomsbury Square, and some not quite so old places in semi-Bloomsbury, named from the titles of Scott's novels: Kenilworth, Waverley and Ivanhoe. There was a hotel on Berners Street, and another, smarter one in Kensington. But still her favourite was the small elegant one in Chelsea, furnished with vases and coloured tiles, where she had been happiest. So many meals, so much talk.

They usually ate their dinner at a Lyons Corner House where 'gypsy' bands serenaded her, or occasionally in Soho at places like Leoni's or Quo Vadis which had once been fashionable. (In Adam's youth, Jo thought disloyally).

They sometimes ate at the Strand Palace, one of their trysting houses, or frequented a little French restaurant on Wilton Road with good cheap food, or a Polish one in Grosvenor Gardens. Over these meals Adam would talk about his past life, people he had known in the war, and some of his past love-affairs. She could scarcely manage to disentangle all the names and places. What could she tell him in exchange? Adam would one day belong to *her* past life.

She had her hair cut very short after having it very long. Somebody asked her if it was the 'gamine' look. For once she was apparently in the fashion.

People were beginning to talk about teenagers – she was glad she was not one. This was the New World of After the War: The New Elizabethan Age.

Adam always talked a lot about the thirties, when he had been young. It appeared to have been a very exciting time. The war too had been exciting, and he had done important service in it. Jo had been only a child during the years in which he was saving the world for democracy – or socialism, as he liked to think.

She voted in the South Kensington local elections, not that any candidate she might vote for would make any different to South Kensington. Meanwhile the economy lurched along, stop and go, but usually with plenty of jobs for everyone. People were on the whole polite. Only late at night on Victoria station were there drunks, and mad old women, and tramps, and unpleasant incidents, and an atmosphere of violence.

The only possible prefiguring of the future was the glowing, vertical, cigar-shaped 'Skylon' that was still on the 1951 Festival of Britain site, and the first tall tower-blocks that were going up, built by the London County Council at Roehampton and Poplar.

Jo continued to confide in her diary:

It would be lovely to have a job I enjoyed – but I suppose it might take time from my inner life. I would still like more peace of mind. If only I could get conflicting ideas to disappear – perhaps someone like me will never attain that, never knowing what to think. Adam is so definite, has ideas and opinions about everything, but I don't think I could ever be like that. It is easy for me to slide into seeing the world as he does – when he is there – but almost as soon as he goes away I am back with different thoughts. So long as I can find more time for writing ... I want to write about the gap between 'love' and 'sex' and how you know when you have both together.

I suppose my character is still much the same – can you change after your twenties? I'm never satisfied; I sometimes sound false, even to myself. I make everything I do a sort of effort of will so I'm never spontaneous. But Adam appreciates me for what he calls my spontaneity! I long to be what I call 'natural' yet nobody else seems to think I'm not! Adam says I am always expecting to be disapproved of. I can be jealous – especially over Hermione, whom actually I think I would like – and I am possessive. I think I'm an idealist. I completely fail to understand the importance of social conventions. I am romantic – but so is Adam – and how! I am prone to self-deception. I'm often not happy.

She closed her diary with a flourish. She could never say quite what she meant – maybe she wasn't sure what she did want to say, but it was pleasant to write a slightly more cheerful diary after the horrors of N99. Her old diary had tended to be full of rhetorical questions which nobody was going to answer.

Surely a world with beautiful countryside and sun and flowers cannot co-exist with ugly urban squalor?
Why should I be privileged to deserve beauty? Just because I want it? But what makes me want it? And does everyone else want it too?
Is it just luck that throws you into a certain way of life?

Jo reflected now that she was not so 'lucky' as the tall, rich, perfect, band-box-emergent, fashionable women she saw strolling down Bond Street. She didn't want to be very rich, though she would settle for tall. Neither was she really interested in fashion. She would just like a few more nice clothes.

Was she 'lucky' that Adam had found her and fallen in love with her? He certainly gave a boost to her self-esteem. Adam said *he* was very lucky, said he had never expected that at forty-four he would fall so heavily and headlong in love again. Jo thought forty-four was pitifully old. She was only twenty-two and could not help feeling sorry for the 'old'. She was therefore sorry for Adam, thinking he might be depressed about his age, needing a small ray of love in his deprived family life.

Of course he was not depressed, and his family life was very comfortable, but Jo was not to understand what sort of man he was until many more years had elapsed – after she had long since passed the youthful age of forty-four.

FOUR

It was a Saturday afternoon in March and Jo had just washed her hair. Stephanie was to come for her at half past five and then they would be off to the Old Vic to see *Cymbeline*. She would almost have preferred to stay in her bed-sitting-room devouring the first of the six library books she had taken out that morning, but felt she owed a duty to herself to make the most of what was on offer. Why else live in London? You could just as well read books in Castlefield.

But in Castlefield, she reflected as she sat, one cheek burning at the gas-fire, drying her locks, in Castlefield, if you felt like having an affair with an attractive young man, never mind an attractive older one, everyone would find out. Castlefield had not changed much in the last hundred years and she and her sister were apt to call it Cranford. As for actually having a lover, apart from the fact that she had never met an attractive man of any age in Castlefield, unless it had been perhaps when she was sixteen and an 'older man' – of twenty-three – had taken her to a concert, well, it was beyond the imaginations of folk in Castlefield. Cranford would have called Adam an evil bounder, herself a wicked woman.

Jo met people at this time whom she would never forget. She

tried to write little sketches about some of them, people met in Kensington at meetings, or at the library, or at 10 Browncliffe Square. Beth Ackroyd, for example, a scholarly woman whose mother was in her late nineties and with whom she had struck up a conversation in the library and had continued on the pavement; Mrs O'Connor's daily help, Evangeline Glossop, who suffered from verbal diarrhoea and to whom Mrs O'C pretended to be deaf so that she need not reply to her endless diatribes.

'Such a good cleaner and apparently indestructible,' she remarked to Jo. Mrs Glossop came up to the top floor only once a week but Jo could see the difference afterwards, or rather smell it: furniture polish, window open wide, crumbs hoovered away. Jo always intended to clean round a little more but a quick tidy and washing-up and shaking of the bedclothes seemed to be all she had time for. She was not untidy so much as unworried about less than pristine surfaces. Once when she was ill in bed with flu it was Mrs Glossop's day. Then Jo learned what her landlady meant about the verbal diarrhoea. Mrs Glossop talked all the time, if not to Jo, to herself, and introduced new subjects just when you thought she had finished and were about to turn away. Politeness kept Jo immobile as in the glare of a Medusa.

There were other acquaintances who might one day be 'copy' for stories, she thought; men she still saw, good old friends, never likely to be lovers. There was Noah who was 'queer', and Justin and Robin likewise, a couple who however lived happily together; Theo, an old Oxford, almost-love who had married young and who farmed in the West Country. There were women too, whom Jo was not especially fond of but who had been thrown in her way. Maureen Higgins, for example, the acme of selfishness, who always had a man doing her bidding and always got her way. Maureen would not be believable in a novel.

But Jo's life in London was not full of attractive strangers, certainly not as full as it had been in Oxford. It was the principle that was important, and the freedom to be yourself. Not that she could have benefited from meeting really attractive young men. Adam stood in the way. Now that she could be herself she was stuck with a lover who urged her on the one hand to enjoy life when he was not there and on the other to remain in love with him and regard everything else as a bonus. She was constrained not to find any other man attractive, and miserable after Adam had left her. Very miserable – but not for long; her keel was re-balanced after a day or two.

The reason Jo was crouched before the fire was that she had no hair-drier; her old one had broken and she didn't have enough money to afford another. She ought to have asked for a hair-drier too when Adam took pity on her after she had described how cold she was in bed at the top of the house in Browncliffe Square. There were so many things she coveted. By listing them in her diary she could put them out of her head for a time.

> Item: A transportable desk, like the one Jane Austen used.
> Item: A portable gramophone. The old one has gone bust.
> Item: A midnight-blue, slipper-satin evening-dress.
> Item: A cravat to wear with my old-fashioned white blouse and the waistcoat that Aunt Elsie knitted for me. Some boots. Possibly a 'Cossack' hat.

With her first month's salary she had bought a handsome long black umbrella from a posh little second-hand shop in South Ken, but the other items, apart perhaps from the cravat, were beyond her means at present. There were so many lovely little shops selling old treasures – they were so much more interesting than the big department stores. Come to think of it, she actually *preferred* second-hand.

Adam had bought her a tiny Victorian pearl eternity ring which she wore all the time, though not on her engagement finger. His taste in clothes was not hers. He wanted her to wear tweedy suits, had actually marched her into Jaeger and bought her two the last time he was in London. She did not like either of them much but wore them for him when he came to see her. She suspected they were the sort of things his wife Hermione wore.

Stephie would soon be here, and they would meet Clare Jackson at the theatre. Jo brushed her hair, which was not quite so damp as formerly, made up her face, checked her handbag, and was pulling on her light-blue three-quarter-length jacket just as she heard the bell downstairs. This jacket, and a fashionable 'duster' coat, were the last two items she had been able to purchase in the sales before she left Oxford, before her grant had run out, and before Adam had taken her on.

Stephanie would not need to toil up the five flights of stairs to Jo's eyrie for Jo was ready for her and would open the outer door herself. She clattered down the lino-covered stairs that led to the top floor, and the carpeted ones in Mrs O'C's maisonette and finally the wider staircase that led down to the tiled entrance hall. It must once have been quite a handsome house; still was, apart from being divided up. Mrs O'C had a gorgeous sitting-room on the first floor overlooking the square.

Jo looked forward to being told all the latest gossip about their mutual friends by Stephie in the interval of *Cymbeline*. Stephanie seemed very happy, beavering away at her research. But then she did not have any problems to do with love.

Stephie had come to the conclusion that her friend Jo was the most peculiar mixture of the serious-minded and the rash and silly. Rash about men and feelings, led astray by her heart umpteen times. During their last year at university Jo had been in love with one man in the middle of February, with another six weeks later, and not much more than three months after that was hesitating about deciding to love Adam Angelwine who had fallen in love with her.

Stephie decided that, like Jo, Adam must be a slave to his feelings, even if they were genuine. She looked on from the sidelines and wondered how such a man could be regarded as grown up. Were all men like this, or was he unusual in deluding himself that his need for sex arose from romantic love? She thought then, in what she called her 'priggish' way, that what was permissible in a young unmarried man was not what you expected from a middle-aged one. But, unsuitable as he was, Adam probably loved her friend more than anyone ever had. Stephie suspected that Jo couldn't truly reciprocate, though she might give a good imitation of it. For Josephine, love had to be full of yearning and unrequital. A real romantic *she* was. Adam Angelwine wanted all of her; her life was to be subsumed in his – though he would have denied it.

Stephie was very fond of Jo, and sometimes wished she could be as open to her feelings as was her friend. Not that Jo was noisily or embarrassingly expressive, though she would occasionally say *outré* things to annoy or impress or irritate, as if she had a picture of herself that she wanted others to see, rather than the real person who might be quietly reading in the library. Stephanie guessed that Jo might actually be far happier reading in the library than messing about with love, though she had never spent quite enough time there, having felt continually obliged to give in to her romantic feelings. She might have been seen as rather giddy by the censorious but Jo was not in Stephie's considered opinion a 'man's woman'.

Jo had once explained to her that the reason for her slightly dramatic way of carrying on was because emotion of the 'getting above yourself' variety was frowned upon by her mother – unless of course it was Mrs Hill's emotion, which was allowable. Quite the opposite from the atmosphere in the Fischer household, which was more dependent upon Stephie's father's whims and opinions, but where nobody minded what you did because they hardly ever asked and did not expect to be told. She could be as eccentric as she pleased – they wouldn't notice.

Stephanie supposed that to the people who didn't know her

well Jo was thought of as a 'lightweight', 'not very profound', but pleasant and full of gaiety. She used to roll her eyes and say she was yearning for a green Chartreuse when about to go out with some young man, or she would show off the orchid the next young man had bought her for a ball and then spoil the whole thing by drinking too many gins. Well, they had all had to learn sometime and Jo had learned quite early on in her time in Oxford, thought Stephie. Jo still enjoyed drinking wine, probably more than most young women did, and still took emotional risks, which some young women never did.

Stephie had been the recipient of Jo's confidences concerning Adam and had listened patiently, not hesitating to give her opinion if necessary. Jo said she had good judgement. She had never actually read Jo's diaries, but Jo would often tell her that she had been rereading them, to 'try and understand myself', confessing that it was sometimes not clear even to herself which young man she was writing about. She'd turn over a page or two – she told her friend – with the same sentiments expressed as one the previous page and then realize that the object of her affections had changed.

Stephie thought Jo had been more ready to be impressed by Oxford than she had herself. Jo had appeared very young in her first term; well, most of them had, though some did seem to be middle-aged by the age of nineteen. Jo was not inconstant or fickle by nature. It was just that she appreciated so many people, saw so much that intrigued her, longed to 'experience' everything. Stephanie considered that her friend had a fundamental bedrock of northern canniness underneath all the froth, for she never neglected her work enough for it to be noticed. Nor did she get into the worst kind of pickle or have to be rescued by being sent away to recover from a 'nervous breakdown'. She was not a depressive, though she might often be anxious.

When they first got to know each other, Stephie would have said that Jo possessed a vivid personality. She was more talkative, more assertive than herself, but they were both capable of long periods of thinking and retrenching. Jo was thin, and her hair, swept up in a thick plait at the back of her head, had been long for years before she had it fashionably cut. She favoured bright colours and strong perfumes and Gauloises cigarettes, and tangos, kept a bottle of Madeira in her room, and flowers everywhere, especially mimosa, all things Stephie thought Jo imagined would be frowned upon by a puritan. She wore very bright lipstick and little scarves, or head-scarves and earrings and rings, for she loved jewellery as well as scents and flowers, and had once confided to Stephie that her favourite party-dress was still pink or pale-blue organdie with puffed sleeves. Or dark-blue velvet. She didn't have the kind of figure that you could show off. Not voluptuous, and too short to be elegant, but her legs were good and her features strong and pretty.

Stephie realized too that her friend appeared to withhold no mystery. What you saw was what you got. Neither was she devious or manipulative, and she was a loyal friend.

Oddly enough, Jo had often liked to be alone, to go on long walks by the canal path or in Mesopotamia, or to an art gallery. But she would say that her perceptions and sensibility – two of her favourite words – were not fine enough. She confided that she could easily see how others might see her as slightly vulgar, and it was true that 'ladylike' was the last adjective you'd use of her.

'My family know that I'll always cope,' she told Stephie. 'I've seen to that.' So she had to cope.

Jo is a survivor, thought Stephie. so many are not. . . . As for herself, had she already been drowned and saved?

She thought she had possibly not 'fallen in love' the way Jo did, but you might say that by the age of twenty she had far more real experience.

Men were always surprised when she took her clothes off.

Stephanie had first met Constantine Mitsoukopolis drinking coffee by himself at the Kemp Café, at the end of her first year in

Oxford. He had kept looking across at her and she felt she'd seen him before. He was by himself, looked older than an undergraduate, subtly not English. She was sure she had seen him working in Bodley. They began a conversation and discovered they were going to the same lecture by a famous writer. The best lectures in Oxford were not attached to a syllabus. Stephanie had so far attended discourses by Lord David Cecil, Isaiah Berlin and Kenneth Clark.

She knew straight away that this man would be the right man for her physically and that she would be right for him. She remembered someone once saying that H.G. Wells was so popular with women because he smelled of honey. Well, Constantine smelled of that: a sort of 'southern island' honey, but sometimes he smelled of toast, not surprising as he more or less lived on it. He was lonely and she supposed she might have given the – untrue – impression of being rather a lonely person herself.

He was of mixed nationality, his mother a mixture of Armenian and of some place in the Habsburg Empire that had changed its nationality many times; his father Greek. But he was to become American. In Oxford he was busy disentangling Balkan wars, spending his time as a postgraduate on a thesis on the Ottoman Empire and its influence. Stephanie found his insights interesting.

Nobody had ever known about him and her. It had gone on for a year and a half – a record for Oxford unless you were courting, which in those days some were. Their affair ended only when he had to leave. She suspected Constantine would become something big in government or in the United Nations. When he went away she did miss the intimacy. During her last six months in Oxford she missed him, but she did not eat her heart out. Perhaps something had been left out of her emotional make-up. He did write to her, though he'd said he might not – they'd both thought it would be pointless. By then he was in the States, and she was in London. They knew that if they ever met again by chance things would continue as before.

Stephanie had been very fond of Costas, and did not forget him. He was twenty-four when they met and he had had much healthy lust to discharge upon her, but when he left, she thought it over and decided that he had probably loved her. Later, she was to feel sure about that. Sex had got in the way for both of them – or had been of supreme importance – you could look at it either way, but it was only the outward manifestation of an inner togetherness. She supposed he was the best thing that ever happened to her. She had never told anyone about him. Not even Jo, though she had been tempted.

She thought Costas might now be disentangling present-day Balkan problems just as he had done theoretically in Oxford.

Stephanie brought her mind back to the present and to Jo who would be sitting waiting for her up in that top floor back.

She rang the bell; immediately she heard the clatter of shoes on the parquet and there was Jo, all ready to go out.

Jo was thinking the following thoughts, concerning her ever-present grumbles. Some of them were the same thoughts as in August.

> Curse Number One: lack of money leading to lack of freedom.
> Curse Number Two: the nature of her employment – also leading
>   to lack of freedom.
> Curse Number Three: or might it be a blessing – the problem of
>   love and marriage. Did she *want to be 'free'*?

It was agreed by the people who had known her as a child that Betty Josephine Hill was ambitious; they had always known she would leave home after her degree. She was an independent-minded girl who had even modified the name she was called by. Jo however knew that her fallings in love kept swamping her independence.

The reason she was – at times – not enjoying herself was still because of Adam. Having done her best to reciprocate by falling in love with him – he was a very capable lover – she found herself an actor in a play she had not written and had no idea where it was leading. If Adam loved her as much as he said he did she would now like to have him completely. Marriage with Adam however was even more remote than marriage with Will had been, as he had already been married twice and had at present a brace of younger children. So long as she could feel free she could put up with the situation but she did not feel free, nor did she feel properly attached. She was not the stuff out of which mistresses were made.

Adam laughed when she used the word.

'How silly,' he said.

Knowing that things would not change was partly the reason she stuck at the job at the Municipal Halls.

Browncliffe Square was to be her home all the time she persisted with this steady respectable job. There were one or two nice men at the office, especially Sammy Solomons who kept asking her to accompany him on Sunday walks taking Green Line buses to Burnham Beeches, or Amersham, or Dorking. There was Hugo Fylman who enjoyed his work, and Claude Haines who lived to write on the ballet, and James Jones, her section head, who was always kind and seemed perturbed that she was so clearly bored.

They were all fairly respectable conventional people, whereas Adam, as a thirties 'progressive', believed in free love. He also however did take seriously his obligations to his children, and Jo reluctantly agreed that they were the more important aspect of the whole thing. He might leave Hermione, but he could not leave Matilda and Phoebe.

He told her to enjoy herself without him when he was away, but at first this was impossible and she suspected he did not really want her to. He had a strong streak of jealousy.

He continued to be with her only every three weeks or so for a long weekend. The whole affair was extremely awkward and had to be kept secret from any members of the older generation, especially members of her family. It was a secret from all but Hermione, Adam's wife, who now knew all about it, and was apparently putting up with it. Jo's own friends knew about it too, but they were young, and uncensorious on the whole. Adam was certainly not going to divorce his wife. Not that he could, in any case, because it turned out he had never been legally married to her but to another woman he had left long ago. His present children were illegitimate. Another example of his having his cake and eating it.

At first Jo simply could not judge him apart from his feelings for her. Did all women go eventually with the man who 'loved' them? Why had she not had Adam's power to persuade others – at least temporarily – that he was in the right?

It would all have been perfect if Adam had not, contrary to his own plans, fallen in love with her. Now she was his object of desire – another person within the field of his extremely strong will.

Jo had already read her Simone de Beauvoir with all her talk of the Other, and how women were expected to be objects and never prime movers. Jo had been a prime mover all right with most of her infatuations – and she must have been with Will, though it had not felt like that. So now she still felt obliged to give back what she could and fall in love with Adam.

She could at least convey a healthy appetite fore sex. It was not difficult, even if she received little profound physical pleasure from his love-making, which was skilled, so it could not be his fault. She was however secretly ashamed of her efforts to please him, when she had even gone so far as to dedicate a few poems to him. They were what her old friend Robin would have called *forcés*, but Adam had not appeared to notice any lack of sincerity.

It had led her to wonder if by dint of effort you could actually fall in love; hoodwink yourself as well as the Other. She did want to love him, even if he did not deserve it, having had plenty of love in his life, from what he had told her. Perhaps it was enough just to want to love? On the other hand she was still flattered to be loved, still enjoying the power she seemed to have over him, though she was aware it might one day pall. Adam Angelwine was not an easy man; in fact she sensed he might be extremely difficult, especially in a domestic setting. It had not taken her many weeks to find that out, and she often asked herself why Hermione put up with him.

Adam organized Jo that first year in London, ordered that impractical young woman – who was yet a strong believer in contraception – to attend a family planning clinic.

Jo read: 'Until contraception can be devised which is foolproof, every act of coitus causes the specific implication of possible parenthood and must be viewed in that light.' This was from one of her favourite 'progressive' thinkers.

She had always been very aware of this, and knew she must visit a clinic so that she could be the sort of person Adam might continue to love. In the past, if she had been sure of not getting pregnant, she would have been less inhibited with some of the attractive men who had lusted after her, wanted her, with no mention of love on either side. They had never been the men she fell in love with, but she did wonder whether she ought to have given in just once. The fear of pregnancy had been too great.

She found a clinic near the Angel, Islington, which amused her, being half Adam's own name, but discovered they would not help her unless she were about to be married. Hastily she concocted a lie about a forthcoming marriage and invented a fiancé called George in Manchester.

They took details of her own income to ascertain what she could pay. How sweet. They had believed her. She wished she *were* about to marry 'George'.

She was fitted internally for a diaphragm. A new one of the right size in a little pink box was produced. She was instructed to put it in and then return to the consulting room. Well, they would know now she was not a virgin. Most girls pretended to be.

Yes, she had done it correctly. Jo was given a tube of 'Volpar' paste.

'After the honeymoon,' they said, 'if there is any discomfort, come back and we shall refit it for you.'

She thanked them and returned to her eyrie feeling vastly relieved. She wished she had not had to tell fibs, but until the world changed that was what you had to do.

Sometimes on Sunday afternoons, when Adam Angelwine was at home in Birmingham, Jo would walk to the Victoria and Albert Museum, a place that inspired her quite often to poetry-writing. It was a calm spot, where she could enjoy beautiful objects without needing to know too much about them.

She felt a different person in her own eyes when Adam was absent, different from the girl she was when he was around or the girl she thought he thought she was. Alone, she was paradoxically older, more independent, thoughtful, creative – happy. Whilst she was walking through the airy rooms of the museum, thinking about the porcelain or the pictures, she could not imagine Adam at all or even that he might walk with her in such a place.

Of course if Adam were in London on a Sunday afternoon she wouldn't be roaming round quiet museums but would have risen from some hotel bed and be engaged in packing away her life with him till the next time.

Then a farewell on the platform at Euston and a slow return on the top of a bus.

The Monday after the Sunday visit to *Cymbeline*, an odd play, and a Sunday afternoon spent at the V and A, Jo came rushing out of the tall house in the square. It was a cool morning and she was in a hurry to get to her job on time. First the Underground to Westminster and then a walk across the bridge. Jo could not imagine what it must have been like in the time of Wordsworth. Now it was not a fair sight even if a famous one. The river was a uniform dark grey with an occasional dredger chugging down from Chelsea or up river. There was a little pier in summer where boats occasionally sailed to Greenwich, and there were trees on this side, but she did not like the South Bank. They said children still bathed in summer near Tower Bridge but Jo did not trust the river. It looked so dirty and unwelcoming, quite different from its transformation into the Isis in Oxford.

Every morning the alarm would wrench her from deep sleep, in the bed with the mattress that sagged in the middle. She never wanted to get up, would have given her soul for another half an hour of delicious oblivion. The mattress did not bother her, for she was young and could sleep anywhere. It was true that she went to bed too late, reading far into the night, but when could she read during the day? Not at lunch time, for she ate her lunch in one of the semi-abandoned Festival of Britain cafés on the South Bank, a place not conducive to reading. Anyway, she needed to walk by the river to get some fresh air.

When work stopped at half past five she would rush back home on the Underground, buying her supper on the way – a few eggs or a tin of beans, or a herring, accompanied usually by a banana or an apple, all of which she would eat ravenously in her bed-sitting room with its sloping roof and view of the tops of great trees. Then she would once again leave her eyrie at the top of Mrs O'Connor's tall house, and go down the attic stairs from her 'top floor back', and through the door of the maisonette below, where Mrs O'C lived with her unmarried sister, who slept at the top of the house in a bedroom next to hers – clearly she was a poor relation.

She would run down the further flights of stairs, to the entrance hall, and go out through the front door. A little walk down the Old Brompton Road would bring her to the branch library. Most evenings she would visit this little library, the kind of place where she always felt at home.

It was a quiet life, but apart from the work, a happy one, solitary except for those weekends – about one in three – when Adam Angelwine would come and sweep her off her feet to the Mount Royal or the Berners or a dark hotel in Bloomsbury and make love to her for two nights before returning home to his wife. Apparently, she had now been told more about Jo!

'She is the only woman in England who would understand!' he said.

At such times, after he had gone away again, all her solitary happiness would dissolve and she would miss him bitterly and angrily until, after a day or two, her life adjusted itself again and she was back on her even keel to luxuriate once more in her freedom, her books, her 'London Fair'.

She paused this morning in the hall before opening the door to the square. Mrs O'Connor always placed her two tenants' letters on the table in the hall and there was nearly always a letter from Adam. Her landlady must have remarked the regularity of this correspondence. Did she think the letters were communications from her mother? Where did she think she disappeared to every week-end in three? She had not yet realized that in Mrs O'C's world people went away for weekends to the country as a matter of course.

Her Aunt Elsie had already visited Browncliffe Square and approved her niece's choice of lodgings. It was a very respectable house and Mrs O'C did not look like a landlady. Jo supposed she was eking out a naval pension, having some vague idea that the deceased Mr O'C had been a commander in the Irish Navy, if such a thing existed.

Auntie Elsie had returned home to the provinces saying she had enjoyed her little stay in London. Jo had taken her to see – and hear – Joyce Grenfell and they had both enjoyed that. Mrs O'C had graciously allowed Auntie to sleep on the *entresol* in a small box-room that was not used by Martha, who was a large young woman from Belfast.

Now Aunt Elsie had stopped sending her copies of the paper from home, the *Millsborough Clarion*, for as she said, 'I can see you haven't time, and you're not going to live up there any more.'

Jo had felt a bit disloyal. Should she have pretended to want to read the doings of her childhood village and town? She had not often thought about it very much in Oxford, but recently after her return from the time spent at her parents' for Christmas, memories had thrust themselves up into her mind when she was half asleep on the tube, or dreaming on the lumpy mattress at Browncliffe Square. She would see her father's garden as it had been in summer with the blue catmint and the white rockery flowers. He had planted a standard rose in the centre of their front garden, reached by some crazy paving, one of whose slabs was not like the other stones but was an oblong with its corners cut off and the following verses printed in curly script:

> *The kiss of the sun for pardon*
> *The song of the birds for mirth*
> *One is nearer God's heart in a garden*
> *Than anywhere else on earth*

There had been lilac in their garden too in May, dark lilac with bright green leaves, and they had a little crab-apple tree that was not like most crab-apple trees for its fruit was more like miniature dark russet apples, not yellow and pink as crab-apples usually were. Father had planted strawberries too, once the war was over and they no longer felt obliged to grow vegetables. In the back garden there were blue Canterbury bells and pink valerian, and enormous white and red peonies. But the flowers she sniffed the longest and loved the best were the rambler roses. They twisted around the 'rustic' fence and over the dustbin. There were pink ones, called Cornelias, and red ones just as pretty, but not so scented.

Like her mother's family Jo was sentimental, and could easily make herself cry. The easiest way was to recite the words of a song her grandmother had taught her mother about a dead mother:

> *Lay your head on my shoulder, Daddy,*
> *Turn your face to the West,*
> *For this was the hour . . . the hour Daddy,*
> *The hour that Mother loved best. . . .*

This still never failed to make tears run down her cheeks.

Her childhood had been so safe and on the whole happy. She had been fascinated by stories of strange members of the outer family who had formed the backdrop to her childhood, but myths had grown up around them and she was not sure whether they were still alive – Cousin Gwen who 'had a drink problem', Great-Uncle Reginald who was rich and mean. . . .

But Auntie Elsie had always loved her and she had felt she should try to make her happy, though her aunt was already a happy woman. As a child she had learned from this aunt how to polish fingernails and whiten their ends with a little pencil; to have a jewel box into which the jewels Auntie gave her were reverently placed; to take photographs with a little Kodak Brownie; to love cats and country walks; to know about gardens and flowers, and above all to enjoy music and singing. To all these feminine tastes she added perfumes. Her sense of smell was her best-developed sense and the day when Chanel No 5 arrived by post from her French correspondent was one she would never forget. She had never smelled anything like it. Only lavender and cologne with an occasional Californian poppy or a Bourjois *Soir de Paris* were allowable in her childhood, or had even been on sale during the war.

Her mother could not play the piano though she had a better singing voice than Auntie Elsie who warbled a soft contralto. Mother's father, Grandpa Wood, had one tune he played repeatedly whenever he came to tea. This was 'Robin Adair'. Who had taught him to play it – and when – was a mystery. He thought he had always known it. He had a good singing voice too, a reedy tenor, and would occasionally sing the words to 'Robin' with his own piano accompaniment. Auntie Elsie sang carols and Mother sang whole arias from Gilbert and Sullivan whose star she had been in the operatic society. But now they no longer produced the operettas her parents loved, only what Mother called rubbish, like *The Student Prince* and *The Vagabond King*. Jo remembered the smell of the programmes from these performances. Aunt Elsie had kept them in the white wardrobe in the Ell Room with all the other photos and operatic society programmes at Holmfield. They were probably still there.

It was odd how many of the family on both sides liked either singing or acting. Granny Wood's sister Alice did what Mother called 'mimo' – she'd walk around, or look in a mirror, with an extravagance of gesture, probably seeing herself in some part on stage. Alice had red hair – or rather had once had red hair – and was 'actressy', like Mira, Granny's own aunt. Great-Grandmother's sister, younger than she, born in about 1860. Mira ran away to go on the stage, ending up, according to Mother, who was vague about the details, in Rhyl in a concert party where she married the pierrot. She thought, Mira could probably sing well too. All that family could. . . .

But all these memories of her family made Jo's stomach churn. she had easily dissembled with Auntie Elsie who was not suspicious, though she worried lest her niece were taken in by, or even harmed by 'men'. It would be much harder to pull wool over the eyes of Mother if she ever visited. It had been bad enough at Christmas. If Mother visited London there would be letters to be hidden, remarks of friends to be monitored.

She had better try to use whatever acting talents she had inherited, for there stretched before her years of dissembling, or to put it plainly, outright lying. If her parents ever discovered with whom she was having an affair, it would, she thought, be a terrible shock.

But she could not consider her whole independent life a sham. She had wanted sexual experience, not a passionate affair. It was Adam Angelwine who had changed it into that.

FIVE

Adam Angelwine was not a tall man, and although he was slim he was strong, a good swimmer and climber. His hair was extremely fair, too fair for an adult, his father had always said. His eyes were his most arresting feature for they were a bright, gentian blue.

Jo continued to consider Adam assured about his opinions, perhaps too assured, in a way that she would never be, forgetting that he was twice her age and that she too could sound very convinced when she wanted. He also appeared full of self assurance, though it was true that he did regret some of his past conduct, he told her, especially towards women.

He did not regret it enough to change it, however; it took her some time to realize that, for he had always said she was the last, that he could never love anyone again as much as he loved, desired, adored, her.

'I am too fond of you,' he said. 'I hate that word – I am always afraid I shall end up in the *News of the World*.' She realized he was not joking. Yet how could all these preoccupations live alongside a scholar, an intellectual?

He had always treated women well, as far as sex was concerned, which the women he had desired had always enjoyed as much as he did, he said. He had not been in love with all his lovers but, even so, with many more women than most men would admit to, and he claimed he had received much devotion.

'I am not romantic,' he had told Jo at the beginning of his passion for her. Privately however she still considered him the greatest Romantic she had ever met, all of course mixed up with sex. He told her that he had kept one 'little girl' – and by this he meant a sixteen-year-old – for three years, and this during his first marriage. Sixteen appeared to be his favourite female age-group. He had been teaching at a university at the time and she was 'just a town girl'. Apparently she had been content to be a kind of slave to him, met him twice a week in a room he rented privately away from his family, but evinced no reaction when he had to leave that city for another post.

Then the war had come and he had resolved to change his habits. He had never seen any of these pre-war women again, apart naturally from his first wife. It was during the war that he had met Hermione, and eventually left his first wife.

Slowly Jo began to feel ready to confront the world alone; even perhaps imagined one day making love to much younger Adams. But the whole of respectable English society was apparently horrified by the idea of pre-marital sex. Most people claimed to believe the theory but it was not how many of them worked out their love-lives in practice. But people seemed scared of the power of sex, and feared for their daughters.

One thing about dangerous Adam Angelwine: she still could not help feeling, paradoxically, safe with him. Was it because he was nearer her parents' age?

She was determined that she would go her own way, would not be stopped from having what they called a sex life. But how could she have once believed that she had no desire to marry? When she missed Adam it was still because she wanted a settled life with him – even though at the bottom of her heart she knew it was actually impossible – even if he were the right man for her to marry, which at the bottom of her heart she also doubted.

*

Jo crossed the Old Brompton Road, and hurried down the Earl's Court Road to the Underground station. As she waited for the District Line train, she was thinking about the books she wanted to borrow from the library that evening. Whatever else was wrong with her life: work she did not enjoy and for which she had no talent, and a lover who had wrenched her from herself, she still loved living in this part of London, that you might, just, call Kensington. Once she was back in the room under the eaves she savoured her solitude. She was never lonely: there were plenty of old friends in London, especially Stephanie and Elinor and Clare, to visit theatres with, or chat to over cups of Nescafé or tea. Living here was a world away from the terrible Forest Top. She had thought she would never escape those three months of living on a ribbon-road under the shadow of hoardings at the end of a tube line. Now that was all over, and would never return.

There were no kindred spirits at work, where Jo was supposedly training to be an administrative officer in local government. There was however still Sammy Solomons, whom she liked, and who was still badgering her to accompany him on his walks in spring, the walks that began at the end of Green Line bus-routes. She decided he was genuine and took him up on his offer, feeling rather daring. Would Adam think she was being unfaithful to him? How ridiculous; she was only going for a walk, and Sammy was quite shy. She needed to get out of London more often.

From the distance of Oxford the post at the Municipal Halls had seemed a good idea; it was solid and secure and not as badly paid as some other posts. She had taken it to please and mollify her parents, not intending to stay there for ever. Her father had wanted her to go into the Civil Service and she had done well in the written papers but fallen down, as all the other women had, at the country house weekend which was not in a country house at all and where the only interesting thing they had talked about in three days had been whether girls should be good, or clever. She had argued insanely for virtue. This was in the spring before Adam Angelwine had suddenly swept her off her feet.

Her work now was even more tedious. Adam said she must master it, make the most of it, and then they would promote her. He was very puritanical about work, but she could not see him doing the work she did. He would never need to; he loved *his* work.

She tried at first to make up stories about the families whose applications for permission to erect garages in a certain south London borough landed on her desk. But there was not really enough time: everybody appeared to want to build a garage. She would come into the office in the morning and there would be a large tottering pile of pink applications waiting for her. She would deal with each one by reference to certain planning regulations and then attach the form to a new one, this time a blue one, and put it on another pile. Often her work was interrupted by the telephone which took precedence over the work on the desk. After eight hours the pile would have halved itself if she worked very quickly, but the next day it was back again to a new mountain of pink forms.

What possible reason could there be for a woman with a good honours degree to need to accomplish – badly – what the clerical officers could do so much better, especially since they had been doing it for years and knew the London County Council planning regulations by heart backwards? The job was supposed to lead to great things in administration. She did not consider herself above it, but was convinced she was so bad at it that it would not be very long before she would be asked to leave. Why on earth had she come here? Because she had passed high in the open examination for the post and it was like a Civil Service job, the sort her father wanted her to have – 'for security'. But it was deadly. As it was, she was always a few minutes late, hating to get up in the morning and having to rush madly to the tube station. By five o'clock she would have been willing to stay another half an hour so as to arrive half an hour later the next morning, but that was something the powers that be would not consider.

She was always pleased to return to the slightly faded grandeur of the Old Brompton Road. She knew that one day she might have another job, and another flat might claim her, but was reasonably content and, when she could forget about work, happy. Especially when she was left to her own devices, and could forget her situation.

She had pieced together more of Adam's's childhood and youth as he continued to tell her the story of himself, but he was still a mystery to her.

On the other hand Adam said *he* understood *her*, said he could be more objective about her than she could be herself. Perhaps he thought that as she had lived so much shorter a time there was less to understand.

She did not believe that he understood her. They were too different. She was to wonder whether what was hidden from view, probably because it could not be detached at the time from so much else of importance, would ever be unearthed by the one who wanted to draw out love from another.

A love-story – love itself – exists in a no man's land between the real and the ideal. Adam's infatuation for her that had begun when she was seventeen and brought her to him four years later depended upon her resembling a certain young woman: the one he had invented.

Jo enjoyed parties if there were interesting people to talk to and not just men trying to get off with her. She did not mind being attractive to men other than Adam but in the first eighteen months of her liaison with him she was embarrassed to have to explain the situation to others. Later, she became more than a little fed up with her apparently single life, at least to the extent of finding several young men 'interesting'.

The first party she went to on a Chelsea barge was a watershed in more ways than one. Here she met people who impressed her. There was a poet, a thin small man dressed completely in black, and there was an interesting woman called Gaye who worked with her friend Clare, and there were the Australians, the painter Julian, and a beautiful young woman called Julia with long auburn hair and an aura of mystery. She was wearing a pale-mauve cotton dress that went well with her greeny-grey eyes and alabaster skin.

Such women in Jo's experience did not often open their mouths, in case their words should shatter the illusion of beauty, or betray a mind less than subtle. But when this Julia opened her mouth she spoke sense.

She saw her looking covertly at her when someone else was speaking; they were all sitting round in the living-room–cum-cabin drinking Merrydown cider, not exactly the type of brew helpful when finding your way back on the gangplanks over the dark water at the end of a barge party. Julia was appraising her, that was the only word she could use to describe the look. It asked plainly: might you be a rival?

She shifted her glance before looking at Julia again. She looked the kind of woman who would be adored by men and who would herself take risks.

One thing that was useful about having a permanent lover was that you could always say quite truthfully that you had been claimed – were 'engaged' – if some other man who did not attract you tried to get off with you. Why she should need this excuse was not obvious to Jo. It was quite true that she felt semi-married, but why should it always be the men who made the first move? She hated hurting people's feelings, that was the trouble. Having an established lover who was not a fiancé, probably gave some men the idea she was easy game. Many men were so primeval and traditional. And what if a man did attract you?

For the first eighteen months of their love-affair, Adam's departures were still painful for her. After two days or so the agony abated and she grew back into her old self, but she resented having to be two people, less so perhaps when Adam took her away from London, to places like Rye or Winchester.

She read in a book about Peter Abélard by Helen Waddell, a book Adam gave her, 'And if it is agony, your going away, I sometimes think that perhaps God will let it be our expiation for whatever is unlawful in our joy.'

Adam had advised her to read many of his own favourites but they were hardly ever hers. He could quote large chunks from Shaw's *Man and Superman* and advised also Voltaire's *Candide*, the plays of Ibsen, and strangely enough Isadora Duncan, *The Good Soldier Schweik* and *The Architecture of Humanism*, by Geoffrey Scott. The only book he recommended that she took to like a duck to water was a collection of medieval Latin lyrics. She committed many of them to memory as she still did with Shakespeare's sonnets.

Adam would not have enjoyed the barge party. For one thing he was too old for them and affected to despise *la vie de Bohème*. But Jo sensed that when she was away from his influence she could enjoy herself even if, metaphorically speaking, the little icon of Adam with the candle under his face, that she carried round with her kept her safe, for the time being, from marauding males.

At the second party on the barge on Chelsea Reach there were several people whose lives she would follow with interest later. Stephanie was not there. It was not, as they would say later, her 'scene'. Elinor Knight and Clare Jackson from Oxford went, Elinor looking faintly disapproving and Clare looking interested. There was also her old friend Primrose; the painter from Australia; their old Oxford acquaintance Noah, already a notorious 'queer' and the fascinating Gaye Hardcastle. There was another man who a year or two later would rent out his flat to her; several other people who would eventually perish young in traffic accidents or cancer. But on the boat, in spite of the cold, they all appeared happy and carefree, still harking back to their student days or to the Festival of Britain. Too young to have become addicted to anything, they were not expecting to become alcoholics after their heavy consumption of Merrydown cider, and wine was far too expensive, drugs extremely rare.

There was such a crowd on the barge that night: friends of friends, some drawn by an invitation delivered to other friends drinking in the Eight Bells, others, like Jo, there with friends from Oxford. Clare was now working in an office with Gaye, who was quite a star on the barge, a plump, blonde woman with a voice like a purring pussy-cat. It was she who had asked Clare to come along the first time and bring a friend. How had Julia arrived there? Did she own the barge?

None of them knew anything about their destinies. They were young, clever, ambitious, well-educated . . . what could go wrong in their lives?

Julia, the beautiful auburn-haired woman, resurfaced a week later at another party. This time Jo was accompanied by an American graduate student of Adam's called Magdalen, who was astonishingly svelte. Tall, with silvery-fair hair, a round face and always ready with repartee, she made Jo feel provincial and dull. Adam had chosen her from a long list. Jo suspected he had gone mainly by her photograph, though he swore he had no intention of seducing her. She was detailed to introduce Magdalen to London.

Jo decided by early summer that she would not stay more than a year at the Municipal Halls. It would not be fair to go before her first year there was up, but she felt she would go mad if she stayed longer than that. Either she had too much to do at work, or nothing. They shifted her from 'Housing' to 'Architects' and she still puzzled over quantity-surveyors' reports and order forms.

The trouble was, what else was there for her to do, without touch-typing, and with only a useless Arts degree? Everyone, even nice Mr Jones, said, 'Why don't you teach?'

Adam was unexpectedly firm about her getting to grips with all this. Perhaps his idea of her was of a woman who easily mastered such details and would rise high in the field.

'But I'm not interested in it. I can't make myself interested – I do my best,' she cried. At such times she felt even more sore about his wife who didn't have to earn her living and who was allowed to have babies.

Her friend Clare said, 'I didn't think *you* were the sort of girl who wanted marriage and babies.'

'No, I'm not, and I don't really – not yet, anyway – it would never have entered my head if Adam didn't make such a fuss about my earning my living.'

This was not strictly true. She had always wanted children one day, even though she wasn't the sort of woman to swoon over swaddling clothes.

'But you do want to earn your living?' asked sensible Clare who was enjoying her work.

'Yes, of course I do, but at something I'm good at. I don't expect I could earn enough from writing to live on, but I wish I could use my brain on something – or that part of it that hasn't yet atrophied.'

She had already written several more sketches about living in London on a pittance but had so far had no success in placing them.

'I expect Adam feels guilty that he can't give you what he would like to give you so he gets cross about your attitude,' suggested Claire.

Jo knew she was right. She was filled with envy, and unhappy over her drudgery. Would she have felt so discontented if Adam had never sought her out? What *was* she good at?

She was trying to find work translating from the French. Adam said he might help: there was some ill-paid academic translation she might do. He asked around, and whilst she was waiting and hoping that something would turn up she applied, for fun, for a job in advertising, not expecting to get it. It was a big agency and she went secretly to the City for a test one Saturday morning. She was still employed and did not want her employers to know she was looking for another post.

The test was fun, more like a test for creativity than an intelligence test and she enjoyed writing copy and putting forward suggestions. What a difference from sorting out building works.

A week passed and then there was a letter from the agency: *Unfortunately the post is no longer available, as the person who was to leave us has decided to stay.* Her heart sank. Then, *However, you did really well on this test and if you wish we could keep your name and details should any other vacancy arise.*

Hooray. At last somebody thought she was not stupid. That was enough to keep her going for another few months. In the meantime, Adam came up with an eighteenth-century French text that needed to be put into modern English. It would not be easy, she saw that straight away. The publisher wanted an example of her efforts so she spent the next two weekends translating a section of the eighteenth-century gentleman's text. It was difficult but not impossible. Adam approved of her doing this. Not that it would bring much cash, for she would have to pay for a typed fair copy.

The publisher replied after about three weeks. Yes, she could take on the task, provided she checked it regularly with one of the editors, who lived in London. She signed a contract and for a whole year this work was to absorb much of her free time.

By the time she had been a year at the Municipal Halls it was November again.

She and Adam were to go to Catalonia the following summer. Adam planned some research in the archives of the Crown of Aragon. Not that he needed help; he just needed Jo to be there for two weeks on end with no interruptions. The round-faced blonde, Magdalen, his post-graduate student, was to continue some of this research the following month when the other two had gone.

Magdalen still fascinated Jo: her accent, her assumptions, her transatlantic directness. But no more than Jo did she appear to have found the right man. She seemed to want to get married even more than Jo did, having been in love for three or four years with an impossible academic. Magdalen was clever and asked her things about her sex life that nobody had ever asked Jo before. But she had read a good deal by now in Kinsey. Magdalen also made Jo laugh:

'One thing I just can't stand are other people's pubic hairs left on the bath,' she announced.

But it was sometimes difficult to know what Magdalen was driving at. She made Jo feel that she too should be doing post-graduate work. Why was she not? Why was she slaving at the Municipal Halls? Because love had got in the way of her work, and if she wasn't careful, love would always get in the way of any success she felt she might achieve.

My life doesn't make sense, thought Jo. I work at a job for which I'm ill-suited; I toil over a translation that will not bring me much money and I see, when I can, a man with whom I can never come first, however much he would like it.

She learned a lot about her lover during that summer month abroad, and she was to conserve the happier memories for ever.

In the bedroom of their hotel on the Ramblas the shutters were closed over their windows in the afternoons, when they had their *siesta*. The room was bathed in the colour of eau-de-nil. Sometimes afterwards, at the end of the afternoon they glided into the warm bath of the Mediterranean, gently knocked on pebbles and gravel by the swell of that tideless sea.

One day they went up into the mountains, passing rocks with pinkish-grey pebbles buried in their faces like doves' eggs. Always the heat, and the blues and greens of sky and land, and the still brighter blues and greens of stiff cotton dresses. Everything seemed enamelled. Their own bodies were filled with wine and salty fish and olives and chicken. Jo knew the restaurant killed the chickens in its own kitchen – poor suddenly murdered birds with their red and yellow innards making glaring jazz-like patterns on the kitchen table. . . .

Adam read to her from the archives of the Crown of Aragon, an account attested by public notary from the lady who in 1319 claimed to have borne King James of Aragon twin sons when he was campaigning in Sicily in 1287. The king said he had no recollection of the affair but *she* remembered all the details, said she was taken by four men of his household to his chamber on Thursday 15 May and described his room with its 'three torches on three candlesticks throwing light on the head, foot and middle of the bed, and the white unhemmed linen, the pillow of Bokhara stuff and the edged coverlet.' The lord king sat on his bed which was low, without legs, and made her sit on the same bed. His shoes were scarlet with pointed toes, and he had a vest of silk. They dressed her or she was already dressed in a gown of emerald green, and wore a turned-up head-dress of the colour of gillyflowers ornamented with gold in the Calabrian fashion, and a belt made with deerskin with a silver buckle. Her hair was dressed in the Latin style and was pleasant enough to look at on account of its sheen. Her skin was pale, her complexion highly coloured, her face animated and pleasing; she was then about twenty-seven years old, medium in height or even small.

She said that the lord king on the evening of Ascension Day made himself known to her, saying: 'Have no fear for I am King James!' and on the Friday morning he said to her: 'Rest assured that no harm will come to you. . . .'

Jo realized Adam was thinking of her. But *she* was not a fourteenth-century lady! Far from it: they had already had one or two silly arguments, even though Adam was on the whole more relaxed than in London.

Later, she could not for the life of her remember exactly what she had said to annoy him, but it had been on a tram when she had possibly corrected some misapprehension he had about what the numbers of 'denier' found in stockings, actually meant. He hated to be corrected – or even informed – about anything. She was usually careful not to try. This was not a matter that really interested her but his attitude made her furious.

After an outburst in which he told her she was being 'schoolmistressy', he sulked until they got off the tram. At such moments she would have liked to walk away out of his life.

She had to say goodbye to him on the station because she was returning to London and work by train and he was going home later by air. She thought how much less grievous partings must have been long ago: a farewell from a rider on horseback, no railway station to draw all the pain of parting into one tight clot and then when the train moved away – snap! the life-force was broken, trailed away, seeped into little red capillaries, railways lines, tears. . . .

But working abroad had been delightful: the sun, the food, the cool little *bodegas* away from the noonday heat, reached down rickety steps where you sat on upturned casks to drink your sherry; the courtyards with their palm trees; the old Gothic quarter; the mountains not so distant, and the sea. . . .

On her return to London one of the editors asked to see her about her translation of the first half of the book. It was 'not quite satisfactory'. She knew she had not made enough effort but was determined not to fail, so the following evenings of her precious free time were spent checking and altering, improving and polishing.

She presented herself at the publisher's office one Saturday morning to see the editor who lived out of London. Mr Wiltshire was a tweedy pleasant man whom she took to immediately, and she wanted very much to make a good impression on him. He was old, but younger than Adam.

Adam came to collect her from the Mayfair office at lunchtime. He looked so old and oddly dressed compared with the handsome Wiltshire, who she knew was six years younger. Adam was not tall like Wiltshire but she was a small woman herself; why should she want a taller man? Jo was shocked at these disloyal thoughts and tried to forget them.

Her efforts at translation were eventually pronounced passable, and she finally managed to achieve the approval of the other, more difficult, editor whose comments had been more critical. It all made her feel she had not made too much of a mess of her life so far. The translation had taken her a year, and it would be another year before it saw the light of day.

She wrote again to the advertising agency but there was still no vacancy. Rashly she decided that if she could not get into the literary world through secretarial work she might get into it through retail work. Books were a commodity she knew something about. A bookshop then?

Mr James went on saying she ought to teach. So did Clare, who had decided to do so. Stephanie was still enjoying herself with research for her Ph.D. at the Senate House. Jo envied her. Could she try to get a grant herself to do a further degree? It was an idea to tuck into her mind. Her old tutor Katie Drines would always give her a good testimonial. For the present it joined her long list of 'Possible Employments'.

Selling books was hardly on a par with administering, or writing advertising copy – or free-lance translating – but it would do for a few months.

She sent in her resignation to the Municipal Halls Establishments Officer.

Clare's friend Elinor was a woman whom Jo could not like, though she tried. She was very critical, made no pretence of approving of Jo's extramarital liaison and denigrated Adam. Clare reported it was because Elinor was shocked. Shocked that such a man as Adam Angelwine should involve a young woman like Jo Hill in his *amours*.

On the other hand, Susie Swift, who had stayed on in France for a time but was now back in England about to join a newspaper traineeship in the Midlands, took it all in her stride. Susie, who now appeared to spend all her spare time painting, was never judgmental, but she was judicious, told you what she thought. In an impersonal way, however, almost as if she was taking it as an example of a well-known human quirk.,

Stephanie said nothing, only listened to Jo when she needed an ear, but Jo did not talk so much now about Adam.

Disapproval did not worry Jo, especially when it came from a woman like Elinor Knight, but she had for some time had nagging doubts over the future of their love-affair. Adam still wrote to her almost every day and she had every possible proof of his physical devotion to her. Why did it not seem to be enough? Did she just not love him enough? She remembered her feelings when comparing Adam with the editor, Norman Wiltshire, and it made her uneasy.

SIX

Almost two years had gone by since Jo moved into Browncliffe Square. A time of busy weekdays, evenings spent toiling over her translation, Saturday mornings passed pottering or shopping or choosing library books, afternoons often at matinées with Stephie or Clare or even Elinor, every weekend in three still spent with Adam. A second winter had arrived and with it, as the fogs came down, a letter from Jo's sister Annette. Hard on its heels came Annette herself, who had decided to come to London for work whilst she painted in her free time. Annette could not possibly manage to pay for a room by herself. She must share a flatlet with Jo.

Jo therefore reluctantly agreed to share with her sister, to leave her eyrie at Mrs O'Connor's, her quiet top room, which was not big enough for them both. The best times had been the solitary hours she had spent there reading – or even toiling with the translation.

This had been before Jo was to leave the job at Municipal Halls. Adam was very disappointed that Jo was about to give up this solid safe job. She felt her situation was becoming intolerable. Really, Adam might as well be her father!

She took her sister to see friends and introduced her to those who were still partying on the old barge. Eventually, they crossed

London to NW3 to look for new digs, and found a large basement at 6 Goddard Road.

Six weeks later they were asked to leave. They had 'not maintained the stove' in the basement to the satisfaction of the owner, Dolly Llewellyn, a retired singer of opera, and she had seen 'a man' shaving at their sink.

The 'man' staying in their basement flat was the painter Julian East to whom Annette had been introduced on the barge and had promptly fallen for. The Merrydown cider might have helped.

Jo was not sorry to leave Hampstead. She longed to return to Kensington. She wrote to Adam about it all and he was dismayed, did not want her to be part of this *vie de bohème* – particularly a poverty-stricken Bohemia.

The sisters moved back to the Old Brompton Road district at the New Year to a shared double bed-sitter at Lansdowne Gardens W8. Adam did not like this arrangement one bit either and never visited Jo there. He had never shown his face at Browncliffe Square; their meetings had all been at hotels, Jo's favourite still the small Pre-Raphaelite-looking private hotel in Chelsea, off Cheyne Walk, where there were always large blue vases of flowers and an air of an aesthetic past. But they never went there now. . . .

In the New Year, after moving to Lansdowne Gardens, Jo found work in Charing Cross Road in the foreign department of Foyles, the – World's Biggest Bookshop – hoping that this experience in retail mode would find her work in future with a publisher.

She would be kept even busier in the shop than in the Municipal Halls on its most frantic telephone morning. The assistants scurried around looking for books for customers, though it was intimated to Jo that, so long as a sale was made it didn't really matter if she found the right book, the one the customer wanted. It was rather like Jo Lyons and the pretty salads.

She decided however that toiling in the shop was much more interesting than sitting in an office. It taught her a lot about people. For one thing you could observe national characteristics, which some people assumed to have been ironed out.

Many foreigners came looking for books in their own languages or came just to browse, especially students, who did not usually buy anything. The French and Spanish and Italians gabbled a good deal to each other and, if they were male, flirted with the female assistants. They were either quite brazen, suggesting you reduced the price of some tome, or cross and easily annoyed, never hiding their irritation.

If Jo asked them in their own language whether they were French, or Spanish, or whatever, their faces became wreathed in smiles. But the Germans and the Scandinavians were solemn, usually erudite, especially in recondite subjects, and they would almost finish the book before they decided to buy it. They flirted with their eyes, preferred to speak English, not welcoming an attempt to speak their own language. The Germans were the bossiest and also the most knowledgeable, the Italians the most lost-looking. She decided the Americans were the cheeriest and friendliest and the most democratic. Frank and friendly, they asked for advice, which she was always pleased to give, and would even ascend ladders instead of letting her do it. The English were on the whole the most polite, and the meekest, the most diffident, the most easily pleased, the least troublesome. The French fussed delightfully, the Germans knew exactly what they wanted and kept her busy trying to find it in the maze of shelves and tottering piles of books.

Jo even came across a couple from Yugoslavia, whose nationality puzzled her at first. Dressed in light-blue suits they asked for a guide to London. She went to look for one and whilst she was away the man found an almost hidden shelf of books in Serbo-Croat. The couple smiled and smiled as they paid for their guide book. It was extraordinary how many hidden shelves there were. Books had piled up from what looked like half a century and there did not appear to be one person who knew the complete stock.

Above all, Jo sold textbooks: grammars, school-books, vocabularies for aspiring travellers or self-educators, often to children clutching book-tokens. She wished the children would buy a story-book. Surely they did not prefer school texts?

The most eagerly sought-after books, after these worthy ones, were books of travel and adventure in every language under the sun. Jo sold French plays, German song-books, Italian novelettes, juggling them with the search for 'a nice book for a Dutch child. Their family helped my husband in the war.'

Once a man looking for a book in Flemish said: 'They tended my father's grave when he was killed in the first war.'

A didactic German lady demanded an improving book in German for a child. Jo searched out a translation of Beatrix Potter.

'Oh dear no,' said the lady. 'Children should read more and look at pictures less.'

Jo got her own back by offering a sober-looking translation of Enid Blyton in German suitable for a nine-year-old. She was sure the poor thing would enjoy it.

There were also some strange-looking sallow men who would converse in undertones behind piles of second-hand French novels.

'I took that away from my wife,' she overhead one of them say.

His companion replied: 'Oh, things get into books nowadays that should never be allowed.' However, they eagerly continued to 'brush up their French'.

The shelf of illustrated medical books was another favourite for another type of customer. There were men – they even wore mackintoshes – who stayed all day to read and had to be politely shown out at closing time. One of these men actually once bought a book. He reminded her a little of Noël Gersheim.

'I do hope you'll enjoy it,' said Jo, which was what she usually said. Then she saw the title: *Psychopathological Diseases*. Perhaps he did.

Every morning they would go down to collect the new books, shiny, and smelling of new paper and print, which Jo sniffed with pleasure. There was always a crowd of 'regulars' waiting for these, ready to pounce. The flow of books was never-ending, as was the flow of customers.

It was tiring, of course; eight hours on her feet with a continual telephone buzz, with requests for 'Gerty', or 'that naughty French book', and once a demand for her to translate a letter from a French hotel that the customer intended to visit.

'My French is a bit rusty, you see. I thought your department might help.'

Jo knew this was not one of the jobs she was supposed to be doing but at least it gave her feet a rest. Patient helpfulness was wearing, but she loved helping people to what they wanted, loved to make suggestions. Books were so much more interesting than food, or forms.

When she had finished her day's work she sometimes took books back to the flatlet with her, for underpaid assistants could buy them at a discount. She spent far too much of her wage on them. In the evening she relaxed and read and hoped that all the people she had met would enjoy their reading as much as she did.

But of course she realised that all this was not a substitute for learning to be one the competent typists publishers needed. In fact her career as a bookseller came to an ignominious end six weeks later.

On one of those long February afternoons, a Friday, a man came into the foreign department looking for the poems of St John Perse. Jo recognized him as the friend of a friend of Clare's, a post-graduate whom she had last seen in Oxford. It turned out he too was a poet and critic. His name was Matthew Francis. She decided on the spur of the moment to take Matthew home with her. Was it that she was so dissatisfied with her life with Adam? Now, after almost two years of Adam, she was going to be unfaithful, for she had fallen for Matthew Francis in a big way.

For the sake of this young man Jo did not go into work the following morning, a Saturday. It was true that she also had a bad cold and a headache. But people could not have days off, however bad their colds, even if they telephoned the reason for their absence, even if they offered not to be paid for that day's work. There was no such thing as sick-leave; there was always another person ready to step into your shoes.

Going into work on the following Monday she received her cards and her dismissal. She knew she had been an asset to the department, but that counted for nothing. Assistants were in constant supply.

Matthew went home for a week or two, but she thought she had found her ideal man, felt she had everything in common with him. He was even interested in her own writing.

He said he travelled with nothing but his typewriter, his toothbrush, and a packet of Durex.

She wrote to Adam, and confessed. Adam was frantic, wrote her a letter of forty pages in reply.

Now she must look for another job.

Matthew, also a northerner, invited her to stay with his family, who were kind but wary. She watched him devote all his energies to his writing, saw clearly that he needed an amanuensis, and wanted a woman for when he had finished work for the day. That work came first for him, did not stop her from sleeping with him when his parents had gone to bed.

She returned to London, to Lansdowne Gardens, and waited to see what would happen.

Matthew promised to come for Easter. She waited in all the Easter weekend, but he did not come. She could have loved him so much, she thought.

Jo found temporary work as a technical translator in an enormous

Ministry, one that faced the building across the river where she had worked during her first year in London.

She wrote an article entitled *Selling Foreign Books*, giving herself a new name. Something had to be saved from the ship-wreck of her second job-failure. To her vast surprise a newspaper took the article and she appeared at last in print. She wrote further articles about her many-sided London job and flat life, another one of which she was at last able to sell. For her own plea-sure she wrote several short stories. Matthew had praised those he had read and she trusted his literary judgement more than she had trusted his earlier avowals of love.

He had liked a short story she had written about walking on Port Meadow in Oxford, near the canal, when a sudden pounding of hoofs had alerted her to horses racing across the field. Her heart had thudded as loudly as the hoofs. Then the animals suddenly stopped and began to nibble the grass. She had passed by a bridge, and then before her was the church that was not a church, a triumph of Victorian engineering – a pumping-station full of great pipes and machinery where there should have been a nave. She averted her eyes, hating any building that was not what it seemed. The atmosphere was what she wanted to convey.

Another 'atmosphere' suffused the story of the child Karen, which she set in Brighton, and yet another surrounded the tale of Kristin which still haunted her imagination. She continued work-ing at all of them. It was no good asking Adam's opinion; they were not the kind of stories he would ever read. Nobody would want to publish them, she thought despairingly.

'I am only good enough for journalism,' she said to Adam, to whom she had eventually returned. He looked puzzled.

Whilst she was doing her historical research Stephie Fischer found the germ of a historical novel taking root in her mind. She kept this to herself. She had to finish her thesis first, and then she would see. She looked around her friends in London, and reflected that if Oxford had lent itself to some people's social mobility, London was an arena for moral responsibility. She had met Adam Angelwine a few times. In many ways she thought him impressive, and he was very obviously crazy about Jo, but she still had reservations she supposed she must call 'moral'. This sounded strange in her own ears for she had behaved as she wanted with Constantine, and had never had any hang-ups about sex. Nor did she find that love-affairs involved 'problems'. She had no religious belief. But she worried about her friend.

Stephie was often to ask herself what Jo would have become if she had never met this professor of hers at the age of seventeen. To her mind there was nothing inevitable about it, if nothing unnatural. Jo was the sort of girl with whom an older man might easily fall in love, especially a romantic man who had a lively imagination and needed to create an ideal young woman, however much he denied it. Adam always claimed he was different from most men, but the only difference Stephanie could discern was that, like a woman, he used the word love for his strongest feelings of passionate sex. You might think that would go down well with women, but it would depend on their age and experience. He must have had many affairs or shorter episodes that he did not dignify with the name love, but according to Jo he discounted these, was almost ashamed of them.

Stephanie didn't think Adam liked her. Probably because she didn't truly like the fact that he had seemingly succeeded in sealing off her friend's options. He was the wrong man for her. If Jo were not careful she would find her future choices altered or restricted in ways she had not envisaged. Stephie had always known that for most women the years between twenty-one and twenty-nine were the years in which to find a partner, a father for her children. Not that everybody found the right one, or made a success of the marriage that followed, but that was the ideal. Many women thought they had found the man they called Mr Right.

If Jo had been less prone to self-deception and Adam had been

113

another kind of man, one less wilful, less clever, less successful, less self-confident, less used to having his own way, younger, unmarried, he might have suited her better. But then he would not have been Adam. Stephanie suspected that he was not the kind of man whose primary attraction for Jo was a physical one. She could see why Jo had fallen for Matthew Francis – and also why she had known she would return to Adam.

Adam had plucked out Jo before she even knew what she wanted, and Stephanie for one could not forgive him for that. It was as though Jo was handing herself over to an arranged marriage, when all she had truly needed was a satisfactory sex life with someone like Will – or requited love from a man like Matthew Francis. She ought not to forgive *them* either, she supposed. Adam did love Jo, acted decisively, and was not ashamed of his feelings. But he was too old, and Jo was not the sort of young woman who wanted a trophy husband or lover.

People had always told Stephanie that she had an old head on young shoulders, which had annoyed her; but she did wish that Jo had a little more of this attribute.

Jo wore a new pair of high heels, used Max Factor pancake foundation, and a bright-red lipstick called 'Touch of Genius'. She kept her make-up handy in a big silk handkerchief for quick renewal.

Adam took her to Paris in May and introduced her to a very old friend, André Bernard, a tall, bald-headed, poverty-stricken Flamand he had known all his life, the son of a friend of his father's, connected with a business partner from Schnechtel Bros., Lille.

André was looking at her appraisingly. She hoped he did not think her too dowdily English, or – the opposite – an over-made-up English girl who wore bright colours. This was certainly more Jo's line. She was to learn later that André had advised Adam to tell her not to prolong the line of kohl at the corner of her eyes too far.

André was homosexual but was clearly intrigued by their relationship. He spent most of the time sitting in a café with them,
demonstrating the wonders of his pendulum.

'I ask it questions – any question – and depending on the left or
right swing – you see – the answer is Yes or No.'

He knew all about Adam's long-ago love-life and had met his
first wife.

'Oh, poor André used to be in love with me,' said Adam, a little
too complacently.

He and André spoke of people they had both known well, and
Jo saw that they both belonged to another generation, to the past.
I like older people, but I am *de trop* here, she thought.

She returned to her temporary job at the Ministry, where she
spent hours over attempts to understand technical writing. She
could hardly put it into English if she did not understand it. After
countless explanations, how a jet plane kept up in the air was still
mysterious. Her office companions were mostly foreign, but the
woman in charge was an old civil servant, a redoubtable feminist,
and Jo quailed before her knowledge. Occasionally there were
more interesting things for her to translate, invariably to do with
people's lives. She read of servicemen's marriages and divorces
but mostly the work was classified and she had to sign the Official
Secrets Act. Why, she did not understand. Were they not now at
peace? But no, the cold war had hotted up.

She and Annette had been six months at Lansdowne Gardens
sharing one overcrowded room, but now there was the possibility
of renting a cold-water flat in a large, shabby early Victorian house
in Pimlico, with their own entrance on the first floor. Their immediate landlord was a journalist who had originally intended to live
in the flat himself. A woman graduate friend of his had rented it
for a year or two but now it was free. Adam said they must make
enquiries about who the freeholder of the house might be, in case
there were repairs needed, or anything went wrong. All Jo could

discover was that the owner from whom the journalist as sub-tenant had originally taken a lease was a strange woman called Mrs Pound whose niece Theresa lived on the ground floor. But Mrs Pound was not the freeholder and it transpired that Mrs Pound's husband was in prison for GBH.

Adam said, 'She must have a lease either from the Church of England or the Duke of Westminster who probably owns the free-hold, since it's all part of the Grosvenor Estate.' The flat was not ideal, for there was no hot water and the bathroom was outside the flat proper on the half-landing, but it was roomy, had a balcony and was convenient for the Tate Gallery, the Victoria Underground, many shops, and the 24 bus.

Annette, with Julian in tow, took the smaller of the two rooms and Jo took the larger that led on to the kitchen. It was at about this time that she acquired her first cat, Cleo.

Before they had lived there more than a few weeks they realised that Theresa was some sort of call girl, and that on the top floor lived Valerie, a tall black girl who regularly entertained male 'visitors'.

Adam knew he could not argue about Jo's choice of abode. For the time being it would be a good base. He bought her a bed which she promptly put on the floor without its legs. Adam did not like this and still preferred to take her to hotels. Perhaps he was just too old to live in this way.

'If I had more money I might live differently,' said Jo.

She had gone back to Adam after three months. Matthew had left London for the time being. She did not regret Matthew – it was all over – but she ought to have been more honest, kept herself away from men for a few months, ought to have been cruel to be kind, and taken the chance of leaving Adam for good. But when she sought him out in May at the Mount Royal, knowing when and where he would be, he was so unhappy, and then so overjoyed to see her again, that she had not the heart to do it. The reunion had been tearful on Adam's part but left Jo feeling even guiltier. She had glimpsed herself in the long mirror of the hotel bedroom and been surprised, then put off, even disgusted, by what she saw: a small tousled naked young woman carried to bed in the arms of a middle-aged man. She saw herself suddenly as an object, in no way resembling how she usually thought of herself. She preferred to be a clothed, reasonably attractive, rational person – with great passions, sure, but not an object, not a plaything. Would she have been better pleased to have made her life with Matthew? Probably, but he was now doing his National Service which had been deferred, and in any case would never *marry* her, she was quite sure about that. He didn't love her, and Adam did.

Either Adam could marry her, Jo went on thinking, and that would be a different kind of life, or he could cut her free, decide himself to let her go to find her own level. She explained to him in subsequent letters how she felt. He thought she was only grumbling, which partly she was. Was it better to learn to put up with everything, or was it disloyal – even to him – to be able to do so? The transitions between one life and another were what still hurt.

Obviously Adam did not feel this, kept his life in those watertight compartments. When he missed her physical presence he would write a long letter, and then, she suspected, probably go back with renewed energy to his work. He said he had not known how his life would be so totally turned upside down.

'It is quite overpowering, a self I do not know and whom you alone have evoked. What have you done to me? What have I done to you? I adore you, come what may, please never doubt that, a love so deep that I have really never known anything like it before and never shall again.'

She thought, he *ought* to have known. His belief in her and adoration of her sometimes frightened her.

Impossible circumstances for an impossible love, poured out on paper, at first day after day, then month after month, finally year after year. He still wrote almost every day when they were parted, often when he said he felt 'incredibly weary'.

117

It was easy for her to say he wanted to have his cake and eat it, which was undeniably still true – but he also suffered. Even if she knew she was not exquisite or extraordinary or incomparable, she liked to hear it. What woman would not, she thought. However ordinary Adam might say his painful longings were, she thought that in their intensity they were not ordinary. When he was with her he sometimes wept, often said he felt frightened, lost.

Once he cried, 'I love you too much – I don't even want to make love to you.'

He had once said that before he ever had any children he had day-dreamed he would have a daughter, and would have wanted one just like her. His own daughters were quite different from Jo. 'But I am glad you are not my daughter,' he had added.

That was surely not why he had fallen in love with her. His life was a success. He had everything that she wished she had for herself – a home, daughters, a career – and a spouse who loved him.

She must live in the present, Adam told her, another of his maxims and one not easy to put into practice.

I must not still be poised between nostalgia and anticipation – or apprehension, she wrote in her diary.

The work at the Ministry would be over by July and she had accepted Hermione's startling invitation to go abroad with her and Adam and their children. Jo had now met the astonishing Hermione, and admired her. She hoped Adam would not be too overtly affectionate to herself during the long walking holiday in the mountains.

'You can make yourself useful looking after the little girls,' said Hermione. She was quite an amazing woman. Jo was determined not to succumb to Adam if he tried to walk off alone with her. Just as Adam had visited Patricia Jackson before coming to see her in Oxford, to make sure, as he had told her, that it was not 'sex' that was making Jo attractive to him, she decided, on the spur of the moment, on the night train as it trundled through Germany, that she would do something similar.

Next to her was a young German who had married a Scotswoman and who was returning home for a holiday with his little daughter. She found him nice and attractive, and they had had a long and pleasant conversation. Then darkness fell and two elderly women on the other side of the compartment were asleep. The child was in a couchette above them.

When the man began to kiss her, instead of being affronted, Jo kissed him back. He covered their knees with his own heavy overcoat, and under this she began to caress him. He did not seem to mind. Later, she wondered how she had thought she could get rid of her sexual urges by ministering to a young man, for she had no intention of allowing him to do anything to her. But it was undeniably exciting, and he was a nice man, and when she got up to go to wash her hands in the *Abort* at the end of the corridor, he followed her and said, 'Can I not do something for you?'

'No, no,' she said quietly. 'I don't want that. I just wanted to make you feel nice.'

'Well, I did,' he replied.

He got off the train with his daughter at six o'clock in the morning at some remote little station in south Germany. Jo waved goodbye to them and went back to the compartment feeling strangely light-headed.

This was something she would never tell Adam about. But she did not even feel guilty.

It was during the first year of their tenancy in lower Belgravia that Jo decided she might as well teach. She could be a student again, study for a year for a post-graduate teaching certificate, with a reasonable grant of five pounds a week, since she had worked for over two years and kept herself. It would make temporary vacation jobs urgently necessary; however generous the grant was, it was not enough to pay rent and food and transport and clothes, never mind

119

holidays. She had helped Adam and Hermione with the children and offered to pay her share but he would not hear of it, and Hermione had money of her own. What a difference that made.

Ever since her experience as a waitress in a Lyons tea-shop, Jo had dreaded the next time she would have to find casual work, but she rather enjoyed working in the sales in a large store in Oxford Street, where she sold terrible hats. Maybe because it was a mercifully short experience and maybe the bookshop had hardened her. She repeated the work at the next sales and sold even more hats, which were almost torn to pieces by the crowds of matrons up from the East End.

She took a week's stint in a job at Olympia, at the Food Fair, selling English apples and celery next to the stall for Bulgarian wine and perfume made from roses. The scent of the roses filled her nostrils all day. Some people found it cloying, sickening, but she sniffed it with pleasure. Here she had met once again that 'resting' actress, Maureen Higgins, who had been at one of the Chelsea barge parties. She appeared very independent but turned out to have a rich boyfriend whom she treated very badly.

Battersea Pleasure Gardens was next, one of the great pools of young labour where graduate and non-graduate, all those who needed cash, worked for a pittance, with no questions asked, just as they had done at Olympia or in Oxford Street. There, selling candy floss during one long ten-hour day, she met a dark young man, a gypsy. He was most polite. All the other permanent workers said 'fuck' before every other word. She had never heard men swear so much in the north.

'You mustn't mind them,' said the gypsy, Barney Smith. 'They don't know any better. Me, my dad sent me to the grammar school. I'm going to university October. Would you like to go to the pictures with me?'

She couldn't – the next week she was back to work, and she decided not to allow anyone for the time being to put temptation in her path.

*

During the pleasant sinecure that followed for the rest of the year, this return to 'education', Jo also registered with an agency that provided young women to look after children, usually the offspring of American diplomats renting houses in Chelsea, or of London 'Society'; rich English families living in Kensington. They were all quite happy for an Oxford graduate to take their offspring out for the day to watch the new '3D' films in Soho, or to help them do their homework, or get them ready for bed whilst their parents got ready to go out. Here, to her enormous surprise, she was pronounced a great success, and was asked for again and again. She had always got on rather well with children – even Hermione's – for it seemed she actually liked them. It was a discovery that at first startled her, so different was it from her idea of herself.

Her favourite children, for whom she had invented bedtime stories, were about to return to the United States. The head of the agency called her in and told her how pleased the family had been with her. It was the first time her work in any post she had taken had been praised.

'You have a talent for this kind of work,' said the lady, a Miss Skimp, in charge of the agency. 'You could make a good living being a mother's help or governess. You have been appreciated.'

Jo was amused. But why could she not give this good impression to other employers?

SEVEN

It was a lovely morning in early spring. The air was warmer now and Jo's spirits were up. She loved the new flat in Pimlico, with no landlady to annoy the sisters, who made more new friends, some of whom were to achieve later fame.

Beautiful Julia Tudor, first met on the barge, loved and desired by every literary young man in London, and eventually desired by Matthew Francis, became better known to Jo. Matthew made a short return visit to London to see Jo 'as a friend', and having kissed her goodnight in her chaste bed in the Pimlico flat, went into the next room to lay siege to Julia who was camping out there as she often did if Annette and Julian were away. Jo decided to go to sleep. After he had departed, letters arrived for Julia from him. Jo recognized the angular handwriting. They were piled up on the floor where her friend had dropped them page by page.

Gaye Hardcastle, who was now Gaye Reynolds, still held court at parties, bewitching everyone with her memorable voice: a sigh, inevitably followed by a chuckle. She had been the first of Jo's women friends to have a child out of wedlock. Adam always said wedlock sounded like gridlock, but Jo noticed that both he and Hermione were critical of women who wanted to bring up a child without a husband. Perhaps they feared lest Jo might do the same.

Much later, after another marriage, Gaye Belder was to become a famous novelist, a household word.

There were many parties now that they could return hospitality more easily; a party almost every Saturday somewhere in London, attended by Australians, Oxford friends, London university friends, friends of friends and old friends who were now married. There were older friends from home, and people Jo met in various schools, and painter friends of Annette, and even Matthew came. Other literary people too: editors, young men with their first foot on the ladder of literary journalism. Will Morgan turned up again, and Jo was pleased to see him. Susie Swift who was becoming quite famous for her water-colours appeared, also Clare Jackson, acquaintances from the Municipal Halls, friends from the university drama society, stray foreigners whom Jo was asked to invite by friends now working for the British Council. Some people she might never see again; others might one day become old friends.

Jo continued to write for her own pleasure whilst also writing realistic accounts of London life. She had a little more time now she was receiving the sinecure of graduate teacher-training.

Once she had decided to teach, she was interviewed. The tutor said, 'You had better get some experience first.' She seemed quite glad to have Jo on her list. 'Do some supply teaching before term starts,' she added.

Teaching the five-year-olds of Bethnal Green, who had been surprisingly well-drilled, and then their thirteen-year-old sisters down the road, was not completely different from entertaining the children of the upper middle classes. Chiefly the difference was the pressure of numbers. But what happened to the keen little five-year-olds with their plasticine and their, 'Please, Miss, can I read to you?' By the time they were they were thirteen they were sullen, hard-eyed and obviously bored.

Jo discovered that what had happened was adolescence.

The 'mixed' fourteen-year-olds of a Westminster secondary modern school nearer home, in fact just down the road, were different again, but were held in check by a sternly religious head-master. Jo was deputed to teach them French, and they put up with her quite kindly. She later saw one of her girl pupils, clearly 'on the game', walking slowly up and down Vauxhall Bridge Road at night.

At this time of her life, to amuse herself, and so that she should paradoxically not forget who she was, Jo tried on various selves. It was like play-acting – but so was teaching.

On Monday she would be the heroine of a novel by Rosamond Lehmann – honest, clear, loyal, perceptive, beautiful, frank.

On Tuesday she would be an Elizabeth Taylor heroine – ironic, observant, quiet, a little malicious.

On Wednesday she would be a rumbustious Joyce Cary woman – full of life, abundant, overflowing, tolerant, generous, enthusiastic, happy, vulgar. Free.

She had not been able to find a suitable novelist for Thursday, Friday, and Saturday, so on Thursday she would be an academic girl: serious-minded, hard-working, a little vague but independent.

On Friday she'd change into an argumentative, assertive, scornful, critical, talkative, possibly political, type.

On Saturday, she became a 'lady': polite, beautiful, with a polished accent, who usually kept her thoughts to herself. (This was the most difficult role.)

On Sunday she was Virginia Woolf: full of impressions that skated up and down in her mind . . . writing, writing . . . critical but also creative, carrying on thought to the end of its tether.

Sunday was the best day.

All this kept her going to the end of the working week. Did anyone notice? It was impossible to teach fourteen-year-old children anything, though one might be tolerated by them: a triumph in itself, but the Joyce Cary heroine seemed to fit in best. Unfortunately, by the time Saturday arrived, Jo had often no wish to be polite and quiet, though she might try for half an hour or so at a party.

This phase did not last long, except that on Sundays she sometimes found she was behaving like Mrs Woolf without intending to. Her thoughts might not be so subtle, but there were plenty of them, and a new notebook to write them in. Was this nearer her real self? It was not a self that was much nurtured by Adam.

Jo met other women who flitted in and out of literary Bohemia. Rich women like Marigold Cassman or Victoria Butler or Nicole Balladur, some living with men, one or two married, some single with many boyfriends. A new acquaintance was one Stephen Carnforth, a friend of Matthew's, who scuttled from Soho drinking-club to Soho drinking-club, laying the foundations of his later successful career.

She wrote about the new 'coffee-houses' that were just arriving, but her early success often eluded her, and many of her efforts went unpublished. She continued her story of Karen, a story written just to please herself, which was a great comfort when she felt lonely.

... Karen was twelve, slim and well-made, a perfect little specimen,' thought Jacintha Brown.... (a young woman teacher at a private school in Brighton).

... She was a bright little girl, Jacintha's favourite pupil. Karen's mother Madeline was smart, often to be found in the bar of the Metropole. The two lived in a mews house near the Lanes. You could see Madeline's taste through the bow-window – puff cushions and a few of the wackier 'antiques'. Karen was the result of an injudicious meeting between Madeline and her about-to-be-divorced husband, in 1942, or so Madeline had hinted when she met Jacintha to discuss her daughter's welfare at the school, and another time in a coffee-shop.

The child and the teacher had met once or twice quite by chance, on the pier, or walking near the Royal Pavilion. Karen wore slacks or jodhpurs, and coloured jumpers. Her hair was tied back in a pony-tail. Oh, she was so lovely at twelve, thought

Jacintha, individual and nice. What a pity she couldn't stay like that. There would be another ten years to wait to find her again after the added bumps and folds of puberty . . .

Karen was friendly with her teacher and they had interesting conversations.

'Do you want to have babies?' Karen asked Jacintha one day.

'Not very much,' replied Jacintha. 'Do you?'

'Oh, yes – heaps.' Karen coloured a little and twisted round on one foot.

'Really?'

'Well, I don't think about it much,' said Karen, implying, Jacintha guessed, that in spite of her disavowals perhaps her teacher did.

I wish I were you, thought Jacintha.

'Stay as you are,' she said aloud. Then theatrically, 'Don't let life shake you up.'

'Is life always doing that?' asked the child innocently.

'Oh – I meant you must do what you want,' said Jacintha lamely. . . .

This sort of dialogue went on in Jo's head when she was marking books or waiting at bus-stops.

The teacher in the story – perhaps Jacintha was rather too fancy a name? – was to meet Karen's father who came once a month to take his daughter out. Would he fall in love with Jacintha? Jo hadn't yet decided. The story was expanding: perhaps it should be a novel?

She told Stephanie about her ideas one evening. Stephie was still busy in the Senate House library and would meet Jo in Store Street. Together they would take the 24 bus to the Pimlico flat. Jo loved her new way of life that gave her a little time to think, in spite of lectures and dissertations and teaching-practice. It was so much more pleasant than the last two years she'd spent working for her living. She'd have to do that again soon but for the time being there was a breathing space, spent writing essays when she was not teaching or observing in schools. She was to find that teaching-practice in a convent was rather different from her supply teaching in the East End. The girls were well-disciplined; there was none of the ribbing and shouting and cheek found in most London secondary schools, but there was no scope for your own enthusiasm.

Jo had discovered however that she enjoyed writing about the philosophy of education. Not as much as she enjoyed writing about books, but it seemed nobody wanted her unfashionable thoughts on women writers.

She and Stephie still did a good deal of talking about books.

'I enjoyed *Lucky Jim*,' Jo said now to Stephie, 'but critics go on as if you can't enjoy both a novel like that *and* a writer like Elizabeth Bowen. Really, I do prefer women writers, but they don't write the picaresque novels that are in vogue.'

'There is *Under the Net*,' suggested Stephie.

'Yes, that's true, but on the whole the women don't get half the reviewing space the men get. They're seen as too 'sensitive', or faintly damned as 'perceptive'. And the angry young men novelists don't seem to me angry about the right things – war, and apartheid, and suicide being a crime in this country, and homosexuals being imprisoned. The male novelists are all involved in horse-play.'

'It's the fashion,' said Stephie. 'They'd say you were asking for nice Boots novels about nice ladies!'

'Perhaps I am.'

'It's the China tea smell of Bloomsbury they dislike,' said Stephie after a pause. 'But really, Jo, there are other kinds of novels you might try to write – more popular ones, I mean. Keep your perceptions for your poetry and write a rattling good yarn. I've been thinking about writing a novel myself,' she confessed with a slight blush. 'Seems a pity to waste all I know about the eighteenth century on a thesis.'

Jo was surprised, had not realized that Stephie saw herself as a novelist. Wasn't *she* supposed to be the writer? She waited a moment and then said, with a theatrical sigh: 'Sometimes I feel that if I can't write as well as Virginia Woolf or Elizabeth Bowen or Elizabeth Taylor, or – oh, I don't know – Theodora Keogh or Alberta Murphy – they're good American novelists – I'd better give up. I don't think I could write a story with a plot, but you never know. On the other hand I rather like writing about writers – I suppose I might become a journalist. It's what my tutor said I ought to be. Of course she meant it as a criticism!'

'Fashion reigns in journalism too, even more, I expect, than in fiction,' said Stephie.

Jo was pondering that they both wanted to write novels, wondering which of them might succeed. Perhaps both – or neither?

Dusk was not so early now and when it came often brought pale violet skies. The moon shone over the side of the square that had faded from gamboge to ochre as they chatted. The pavement under their balcony was quiet but there was activity not far away as people went about their business in Wilton Road. In spite of the drawbacks – chiefly the lack of hot water – Jo loved living in Coventry Square. The atmosphere was a mixture of the purposive and the unaccountable.

'Oh Stephie, you *will* write – and publish, I feel sure. At present I'm torn between two ideas. I told you about the little girl I was writing about – Karen?'

'Yes. The relationship between the child and the woman sounded interesting.'

'Well, I'm also writing about an imaginary man.'

'Aren't all your characters imaginary?'

'Yes, of course, but this one is the invention of the character in the story. It's about romantic illusion. The woman thinks he exists but he is not really there.'

Stephie looked mystified.

128

'I mean, he is partly a figment of her imagination but he does exist in another realm. He must die, and she must suffer – and so he disappears from her imagination.'

'Goodness Jo, that must be terribly hard to convey.'

'Yes, but the reality of the man – I call him Kristin – is in her head. She grieves for him till she recognizes his illusory quality – I can't decide whether she is going a bit mad or not.'

'What is it *really* about?'

'About the truth that romantic love is a myth that will always die and that it needs hope to live in a different way. I just want to convey a dream-like atmosphere and then have my heroine come down to earth and begin to live with a real man. But there's a lot more. I've written bits of it all over the place. I've also been trying to write a realistic story about quite a different boy.'

Jo stopped. In fact she had been recreating Adam's childhood for herself in fictional form and it was probably too close to the truth. He talked so much about himself – but Stephanie would not be interested in that. She sensed Stephie still had reservations about Adam, probably did not like him all that much. Not that she had seen a great deal of him recently, only once or twice in Bloomsbury when they had both been near the university on Saturday mornings and had bumped into each other in Dillon's bookshop in Store Street. The trouble was, if Adam had not loved her, and drawn out a response from her, *she* might have had just the same reservations.

Stephanie thought, Jo is yearning for a platonic lover; this character Kristin in her novel sounds like one. Also, had she realized how like the word 'Christ' the name 'Kristin' was? The realistic story might not be in Jo's line, if she were to be truthful. Better stick to the realism of non-fiction.

Jo was now on another tack, felt she might have been boring her old friend.

'I went all by myself to Leoni's yesterday,' she said, pouring tea for them both. The kettle had taken ages to heat up.

'For a meal?'

'Yes. People always say women daren't go to restaurants alone, but I thought I would. The waiters were very nice. I read a book and had half a bottle of red wine.'

'Do you think they remembered you from the times you've been there with Adam?'

'I suppose they might have done, but I enjoyed myself.'

'You've always been a feminist, Jo, you know.'

'But why is it so extraordinary for a woman to go by herself for a meal? Even people like Marigold or Victoria never do that.'

'I don't know Marigold and I've seen Victoria Butler only once, but I'd guess they are men's women.'

'And I'm still not?'

'No, you are not, Jo. Perhaps I'm not either.'

'I'd rather have been born a boy!' said Jo rebelliously. 'I know that sounds childish. It's true enough though.'

Stephanie changed the subject. 'How's the old diploma going on, or whatever it is? I looked for you and your purple coat in the SOAS canteen the other day but you weren't there.'

Jo had bought a lovely warm purple wool coat in Selfridges' sale, the first substantial item of clothing she had been able to afford to buy for herself for months, if not years.

'Oh, some of it is pretty elementary stuff but they're good on teaching you how to teach your subject. I've chosen the philosophy option so I can wallow to my heart's content in Matthew Arnold.'

'You ought to have read English. I bet it's not much fun teaching the average Cockney French.'

'You're right there – but I like teaching the intelligent ones. I suppose one might do just a *little* bit of good,' Jo said wistfully.

'Better than earning your living advertising Kellogg's corn flakes,' replied Stephie, who had been relieved when her friend had not gone into advertising.

'What's on at the Academy next week?'

'They're showing *Les Enfants du Paradis*. Shall we go?'

'I've seen it at least seven times,' said Jo. 'I'll never have enough of it. They've advertised an Edwige Feuillère film in the not too distant future – I'm longing to see that.'

Jo had waited at the stage-door when the French actress had played *Phèdre* in a London theatre, and the goddess had actually spoken to her.

'What are you going to do in the summer? Will you go home?'

'No, I'm applying for a job for six weeks I saw advertised in the *Statesman*: some long-established worthy holiday outfit that has centres all over the place. There's going to be one based in an Oxford college so I thought six weeks there would keep me, and Julia can borrow my room here.'

When she went away for those six weeks in Oxford after her summer term ended, to earn a bit of money, Adam would be in that city towards the end of her time there. She did not tell Stephie this.

'Any nearer finding a permanent job?' Stephie asked.

'I've applied all over the place. I thought I ought to pay back my debt to society by working in a poor area, but I'd be no good in a Sec Mod. You've either got to be a sergeant-major or a saint. There's an East End grammar school with a progressive head-mistress that my tutor thinks might do for me.' But she looked worried.

'That sounds more like you,' suggested Stephie.

'The trouble is, when I was at school I was all for freedom and being progressive, but since I've begun to teach I seem to have changed. Not that I'm authoritarian – not much good at keeping order anyway, because I don't *care* enough, unless I sense the children like me, and then I think I'm a good teacher. There's a trap there too; middle-class people romanticize the working-class and dream of changing their lives, but I've found very few from any class who are really interested in language and literature. If the pupils learned how to *work*, English schools would be transformed, but they can't be made to. Not that I blame them. Why should they learn French? Spanish would be a bit more sensible – that's where they're all going for their holidays now.'

'But you still hope to open a few windows in the minds of the bright?'

'Well, there's a Proust exhibition on next year – I might take some sixth-formers. I find if you're enthusiastic about things, it's catching, but only with people like yourself. Of course they might be found anywhere.'

'You'll end up preaching the value of hard work like your mother.'

'I do believe in hard work. It's just that none of the jobs I'm offered seems to have anything to do with my real self!'

'Teaching children must have, surely?'

'Yes, more than the other things I've done, but most of the time I'm not teaching what really interests me. If I thought I could make a difference – as you might with your own children from the beginning – it would be different. On the other hand, I do like teaching the really bright. I always learn a lot when I have to prepare translations or proses, or introduce them to literature – like this Proust exhibition. There were some nice girls at the convent where I did my teaching practice, but there wasn't time to go into things very deeply, and I had the feeling some of the staff there wouldn't want me to.'

'Still, you're happier now aren't you, than you were being an admin officer or whatever it was, or toiling in the book shop?'

'Yes, I suppose things are looking brighter. I do know *something* about my subject. What about you, Stephie? You never say much. How's the thesis?'

'I'm not really worried about the thesis, it's just that I can't see myself as an academic. The three years won't go down the drain – don't worry – I shall finish it next year and I keep getting these ideas for a really long historical novel. I haven't mentioned it to anybody else – it probably won't come off – but that's what I'd really like to do.'

'I'm sure you'll succeed. I just have the feeling,' said Jo, looking at her friend in this new light. Stephie seemed quietly confident, whatever she said. 'I wish I could write the sort of novel you have to know about lots of things to write. I seem stuck in my own imagination; I enjoy thinking about Karen and Kristin, but sometimes I feel despair about it all.'

'It's much harder to write a literary novel,' comforted Stephie. 'Have you sold any more articles?'

'The editor of *Reality* seems interested in my little piece about national characteristics. I tried them with coffee-bars but they weren't interested. If I don't get more things published whilst I have a bit of time, how shall I manage when I'm exhausted by teaching?'

'Well, you've got the translation under your belt.'

Stephie never asked how Adam was. The nice thing about her friend, thought Jo, was that she would always give you her opinion if you asked her but would otherwise keep mum. She wondered again about Stephie and men.

'I met a journalist friend of Susie's the other day,' said Stephie. 'He's quite clever, I think, but not my type. I must introduce you – or get Susie to. I think he really wants to be a literary critic. He might help you place an article or two.'

'I think I've seen some of his stuff in *Reality*,' said Jo.

'Do you still hear from Matthew?'

'Oh, he writes to me now and again. I don't think he got very far with Julia. I expect he's away in fresh fields now. I've a very high opinion of his intellect though, and he really can write. When I read his poems I know there's no hope for me!'

EIGHT

Jo did not know it but she was only to stay one more year at the flat in Coventry Square, Pimlico.

The six weeks' stint with the holiday organization taught her that adults were worse than children when you had to be in charge of them. She was also responsible for the financial side, for banking a large amount of money each week. There were three groups of holiday makers in all, each staying a fortnight, a new one arriving every two weeks. Jo was asked to lecture to each group once. She organized trips to Stanton Harcourt and Blenheim as well as conducting tours around the city, and walks in Port Meadow, and on Boars Hill. She liaised with the bursar of the college about the meals they were to provide, and answered a hundred queries a day from puzzled middle-aged people, some of whom were foreign, mainly Dutch.

In the middle of August a group of four young French people arrived who did not seem to possess any English vocabulary between them. What would the holiday company have done if she had not spoken French? she wondered. Before Adam came to work in Bodley, she had a short affair with one of these French students, embarking upon it quite determinedly, out of a mixture of exhaustion and boredom. Even after the failure with clever beautiful Matthew, she realised she must still be trying, almost unconsciously, to escape Adam. He arrived after the French had left.

Jo had been offered a permanent teaching post in a grammar school, in the East End, beginning in the autumn. She felt her life would soon all be measured out, if not in coffee-spoons, then certainly in preparation, and marking, and journeys by Underground, always late, always in a rush, with the *Manchester Guardian* to finish before her journey's end, by which time she would have put her make-up on at Bromley-by-Bow. She took up this permanent post a week after her holiday job ended.

She enjoyed the journey to school, even if she was always late. Fortunately the eight o'clock dash of cold water on her face in the kitchen didn't appear to affect her complexion, and her rush down the stairs, followed by another dash to Victoria station, kept her thin.

She worked for a year, and learned that she was not a natural disciplinarian and that she liked some pupils and heartily disliked others. Some of her pupils liked her whilst others thought she was obviously odd.

One, a certain Jean Robinson, volunteered, 'I don't know what it is, Miss, but when you talk to us it's like you were my mum and you said, "Run down to the chippie, love, will you?" '

She was clearly not dignified enough.

Early in the following year Adam announced that he had found a new post in London, and that he could now live part of the week with Josephine. Hermione would be delighted to leave Birmingham, and he was looking for a house for her and the children – and himself, of course. One of Adam's little girls was now away at boarding-school and the other would soon follow her. Hermione didn't want to live in London: she wanted an old house in the country. He would go to her every Friday evening until Monday morning, and stay with Jo during the week. At last, he said, they would be together!

After four years, Jo's feelings about this were mixed. If only it had happened earlier, before Matthew and her other little infidelities. She would have to leave Coventry Square, which was sad, though by now she was a little tired of Julian and his drinking. It would be bliss to have her own flat – shared with Adam from Monday evening till Friday morning.

Why did she feel she would rather have a place to herself? Was it not wonderful that at last she and Adam would be like a married couple? But they were *not* a married couple and never would be, as far as she could see. She did not care about living in sin, but she did care that her parents and family could never visit, unless Adam confessed all to them. She had no intention of doing so herself.

Now that she had a permanent teaching job she felt a little more able to plan. But even now, she never had any money over at the end of the month. The school had told her she would have to accompany girls to Paris and to Germany and had already asked her to learn Spanish. She was enjoying this.

Adam was now looking for a small flat for the two of them, and it turned out that he was looking not far from Goddard Road.

Jo could not help feeling that this was not a good augury. Her journey to school would also take longer.

After listening for hours to Adam who talked a great deal about himself, and his past life, Jo felt she could have written a book about him:

ADAM ANGELWINE
by B.J. Hill
Chapter one: Childhood and youth.

she wrote idly one day in an exercise book ...

Adam's grandfather Angelwine had arrived in England as a child in 1855 and had founded a very successful family business.

Adam had given Jo a postcard photograph taken for some Edwardian Christmas, the photographer's name scrolled in gold at the bottom right-hand corner. It showed himself on his mother, Lydia's, knee. His mother was not smiling, but was wearing a dress with two hundred tucks, and much gold jewellery. The blond goggle-eyed baby was in a long white starched dress with lace insets. His eyes were most likely already a brilliant blue but no photographer of the time was able to reproduce that colour, the colour that would remain all his life.

Jo embroidered the story of Adam in her mind, jumping off from this photograph and many others, and countless long talks with her lover, weaving in all he told her about himself. Apart from anything else she still found him clever, and interesting, though he continued to baffle her.

One day he said, 'I once wrote a bit about my early life. You can read it if you want.'

Jo felt sure he had written it originally for Hermione.

They were sitting over coffee in the lounge of a large London hotel before going up to bed and to long sessions of love-making. Adam was back on the subject of his family. His father had been called Arnold Angelwine.

'What did he look like?' Jo asked.

'He was the tallest of seven brothers, and the most intelligent. When he was a young man he sported a curly waxed moustache and he always wore or carried a panama hat in summer. He'd travelled all over the globe.'

'Do you look like him?'

'Not in the least; his eyes were brown, I have my mother's blue eyes. He was quite dark-haired too.'

Apparently Arnold was of a proud and unmalleable disposition.

'His father, my grandfather Daniel, told him to make his own way – there were three more hopefuls after him in the line. I'm sure my grandfather knew my father was the quickest-witted. Father lost no time. He left school and got himself apprenticed as foreign traveller for a large Jewish textile firm. Sensible at first to be a spoke in the wheel of Schnechtel Brothers: Hamburg, Lille and Woolsford. He was a good linguist – he had a sharp tongue in many languages.'

Like you, thought Jo.

'He soon became the manager of a large export house, and he was eventually made a partner. Then he founded his own business.'

From what he said, Jo guessed that Adam was not unlike his father and grandfather in temperament. His paternity and back-ground might not explain him completely, though at different times he would both assert and deny that it did. Adam said that Hermione might believe it did, but *she* knew little of the reality of a family of the aspiring business-class, precariously balanced by virtue of brain-power and the inheritance of certain skills on the bridge over the abyss which separated the Angelwines from the toiling poor as well as the idle rich, or rather the gentry Hermione had sprung from.

He loved telling and retelling the tale of his first day at prep school. His father had wanted the best education for him, so sent him away to school.

Jo discovered quite a lot about this in the account he gave her to read. At the age of nine, having arrived at his first boarding-school, he had been more interested in his discovery of the school library than in making friends with his fellow pupils. He wrote:

. . . On my second day at the school I rediscovered the works of Henty and took out a volume on Gustavus Adolphus and the Thirty Years War. This kept me happy, once I'd finished my prep. The romance and colour of the past had always attracted me – such a contrast with home I always thought.

The food was plain and the life Spartan. The boys had to make their own beds and clean their own shoes. As time went on, the hearty school life absorbed me – we played cricket and football and had a new swimming bath, the HM's pride and joy, where I was soon taught to swim.

She asked him later whether it had been a progressive school.

'For its time it was very modern, yes. Father always wanted the best for me, the most up-to-date. I learned to roller-skate and play chess, and I was taught the elements of carpentry and photography.'

'I supposed you were good at everything?'

'Well, I was quite practical – yes, good at doing most things, I suppose, and I really enjoyed myself thoroughly there.'

'Was it a religious school?'

'Religion interested me not at all – there were prayers but boys were not encouraged towards introspection. "Keep 'em busy" could have been the school motto,' he went on. 'I started a stamp collection. Two years of the place had made me become an extremely self-reliant and independent boy. But there was something missing. I suppose it was the life of the mind.'

Things had changed when his father sent Adam to another school when he was eleven, this time one in the gentle south of England.

Jo read what Adam had written about this. One day she might want to remember all the details he was wont to give her about his childhood and his youth, to explain him as a 'character'. She would like to have a copy, to have something to keep of his own words. It was not as if she did not already have stacks of love-letters, all written in Adam's beautifully neat handwriting, but she wanted to try to understand him by learning more of his past. Eventually he sent her several more pages of reminiscence enclosed in one of his bulky letters.

I remember going up the oak stairs on my first day at this new school. Before following the head's wife into the dorm, I paused to look out of the window on the half-landing at rolling hills. I could hear some boys shouting, but when I followed Mrs Head into the dorm everything was quiet.

I was shown my bed and the woman said: 'Bangers for tea today.'

I was unpacking my trunk when another lady came in who introduced herself as Mrs Harris.

'I look after your clothes for you and do your darning, but when you've been here a year you will have to do it yourself,' she said.

This surprised me as boys had done most things for themselves at my old school. I went down to the common room. Somebody was talking about his brother who had just been demobilized from France.

I said: 'My cousin was over there,' but they didn't listen.

I knew that boys' older brothers had often been killed. Fortunately all my own family had returned home safely.

Well, it was all right here, except that I missed my old friends and felt a bit lonely. But there was a lot to do; it would soon be tea-time and they had told me I had to see the Chief Beak in his study at six o'clock. This didn't worry me.

I wondered whether I'd be able to swim here. By craning my neck out of a window I could see a deserted open-air swimming pool at the back. After tea I set my things up and put *Gulliver's Travels* next to the Bible I had been asked to provide. I sat on the bed and thought about maps and whether they would teach me about them. At supper I was squashed between two bigger boys with round faces and different accents from mine. They had talked about football and somehow I knew they would be good at it. The tea was nice – hot and dark, and there was lots of bread to eat. I found I was quite hungry. They said grace in Latin and that was interesting. It was all a bit of a jumble though, not like the stories my uncle had read me about boys away at prep schools in the south.

Suddenly I felt very tired, and just as I was looking forward to a good sleep Mrs Harris came in and tidied my hair, tweaked my tie and said the headmaster would see me now.

Then it was: 'How do you do, Adam? I hope you'll be happy with us. You've met my wife? Excellent. Don't hesitate to regard her as a second mother.'

I didn't think she was a bit like my mother. She looked older and smelt of bread, not scent. And she had bigger bosoms. But the headmaster was swivelling round slowly in a funny sort of chair like the one they had in father's office. He looked at some papers, whilst I looked out of the window, though it was growing dark. It was a bit like my interview, except Father wasn't there. Then the head said:

'Well, Angelwine – Adam – I expect you to be one of our scholarship boys. Any idea where your father wants you to go?'

It seemed a bit odd since I'd only just arrived, to be thinking about where to go next. My father hadn't said anything except that Quaker schools were good, so I replied:

'I think a Quaker school, Sir.'

'What do you like to do in your spare time – er – Adam?' He repeated my first name – though my grandfather had told me that southerners always called you by your surname. But the headmaster was quite nice. I wondered though why he hadn't been in the war.

'I liked following what was happening in the newspapers – I used to follow the military campaigns. In the war, I mean,' I replied, and then wondered if I had been indelicate.

'Yes. Why?'

This took me by surprise. 'I like to know why things happen,' I said. 'I like old buildings too. And playing chess,' I added hopefully.

'Good, good.'

The headmaster seemed to be thinking about something else. Then he swivelled the chair round to look at me more closely and said:

'We want you to be happy here. But we expect you to work hard. Nothing good ever came from laziness.'

'No, sir.'

That was a nice relief, because at the other school they'd always been telling me to stop reading and do something useful.

'That's all,' said the head, and put his hand out without rising. I proffered mine and he shook it.

I turned to go. As I went out, the man said:

'Eleven years old now, er Angelwine – Adam – a few years here and I think you'll be pleased – and please us.' I thought it a rum sort of speech.

I walked back quickly and went into the games room where boys were playing table-tennis or trying to roast conkers in front of a very small fire. Nobody seemed bothered about me, so I went to a bookcase in the corner. A big boy with red hair made a rude remark, something like: 'Another of Lindsey's swots, I bet,' but I didn't take any notice because I didn't really think they were talking about me, and anyway my Uncle Albert had taught me how to fight. Even though I was small, my muscles were good.

I sat at the table and thought about the morning and saying goodbye to Mother. She had looked a bit, well, sort of guilty, which was funny because I couldn't wait to be gone. I was sorry that I couldn't feel sorrier about going away again. But then the journey in a train that smelt as though it had last been used for troops, and the excitement of seeing a real cathedral in the distance had made me forget home. I only wished I was going further, except nobody could cross over to France yet, and Father's Flanders business connection was still dangling like a severed limb, in limbo, even though the Hun had been licked. My father had been just too old to fight in the war but, as well as my cousin Edward, some of my mother's relations had fought over there. Naturally, Father had had to stop his travelling for the duration to help his old father out with the business. The government had asked other members of the family to start manufacturing gaberdines for officers. The weavers said the colour right made them sick. . . .

I nodded over my book. . . .

In the morning I was woken by a bell telling me to get up, dress,

brush my teeth and wash my face. Later, when I was twelve, I'd
have to take a cold shower every morning.

It all seemed quite ordinary, till Parkinson had a fit. It was whilst
I was sitting in my new form-room waiting for the Latin teacher to
enter and begin the first Latin lesson. Suddenly there was a sound
like a tap emptying down a plug-hole with a gurgle, and then close
on that a scuffling and kicking. We all turned round. A small ginger-
haired boy with freckles was writhing on the floor and foaming at
the mouth.

A few people began to giggle. A tall boy said: 'Send for Matron,
Taylor.'

The bespectacled boy sitting next to me ran out of the room. The
other boys crowded round the unfortunate Parkinson. I felt
disturbed, but felt I should not need to be brave. Curiosity prompted
me to stand up and peer through the crowd of legs. How could a boy
like myself be moaning on the floor? And if he were moaning on the
floor he would have hurt himself when he fell. I looked at
Parkinson's knee, which was writhing around jerkily and thought
how ugly it was, but it must feel uncomfortable lying on the floor. I
took off my jacket and thought how to get it under Parkinson's head.
I tried to push my way forward, but as I was smaller than most of the
boys I couldn't be seen and couldn't push enough, so I put my fingers
to my mouth and did an Uncle Albert whistle.

Everyone turned round in the hope of further excitement.

I pushed my way through the others and knelt down and saw the
boy's knee, now with a red bump on it. As no one else was doing
anything, I rolled up my jacket, tugged Parkinson's head up – he
felt heavy – and slipped the jacket underneath his head. The boy
wasn't jerking so much now, so I stood up and the boys looked at
me curiously.

A silence had fallen as though I had done something wrong. A
voice from the door said: 'Back to your desks,' and Mr Wood the
Latin master strode forward. They shuffled back to their desks and
then Mrs Davidson, the oldest member of the household staff,

bustled in with the head. Parkinson was, it seemed, well enough to be moved.

'Who made that disgusting whistle just now?' asked Mr Wood.

I put my hand up.

'You, boy. Who are you?'

'Angelwine, Sir.'

'And are you in the habit of emitting low-class shrieks?'

'No, sir. I wanted to put something under his head.'

I looked at the body of Parkinson, now being borne away by the two adults.

'I thought he might be more comfortable, sir. With my jacket,' I added.

'Did you need to whistle for his comfort?'

'No, sir. But no one would let me through. I did it to call attention to myself.'

'He did it to call attention to himself.' Some of the class tittered.

'Are you new here, Angelwine?'

'Yes, sir. I arrived yesterday,' I replied.

'You may sit down. Let us hope your Latin is as strong as your whistle. Hands up those who have done no Latin.'

I, along with a few other boys, put my hand up.

'Right.'

Mr Woods threw some books around, exhorted us to keep them clean and began on the first declension.

In spite of not having done any Latin before, I found I could follow quite easily, so that when Mr Wood asked for 'The table is beautiful,' I produced the right answer and mentally invented: 'Parkinson is not beautiful.'

I looked up 'not' at the back of the grammar.

'Please, sir,' I asked, 'Is "is" the same word in Latin as in French? Is "was" the same too?'

'No, Angelwine,' said Mr Wood. Some boys sighed and the bespectacled boy who had gone for assistance looked more closely at me, the new boy.

I put my hand up again: 'Then, please sir, could you tell me where to find it?' I asked.

'Look on page thirty-eight,' replied the master, glad to see, I suppose, that in spite of infringement of protocol, someone showed a spark of interest.

'And,' he added, in case I should seek to rise above myself, 'tell me what "the pupil was not good" is.'

I looked up page thirty-eight, made a swift calculation and replied: '*Discipulus bonus non erat.*'

'Good,' said Mr W.

He looked more closely at me. In those days I was good-looking, fair-haired, with bright blue slightly hooded eyes, and a full mouth.

The boys groaned. I took no notice. Mr Wood beamed at us all as he gave us our prep.

My next-door neighbour whispered: 'You've got him in a good mood.' I remember practising a shy smile.

My neighbour must have decided he had better get to know this new prodigy, for he stuck close to me like a limpet for a few days. Within a week I had been promoted to another Latin class; by half-term to the next but top class, and by the end of the term to the top class. Here I immediately became 'Top Boy' in pretty well everything. I was never complacent however and I always worked hard in the true spirit of the Angelwines. Father always demanded value for money, and my attitude probably pleased him.

'No time for airs and graces,' he would say, and at first I had concurred, though I was a little worried that the subjects I could not shine in from hard work alone – playing the piano well, for example – were seemingly beyond my ken. My mother did play at home and I had always enjoyed listening to her playing and singing before realising eventually that her technique was not very good. We Angelwines were self-sufficient but I had longed for brighter conversation, more informality at home and less of Father's constantly reiterated: 'Don't!'

I did not know how to express this need and if I had they would not have understood, and would have been hurt. . . .

He is writing through the eyes of a child – he writes well, thought Jo. I wish I had known him then, or that we were of the same generation. His ancestry, and his father's ambition, his mother's difficult nature, and his own childhood, must account for part of his character.

She read on:

Father was becoming successful. As he made more money after the war, when so many firms failed, he travelled for pleasure, liked to swagger down the *grands boulevards* in Paris. Soon after I had started at the new school he decided to leave the suburb where I had been born, and to take the family to live in the countryside in a much larger house.

This pleased me, though the countryside around my new school was eventually to please me even more. I loved its gentler southern hills and valleys and orchards far removed from the harsh north.

Not everything about my new school, however, pleased me. I would say it made me into a lifelong iconoclast. For I loved disputation and defeating an opponent in argument. If the opponent was an adult and had recourse to loss of temper, I regarded it as a triumph. Injustice and irrationality aroused me to contempt.

As adolescence approached, Father's own domineering temperament began to annoy me at home. Father had wanted me obstinate, opinionated, and conscious of my own superiority; so I would be, and would turn these weapons against Father himself.

But my father was made of sterner stuff than headmasters and since neither of us would ever compromise, the reconciliation which I would privately have liked never came. I discovered that I possessed a capacity for rage, and an extremely sharp tongue. Like Father, too, I was proud. I could not feel natural and intimate with Mother either. I sometimes tried to intervene in the squab-

146

bles between her and my father. She was not an easy woman to please.

If my life at home became more and more like balancing on an emotional precipice – and my mother and father were quarrelling more and more at this time – some of the masters at school cheered me up. In spite of my rebellions I appreciated the selfless way some of the masters worked for their pupils. The books I could borrow from them were full of delights. I read Scott, and volumes of topography and architecture, read Dean Inge and the poems of Tagore and even perused a manual of bell-ringing. The masters' and the head's tastes were represented in their own private libraries and to these books we boys also had access. The headmaster read the older boys ghost stories every night, or perhaps tales by Stevenson and Buchan. It was an enlightened school for the time, but I hated authority. In spite of this, I was learning the delight of learning for learning's sake. I was regarded as 'brilliant' with 'abnormally acute mental equipment', if at the same time 'difficult', 'argumentative'. I was told I was a 'neurotic introvert' – the words had just come into fashion – and a little 'unstable'.

But I enjoyed myself cycling to churches, and started to make brass rubbings in some of them. . . .

Jo looked up and realised she had better prepare some work for the morrow. Truly, Adam's life interested her more than her own work.

She read the final instalment in bed. It was as fascinating as a novel. Back in the north again at his next school, which he began to attend when he was thirteen, Adam was introduced by one of the masters to opera. Teaching at this school took place in an atmosphere of equality and ease, except in religious lessons which Adam regarded as a forum for debate. Other school-friends had become important by then, especially those who had civilized and intellectual parents and lived in a world not principally concerned with the making of money. His father and mother might play bridge – and introduce their sons to the game; his father might mark out a tennis-court at the new house; but there was nothing really intellectual there for Adam.

'Life is a moral gymnasium,' he confessed he often thought. But he was unhappy at home, isolated and, he imagined, misunderstood.

Reading between the lines Jo saw that he recognized, as did others, that he had a good deal of energy and a very strong will. He looked for, and found, in knowledge, and above all in learning about the past, the sense of harmony he realized he could not find elsewhere in his life; he discovered it in places easily reached from this new school: in churches, in old manors, in ancient fields.

Church architecture became his adolescent passion. He learned with delight of monastery life, and took ever more complicated brass-rubbings. Out on long bicycle-rides in the holidays he discovered the history of the county in which the school was to be found, explored Wharfedale and Nidderdale, Fountains Abbey and Bolton Abbey. The ruins of the past came increasingly alive. Local history, historical evolution, were his new passions.

Life was pleasurable. He was both active in his enthusiasms and meticulous in executing them. His painstaking drawings of the details of abbeys, his wide and yet deep knowledge, all of which he had acquired for himself, were to be his trademark. His school reports, as far as work was concerned, were always good: 'Adam writes a fluent, succinct, and elegant prose.' 'Adam is gifted in mathematics.' However his powers of logic were, they considered, overdeveloped.

He was too critical of others, insisted on pushing every statement to its logical conclusion. He was not particularly popular and the reports on his character were never as glowing as those on his work.

Jo got to the most interesting part a little further on. When he was fourteen Adam, already intellectually fascinated by the mysteries of sex, and even more intrigued by it than most boys of his age, began a loving relationship with a boy in his form, who also happened to be one of the three companions who shared his dorm. He was a dark young Scot called Francis, with no intellectual pretensions.

Night after night, for over two years, they slept together naked, to the horror of the other boys, who however never told on them. Strangely enough it was not sex he had with the boy, though they kissed and cuddled.

Why did Adam do it? Because he needed to be close to someone?

He said he usually felt restless, 'not knowing then that I would always feel restless unless I was in some way emotionally "fixed".' It must have been, thought Jo, the same need for harmony that he had already experienced in his architectural researches. He was a needy youth.

His friendship with another boy, an extremely clever young man, two years older than himself, was quite different, and Adam grew up intellectually under his tutelage. The sixth-former, from an intellectual family, amused himself by educating Adam, and invited him to meet his own father. In this family Adam found an ambience very different from that of the Angelwines and one much more to his taste.

Then, for no reason that he could clearly recall later, but in a sudden fit of irritability, he decided to leave the school at the same time as his intellectual friend did, telling his father he simply would not return there.

He had no idea what he wanted to be, unless it was to be an architect, which did not please Arnold, who thought architects were lowly clerks in offices.

Adam spent the summer playing tennis and reading.

His father was wild. In September he stated: 'I've made arrangements for you to start at the best grammar school in the city on Monday week.'

Adam was just as furious as his father and continued to be so for the two years he unwillingly attended the town grammar school. He disliked his new school companions; even his father said he was a snob.

To his old friend, now at Oxford, Adam had written: 'They are from a self-centred and aggressively anti-social lower middle class, self-assertive and ill-mannered, devoted only to "getting on".'

The friend demurred a little, never having understood why Adam had left the school they had both liked.

'It's true their lives are concentrated on their families rather than on a community,' he replied, but Adam was angry.

'That's why I believe in boarding-schools. Imagine what I'd be like if I'd never had the experience of leaving home when I was young.'

But he was awarded an Oxford scholarship, and went up there when he was eighteen to start his first Michaelmas term.

It was all so unlike her own life, thought Jo. Was it just the difference between men and women, or was it because Adam was so much cleverer than she was? Or that they were temperamentally so different?

Adam had always said they were alike but she had never believed him. She still had the impression that to him everything seemed cut and dried.

The next time he came to London she asked him to continue the story. She presumed it was not yet finished, that she herself might be part of it? This unsettled her. She did not want to be part of anyone else's development.

Over another meal, this time at the Strand Palace, which he always regarded with amusement as the sort of place his father might have frequented in his youth, Adam told her about his first venture into the land of girlfriends. When he was seventeen he had the use of his father's car, employing it occasionally to pick up girls. He felt much older than seventeen, played the young master, went to hotels for drinks, led what he thought was a sophisticated sort of life, even if it was provincial. Not that he managed at first to get anywhere with the young women he took out and played tennis with.

He had already reaped the benefit of the many continental holidays indulged in by his father, become blasé, adopted Gallic mannerisms and attitudes. Like his father he began to prefer the 'Continent' to England. Arnold in his travelling days had known Vienna and Paris and Bucharest and Berlin, and Adam already knew Paris well. He was often there in the company of his father's previous business associates, and thought he knew it as a Frenchman, not as a tourist.

The year before Adam started at Oxford Arnold had taken his family to Switzerland and there Adam had been in the seventh heaven. There, day after day, everyone swam and boated and danced and ate and drank, and he found the place perfect. He went around with two young Frenchmen, and made the acquaintance of the mistress, aged about twenty-eight, of a rich *vigneron* who allowed the young men to take her around for weeks. She flirted with them, provoked them, and allowed them a few liberties, though never the final one. By the end of the holiday Adam had no more interest in the girl other than as an object of experiment, for she seemed to have no genuine feelings, and he was put off by her vulgarity in spite of his desire for experience.

Women appeared to be another species, one he wanted to understand but despaired of ever understanding. But one of the happiest experiences of his life was to envelop him on holiday during the summer in which he reached eighteen, during his second visit to the Alps.

It was to be only the first of countless episodes of love with many different women. . . .

Jo thought: it was our mutual love for France perhaps that brought us together.

Jo said to Stephanie, 'Adam had all this life before I was born! For years and years and years! Why should he want to begin it all over again with me? Is it that men like him are never satisfied?'

Naturally, Stephanie had not read any of his 'History of Myself'. She knew he wrote long letters to her friend, and Jo had intimated enough for Stephie to understand what kind of man she had long been involved with.

Stephie realized that Adam was still genuinely in love with Jo. She said:

'He sounds to me like you once said he was – a romantic who denies he is one, and who feels impelled to make a god of reason.'

She thought, I would not want to get entangled in the life of such a self-absorbed individual, however brilliant, however much in love with me he said he was – and truly was.

Aloud, she said: 'I think you ought to write the story of the life of a man like him. You know so much about him. It would be much more popular than your tales of Kristin and Karen.'

Jo was hurt and Stephie saw she had been tactless.

'I meant that his life would lend itself to a realistic novel whilst all your imaginary stories would be more literary.'

'Yes, it's true,' said Jo with a sigh. 'Adam is not a literary person. But I just could not write about him. I feel I'd traduce him. I don't understand him well enough even now.'

No, he is part of your *real* life, thought Stephie, the part you often seem to want to deny.

Just before she moved herself, her possessions, and Cleo the cat in her basket, over from SW1 to NW3 Jo was asked to take a group of adolescent pupils to Paris for three weeks. This was apparently a policy of the school whose progressive headmistress thought it a good idea to 'gentle' young East End women through visits to the middle classes abroad.

'We couldn't really let them loose in Cheltenham, you see,' she explained.

Jo took this with a pinch of salt. As far as she was concerned, she would do her duty – she knew she could stay on the Avenue de Clichy with Françoise, one of the Frenchwomen she had met in Oxford the previous year, and she would enjoy her free time. It might be quite interesting too, teaching English in a college in Montmartre.

The girls she was to accompany and keep an eye on were aged fourteen or fifteen and she knew most of them, for they were in her fourth year B stream. The girls in the A stream she did not know.

In her mid-twenties, Jo was not a nervous person and viewed the prospect of being responsible for these girls with reasonable equanimity. What she had not been prepared for was actual delinquent behaviour.

One Carol Jones, of the A stream, was to be the cause of much embarrassment, and a sudden departure.

After she had been enjoying herself in Paris for about a week, Jo was called into the office of the *directrice* of the college to be informed that the lady had received a telephone call from one of the host families, complaining of the disappearance of all her week's housekeeping money. The woman did not want to accuse her daughter's guest, but really there was nobody else who could have had access to it. That morning, sniffing a strange odour, she had looked under Carol's bed and found a suitcase stuffed with expensive cream-cakes of every variety.

Jo had to interview the hapless girl in the presence of the hostess and the *directrice*, and to switch from French to English since Carol had so far refused to open her mouth and utter one word in the language she was supposed to be practising.

'I bought them for my mum,' was all she would say to Jo.

'But, Carol, where did you get the money from? Did you take it from Madame Dujardin's purse?'

There was a sulky silence.

Meanwhile, the *directrice* had got her senior English mistress to book a telephone line to London to speak to the East End headmistress. Jo was asked to explain things to her.

Miss Robertson was dismayed but did not seem too surprised.

'You will have to bring her back,' was all she said.

The next morning, Jo and the silent Carol were on the bus to Beauvais, then the plane to Lydd, the cheapest flight, and finally a bus into London, all of which time the girl sat and read *Woman's Own*. She did not look in any way ashamed. Jo did not try to ask her more; she knew she was to be met at Victoria coach station by the child's form teacher.

What did amaze her on their arrival in London was the whispered revelation by Miss Hume, who was accompanied by a probation officer, that the child's parents were both registered blind and that Carol had never before left home.

'Why was I not told?' Jo asked. 'I ought to have been made aware that there might be problems!'

'Oh, we always hope things will go well. To expect problems is often to court them,' said Miss Hume complacently.

Jo slept that night at home in Pimlico and returned to Paris the next day. The child had obviously not realised how embarrassing – even criminal – her actions had been, not only for Jo but for the other girls.

What else could happen now?

Fortunately the rest of her time in Paris was uneventful. One girl threw her arms round her and said she loved her; another began to speak quite good French, and Jo taught the French girls 'Greensleeves'. They appeared to enjoy her English lessons as they departed from their set textbook.

What retribution was dealt out to Carol was never revealed. She remained in the school. Was she a kleptomaniac, disturbed or just morally stupid?

Jo decided she must have put her love for her handicapped mother before all other considerations. She was never to offend again.

The new flat had been purpose-built in the 1930s. There were about forty small flats in a large three-storey block on a pleasant road. Theirs was on the first floor, not large, but with a sitting-room, bedroom, kitchen and bathroom. Adam had paid key money to the agent, thus making it a 'furnished flat', something Jo would never have been able to manage herself unless she had won on the new premium bonds.

There were some not very exciting bits of furniture left by the previous couple, a table at which to eat in the sitting-room, a bookcase – but Jo needed more than one now – and one small electric fire. Even with this it was much warmer than the cold-water flat in Pimlico. There was no proper central heating, and the windows were steel-framed, but the ceilings were lower than those at Coventry Square and it was cosier, if not so stylish. The bath-room was the greatest improvement, with constant hot water from an immersion heater, and a large clean bath. Jo felt it was luxury. As a child of twenty years before she had enjoyed an even nicer bathroom and big roaring open fires, but this was London and you couldn't have everything.

Adam said he was going to repaint it all. He had moved Hermione and most of his possessions, along with Phoebe and Matilda, to the Kent countryside and kept to his plan to stay in NW3 only between Monday and Friday.

In the one bedroom there was a vast wardrobe; in the tiny hall, a mirror; in the kitchen a minute fridge and a wooden draining-board. Adam cooked on a Thursday evening; he was better at it than Jo. She explored the area before he arrived and discovered Grodzinski's bakery up the road. It was always open, even on Sundays, and there were one or two of the new coffee-bars too, which were now spreading to the smarter suburbs. Further up the hill was a cinema where good films were shown. Down the hill, just as near, a lovely little branch library.

Jo was uneasily aware that these agreeable surroundings were pleasing her even more than the future proximity of Adam. Naturally, he would have had to live somewhere, even if she had never existed, and she supposed that, for him, she was in a way a bonus. He was not 'keeping' her, apart from the initial key money deposit; she did earn her living.

She hoped her little black-and-white cat would settle in well. Jo loved Cleopatra who had been given to her by the mother of a friend. Cleo would now have a garden to explore, rather than a walk from balcony to balcony along her side of the square, when several startled tenants had told her of the cat's sudden arrival at their windows, though they had not appeared to mind.

Adam was to come to London for a few days at the end of August. Then, having settled Hermione and the girls in their new abode, he would come for his four days a week to Jo.

By this time Jo had begun to teach Spanish, and that summer had been again to Spain. Victoria Station now led to Spain as well as to France, led to long, hot journeys in cheap compartments with the first sight of the south at dawn as mile after smooth mile delivered her past reddish earth and cypress trees and then lagoons to the Spanish frontier, and another railway-gauge, and dusty platforms where thirsty youths drank water from fountains.

Barcelona: heat on noonday squares, warmth of Ramblas nights. The dark Barrio Gótico, the even darker impression of dark blue in the vast Santa Maria del Mar with the melons piled in the streets around. She was to spend a month there in a doctor's family. Not that Catalonia was a particularly sensible place to stay if you wanted to learn Castilian but she had loved the place before with Adam, and wanted to see it again.

After the month was up she went over the Pyrenees in a bus to Perpignan and thence to Toulouse where she met Clare Jackson and Susie Swift, who wanted to look at cloisters. Stephie had said she could not manage it this year.

On her return, as a final fling, before Adam's arrival, Jo had had a one-night-stand with a man called William Appleton. Why, she was not sure. It was more like the encounter in the train; exciting, quite pleasurable. Nothing to do with love. A relief, she supposed.

Then the autumn was upon them both, and Adam was there,

and there would be suppers together and once a week a visit to the cinema up the road.

She thought, I might as well be married!

As long as she lived with him she knew she would be faithful.

INTERLUDE

In the February of 1957, after living with Adam for less than six months, Jo had a great shock. She discovered she was pregnant. She remembered well when it could have happened. She had been living with Adam for only two or three months but with the feeling of being 'married', and therefore being more likely to take risks. Four years of contrivances had wearied her. Surely there must be some way out.

Once the possibility arose however, Jo knew there *was* no way out. Her parents would be devastated – she could not do such a thing to them. Premarital sex and an illegitimate child were the two worst sins in the calendar of respectable parents. There would be no sympathy at all. There might have been if she could have married the father, but that was clearly impossible.

She telephoned Julia, who knew about these things, and arranged an appointment with a suave-looking doctor in West Brompton. First, he said, he must ascertain that she really was pregnant. Until she knew for sure, she nursed wonderful daydreams. In spite of everything, how she would love to have this child. If she were rich, and lived abroad, or could do it secretly. . . . She did not even think very much about Adam as the baby's father; it was the baby who set her off dreaming . . . her baby.

Adam said she must make her own decision.

What she wanted to say was: '*You* tell them – *you* speak to them and then I can have it – you started all this!'

But she knew he never would. A child would also make her even more beholden to him, and her future would be arranged for ever. She had no illusions about children. But she would rather destroy an embryo than have a baby who might have to be adopted. That would be beyond her. She knew it would also be beyond Adam too, though she might force his hand in this way. Then she thought of Phoebe and Matilda, who were alive and needed their father even if he had other fish to fry for part of the week.

This was 1957 and abortions were illegal. Also expensive, if they were to be done safely, which meant by a qualified doctor.

Ten years later, but then only if she were lucky in her doctor, Jo might have done legally what she had to do that February evening. Even at the last moment, if Adam had told her he would abandon all his other obligations to marry her one day, she might perhaps have changed her mind. But she knew he could not, must not, did not really want him to. She was unsure that she would want to marry him, though she sometimes told him she would.

She wanted the baby, not the marriage; the baby who would mean telling her parents, disrupting – even ruining – her mother's life, and she could not face it. It should rightly be Adam who told her parents, but he would be either too guilty or too terrified to do this, and she did not ask him.

The operation cost £80, which the clearly scared Adam was glad to pay. The surgery was on the third floor of a block of mansion flats. First, she had to go for an interview and a check-up one Tuesday morning. It was the school half-term: Shrove Tuesday.

She went alone, and the middle-aged doctor gave her an internal examination. Yes, she was certainly pregnant. Only seven weeks though.

How could he tell? Perhaps he was just saying she was, to get the £80.

Could she come round on the Friday evening three days later when the doctor did his operations with a nurse assisting? It would all be over by the weekend, so she need not miss work.

She felt she had to get it over and done with, closed her mind to any further day-dreams. Several of her friends had done the same, so she was not frightened, although her knowledge of illegal abortions culled from novels ought perhaps to have made her so. Stories of terrible pain, of bleeding. . . .

Adam left her at seven o'clock at the mansion flats, having given her the money. Jo went up in the lift, hungry because she had eaten no dinner. They were waiting for her in a room with an operating table. The nurse looked middle-aged too, competent.

She felt a prick on the wrist before succumbing to the anaesthetic; then she woke to hear herself telling the doctor he was a benefactor of humanity. The operation had been accomplished quickly and, he said, successfully.

He took her home in his own car and she was sick on the way. The result of the anaesthetic, he said.

Adam was waiting for her, looking extremely nervous. Jo went to bed and rested the next day, when Adam went over to Hermione for his usual Saturday and Sunday in the country. She had no pain and had lost very little blood. Clare Jackson arrived on the Saturday morning and Jo was surprised. Apparently Adam had asked her to look in and check that she was all right. She felt quite normal, very relieved, anxious to put the whole thing behind her, and to thrust any deeper thoughts or feelings away from her conscious mind.

She returned to work the following week.

It had all been conveniently managed and for the time she felt no regret. She knew that, like Adam, she had wanted both to have her cake and eat it. Unlike him, however, she was a woman, and life was not so easy.

But it must never happen again. She would refuse to undergo

another operation. If there ever were a next time, with matters still as complicated as ever, and if she still could not have a baby, then it would be curtains for their affair.

Then she thought: but even if there never is a next time, what I have been forced to do is to involve myself in a choice. I have drawn a line under our love. Nothing will ever be the same again.

It would take another eighteen months for her to realize the consequences of that choice.

She was to suffer far more from the death of little Cleopatra who was knocked over by a car starting when she was asleep underneath it. Jo was at work. Only when Cleo did not come to greet her as usual and the caretaker of the flats came out with a long face, did she realize what had happened. She should not have had to be away at work, was her first thought. Cleo was like a baby and you did not leave babies out by themselves. She was responsible for her being killed. She rang Adam who was away at a conference.

'I thought it must be the cat,' he said. 'You would not ring me for anything else.'

She cried all night.

TWO

Stephanie

1957–1984

NINE

On a cold January morning, a few days before Jo realised she might be pregnant, Stephanie was just about to set off to the Underground station on her usual journey to the Senate House or the British Museum when the postman arrived.

Often he was late, and she missed seeing if any of the letters were for her until she returned from work in the evening. This particular morning he stuffed through the letter box the usual mixture of boring medical advertisements for her father and letters from her many friends for her mother. Lamorna Fischer was not yet up; she always enjoyed a cup of tea in bed before a long hot bath, and her husband was away in the West Country travelling around, talking up pharmaceuticals to doctors whom he hoped to influence, or interview, or interviewing hospital managers or administrators.

Stephanie bent down, put the letters on the kitchen table, flipped through them, and then saw that one of them, a blue airmail letter, stamped New York, was for her.

She took it up quickly.

The name of the sender was on the back: Costas Mitsoukopolis.

It had been months since she had received a postcard from him – from Norway of all places. She was pleased, looked forward to reading it.

She added it to the papers in her briefcase, shouted 'Goodbye' to Lamorna, who made a feeble reply, and was off out of the door. There was a light powdering of snow already on the garden and the road.

On the tube she opened the letter.

My dear Stephie

I find I am detailed to work at a research outfit in London from mid-January. Woburn Square, near Russell Square, not far from where you labour, I guess. My masters have also found me a place to live in Bloomsbury Square. It sounds very English, and is a kind of sublet apartment, what you call 'flatlets'.

May we meet? I would love to see you again. I never expected to, you know. I enclose my phone number, just in case you have changed yours {which you once gave me in case I was in London for the vac}.

I shall understand if you don't want to meet again. I expect a lot of water has passed under the bridge since we last wrote, and even more since those days in Mesopotamia or in Walton Street?

We can exchange all news later.

Your old friend
Costas.

Stephanie found her hands were trembling. She had not allowed herself to feel too unhappy when Costas Mitsoukopolis left at the end of her second year in Oxford, almost six years ago, though it had hurt, and she had been very upset when he went away. But she had deliberately tried to banish his image from her mind. They might never meet again. He had his life and she had hers.

A clear picture of him was suddenly in her head as she went up in the lift at Goodge Street; she felt excited and happier than she had for a long time. He had not forgotten her.

In the depths of her mind she had really known that he would

166

not forget her. But that was different from his wanting to see her again. As for all that water flowing under the bridges, she paid little attention to the passing of time in her own life, which was surprising for a person with a history degree, for whom time ought to be of the essence. In a curious way she felt that Costas, whether absent or present, had meant enough for her to carry his image with her and remember for a lifetime. But you could not expect a young man to feel the same.

He was not so young now though, and she was free of any other entanglement. Not that she expected things to be the same between them but it would be so – *reviving* – to see him again. She would be able to recall shared time together whether she let him know or not that that was what she was doing.

Costas was still working, as far as she knew, for the United Nations, visiting trouble spots, analysing problems. There were plenty of those: Cyprus, Israel, the cold war situation, terrorists of one sort or another. She had never pestered him for details of his work in the few letters they had exchanged during the last few years. He would tell her what he judged she ought to know. This was not because he had any opinion about women's lack of inter- est in political situations or in current events, but because he did not write long letters. He would have answered any questions she cared to ask, and she had not cared to ask.

As Stephie sat at her usual desk with the usual pile of refer- ences before her, she knew she must rouse herself from the eighteenth-century torpor that had accompanied the last year or two. She had done a lot of work, yes, but the academic detective work had not excited her as much as she had hoped. Nobody would know that, for she was a capable writer who knew how to interest a reader, though she sometimes suspected that academic readers might not be so impressed by her style as by her clever delving into the dusty past. What had she to show for the last four and half years? Well, here was her thesis, which would soon be finished, and which she must now have retyped.

She had another special notebook in which she wrote ideas of her own, using some of the material of her researches. All these notes she had made were for the projected novel, set in the time of Queen Anne, a period that in Stephanie's experience few readers knew much about. They had vaguely heard of William and Mary and James II but then skipped to the Old Pretender and his son Bonnie Prince Charlie. Not much was ever said at school about Queen Anne or the great battles of the time, or the rest of the century, before the French Revolution suddenly appeared in 1789. She had learned more in the past from Thackeray's *Henry Esmond* than from text books. She had begun to nurse other ideas too. *Anna Victorix* her provisional title, was not to be her only novel. She planned stories set in other countries of Europe.

Curiously enough, none of her enthusiasm for her own writing faded when she thought of Costa. The writing was something quite separate, which might interest him, or might not. In any case, a whole lifetime of research was before her.

Dear Costas

I am so pleased you are to come to London. How long for, do you think? Do they usually tell you? The research institute you mention is quite near where I work, also in Bloomsbury. Let me know when you arrive – the phone number is the same as ever. I can treat you to a good meal at Bertorelli's, though I suppose UN officials are used to far grander restaurants.

With love from

Stephie.

There was only a fortnight in which to await his arrival and Stephie found herself unusually anxious. It had been so long since they had seen each other and she was uncertain what might have passed under *his* bridges. Many women? A wife perhaps? Would he still find her attractive? She was certain that her own feelings

168

towards him would not have changed. She would find him the same as he had always been. Madly attractive. Yet that certainly might be dangerous. She had better not betray any indecorous enthusiasm unless he did so first. But she was so happy that he was coming to London and that he wanted to see her! She tried not to count the days before he would be in London. She was so excited; it was unlike her.

How had she managed for six years not to miss him, not to think about him constantly? Well, she had. She gathered her wits and saw that she must be rational. If she had managed for so long to be reasonable she could go on being so. She resisted day dreaming about their reunion.

He telephoned on the Friday night, having, he said, slept off his jet-lag. He sounded just the same except for a slight American accent, and they arranged to meet outside the Senate House at seven o'clock on the Monday after they had both finished work.

That evening there was a slight powdering of snow on the pavements and a few lights were still on in the Institute of Education. Stephie wondered for a moment if Jo might still be there. No, of course she wouldn't. Thinking about her own past she had lost track of time. Jo had been teaching in the East End for four terms now, claiming she enjoyed it more than the previous practice term in the convent.

Stephie came out of the covered entrance to the vast building. No wonder Orwell had used it as his Ministry of Fear in *Ninety Eighty-Four*. Her thoughts were skittering around; why think about Jo or Orwell now?

She took a deep breath and looked over in the direction of Gordon Square. They were threatening to pull down some of the lovely Georgian buildings that were left and a crane was silhouetted against the January sky.

Then she saw him striding swiftly towards the Senate House steps, swinging a briefcase. He must have just left his job; what the Americans called a 'think tank'.

'Costas!' she tried to shout, but her voice came out muffled. But he looked in her direction and waved. She stood stock-still and waited for him.

When he came up she saw that his heavy overcoat was pearled with drops of melted snowflakes. He stood before her, smiling, took off one of his gloves as she put out her hand to shake his. The contact between their skins seemed quite natural, was like putting on a familiar glove that had been lost.

He raised her hand and kissed it. He had always had 'foreign' manners; obviously America had not altered them.

'Your hand is so warm!' he said.

'Would you like me to take you out to dinner?' she asked him. 'It's not far.'

'How will you get home? It's a cold night.'

'Oh, there is the Underground – it goes on till midnight.'

They walked slowly towards Tottenham Court Road, crossed it and walked towards Charlotte Street.

The street was not well lit, so that when they finally entered the restaurant the light dazzled them and they stood silently for a moment, looking at each other.

'You have not changed!' he said after the receptionist had taken their coats.

They were led to a table at the back on the ground floor. Once they were seated Stephie allowed herself to look at him again. He was perhaps a little filled out, but the hands were the same, with the dark hairs on the back, the hair on his head still dark too, and curly. It was just as if the intervening years had never been.

He must have been thinking along the same lines for, after several minutes of utter quiet, he said:

'Six years – why did I not come before?'

He appeared to be asking himself the question rather than her, but she replied:

'Never mind – here you are!'

He did not seem to take this as anything untoward, had never regarded her as 'forward'.

Indeed, he said in reply, 'It is so good to see you – you must tell me everything that has happened to you! But perhaps I do not need to know,' he added quietly.

'Well you can start by telling me what you have been doing. My life is very tranquil. I've nearly finished my thesis. I still live at home.'

'My life is well organised,' he said, 'but a little boring!'

'How can international relations be boring?'

'Well, I suppose it is exciting in some ways. It uses the top part of my mind, not the other parts of my brain.'

He ate his melon deftly and they toasted each other shyly in Soave. She no longer felt nervous but could see that he was, a little.

Suddenly she knew that there was only one way for them to be back together completely. Perhaps he was thinking the same and wondering whether she would want to resume the old relation-ship. But she could say nothing until he gave her a clue to the direction of his thought. He was looking at her steadily as they waited for their veal escalope, which arrived at last with its slices of lemon.

'Do you often come here?' he asked her.

'I don't eat out all that much, but when I do I come here, usually with Josephine or colleagues from the history department.' She knew he was trying to find out if she came with a man, a steady boyfriend.

'Ah, I remember you talking about little Josephine, and I believe I met her once or twice,' he said. 'Not that I know any of your friends well, but I do remember her.'

After a pause, Stephie ventured: 'I suppose you eat in all the posh restaurants in New York?'

'I don't really enjoy such places – this sort of restaurant is much nicer. *Plus intime.*'

'It depends on who you are with,' she said boldly.

'Yes.'

They were soon on the last course. Costas did not drink very much but he poured them both another glass of Soave.

'You must have a glass of their zabaglione – it's delicious,' said Stephie.

'You have a sweet tooth, Stephie, I remember!'

She was suddenly back in Walton Street on a summer afternoon of his last Trinity term. They had bought ice-cream cornets and were eating them in bed. It seemed such a long time ago; he would have changed. But now, as they waited for their dessert, he was saying something earnestly.

'I expect you will have changed a bit, Stephie, as I have. I mean, I shall never forget Oxford, and that means I shall never forget you – but I'll do as you wish – whatever you want. It may be enough to be together as friends.'

'I don't think I have changed very much,' she said. 'Except that I've got older. But I'm sure you've had a much more exciting life than I have in the last few years – so perhaps *you* are different?'

'When I knew they were sending me to London,' he said, 'I thought it is time – it's destiny. I never wanted to push things one way or another, you know, there was so much I had to do in life. But, believe me, I did look forward to your letters though I'm such a bad correspondent myself. You must tell me all about your research.'

'I've nearly finished my thesis but I've got ideas for another career. It sounds portentous saying it like that but I want to write novels.'

She twiddled the stem of her glass and looked down, feeling suddenly shy. She did not usually talk either about herself or her work except occasionally to a friend like Jo or Clare.

'I mean … I have started to write … a novel.' (And seeing you doesn't take away my ambitions – it makes them all seem more possible, she was thinking.)

She thought, but the only way of getting back to where we were, to our old selves – and it won't be 'back' but something new because we are new ourselves in a way – is by showing each other what we feel through passion. You can't talk about that as it might all have evaporated.

But as she looked up at him, as the waiter brought their zabaglione, she knew she would follow wherever he led if he wanted her. You never knew the truth of your feelings till you were back in your body. And bodies had, she had been told but had never quite believed it, an unaccountable way of their own, so that desire might fail.

'I'm so glad. You will write a splendid story. I won't ask you what it is about till you have finished it!'

'Now tell me what you have been doing at the UN,' she said, making an effort. It would soon be time to go and she must leave it to him where and when they met again.

He elaborated on his travels, in the tight spots he had been in. She had known about the war in Greece that he had been involved in during his teens before coming to Oxford on a scholarship from the British Council, but now he told her how he had narrowly missed being shot by a terrorist in Cyprus, three years ago, which accounted for a gap in his letters.

Where else had he been?

'I have to go back to New York in October. Till then I stay here most of the time. But they might want me to go to Rome as an observer after this new Europe thing is signed.'

'You mean what they are calling the Common Market?'

'That's it. How well-informed you are. The United Kingdom isn't keen. Personally, I think one day it should be a council of the whole of Europe, if only the Hungarians and the Czechoslovaks and the others could be members – not just a trade thing. Not much hope, though, with the Soviet stranglehold.'

'There's such a lot wrong everywhere – don't you find it depressing?'

'There'll never be a perfect world,' he said with a smile. Then, 'Look, Stephie, I mustn't make you late home, but can we arrange to meet again soon?'

'Yes, Costas – whenever you want.'

He looked at her searchingly. 'Then I think I shall like to entertain you. There's a little restaurant attached to my block of apartments – I mean "flatlets" – where we could eat. They even bring up meals on trolleys for hotel guests. Saves having to go out on a cold evening.'

'Do you have any appointments – meetings and things – in the evening?'

'No, I don't have any duties after six o'clock – not so far anyway. When could you come? Tomorrow? Or must you work at home?'

'I can meet you outside the Senate House as we did today,' she said. 'I know where you are staying – it's not far. Or I could come straight to the hotel.'

'I shall meet you. I shall come for you at seven again, and if it is raining I shall have bought a big new English umbrella – but no bowler hat!'

They went out together after she had let him pay. As he had explained, he was well off monetarily now.

As he said goodbye outside Goodge Street, he murmured, 'Perhaps the restaurant will serve ice-cream!'

She returned home in a dream of happiness.

The next morning Stephie was determined to carry on as usual. She was excited, but she refused to pursue a day-dream. If Costas still liked her – and he appeared to approve of her – he would not want a woman who thought about nothing but him!

She had always been able to separate her work in Oxford from their clandestine Walton Street meetings. She had not found it hard to do this, for she had not the kind of possessive temperament that needed constant reassurance or expected a lover to concentrate all his thoughts upon her.

By five minutes to seven that evening she was waiting on the pavement in front of the Senate House. The moon was high in the sky, amongst clouds like scoops of cream. The rest of the sky was dark; no more snow had fallen that day, but that from the day before was now a stiffened rim of Christmas-cake icing. The air was still cold, perhaps it was too cold now to snow again.

He came towards her, hands in gloves, a fur hat that she had not seen before, on his head. She waited; he was quickly by her side, took one glove off, took one of her hands and tucked it into his pocket where his own hand enclasped hers like a warm paw.

'I shall not raise my hat! Careful – don't walk on the snow, it's frozen hard. It's not far.'

They walked across Russell Square and then turned right along Bedford Place and along the side of another smaller square. There was a statue in the centre of the square's gardens and the plane trees were motionless in the moonlight.

'I think, a warm drink,' he said. 'Then they will bring up a little meal to my apartment if we order it down here – the hotel and the restaurant are owned by the same management as the apartments. The food is not so bad. If you would like that? I know hotels are notorious for unexciting food.'

She had been dreading a stiff formal meal in the hotel dining-room.

'Lovely!' she murmured.

'I'll order for us. Would a mushroom omelette be OK, or are you very hungry?'

'That would be a good idea. And ice-cream?'

He laughed. 'Not too cold for ice-cream?'

'No, I don't think so.' They went into the bar.

'As we are in England – though not in Oxford – would you like a *very* dry sherry to remind us of old times? I think I would.'

'That would be just right,' she murmured.

It was nutty-flavoured, warm, and even her feet began to thaw.

They sat at a little table and he looked at her silently as he drank his sherry.

'Oh, Stephie,' he said finally.

They went up in a little old lift.

The hotel had once been an early eighteenth-century house and there were low-ceilinged twisty corridors leading to the private apartments. She followed him down them.

He opened a door at the end of a short corridor. He had left the standard lamp shining in his room, and the curtains were drawn. They faced each other, he put out his hands and took both of hers in his.

'I suppose we *have* to eat?' he said.

Stephie laughed: 'They'll be bringing our omelettes up soon.' But his touch had made her shiver.

'You are quite right, they will. We had better sit down.'

Stephie saw that this was indeed the sitting-room. The door opposite must lead to the bedroom, and possibly a bathroom. Here, there were two armchairs drawn up to face each other on each side of an electric fire. It was the turn of Costas to smile.

'There is central heating, but I suppose they worry lest their visitors might not be warm enough, hence the extra fire. I find London quite cosy. How did I ever manage in Oxford in that basement room!'

'It was just as cold in college. I bet they still have those one-bar heaters. We used to have to take baths to get warm. But we were young, I suppose.'

'Well, you're not so old now. I can't tell you what I felt like when I had my thirtieth birthday last year – the years have just crept up. But it's not quite seven years, only six, since we were last together, so I can't claim all the cells in my body have changed.'

His voice *had* slightly changed, had that slight American twang to it. She looked at him and put her hand out to him.

'I still feel the same,' he said.

Just then there was a knock at the door and they both jumped up as if they were misbehaving.

'Come in!'

A waiter pushing a trolley made his ceremonial appearance. There were two plates covered by silver dishes, a coffee-pot, white cups and saucers, and two fruit-dishes, obviously for the ice-cream, which was under a little dome.

The waiter, only a boy really, with several spots on his cheeks, placed a lacy cloth on the small table by the window, set it with large pieces of cutlery, then removed the dishes on to the table.

'Will that be all, sir? I did not bring up any wine as you had not ordered any.'

'Did you want wine, Stephie?'' asked Costas.

'No, thank you – the sherry was enough. And there's the coffee.'

'Thank you, that will be all,' said Costas and the waiter clanked away with the trolley. They peered under the silver covers.

'A nice mushroom omelette, and I see some bread. I hope it's enough.'

They were both hungry and ate everything up.

'The ice-cream will be slightly warm perhaps,' he said.

Stephie was glad that Costas had not felt it necessary to ply her with wine. She remembered Jo telling her how Adam Angelwine used at first always to make sure she was nicely tipsy when they went to hotels.

But this was the first flatlet Stephie had ever been in accompanied by a man. She wondered vaguely how many women Costas had shared rooms with. It did not really seem to matter.

Costas looked nervous, and she decided, after the ice-cream, which was a mixture of chocolate and coffee, her favourites, to pour the coffee. It did not look too bad, though Costas must be used to wonderful American coffee. So many of her friends would return from America saying how dreadful they now found English meals and drinks, after being exposed to Chicago or New York fare.

To break the other sort of ice, and put them both out of their misery, she put her hand again across the table to him.

'As good as the Oxford ice-cream?' she asked.

He put her hand up to his cheek. 'As good – for me. Drink up.'

She did so and then they both stood up and in a sort of dream she saw him open the door to the other room. A remembrance of the old Walton Street basement, dusty and book-filled, flashed across her inner eye.

Here was a neutral sort of room, but there was a large bed, turned down ready for Costas's slumbers by the maid he had told her cleaned every morning and came in before dark to turn down his bed.

A gold-painted radiator was located under the window. The light came in from the other room; they did not switch on the bedroom lamp.

They held each other close for a moment and then he took off her shoes for her. He had already changed into loafers and now he slid these off too.

'Quick – don't let's get cold!'

They tumbled under the yellow eiderdown and at last held each other tight, arms round each other's necks, then an entanglement of toes and feet, and the warmth of their two bodies that fitted so well together.

It felt comfortable; it felt almost as if they were both still students; it felt just as it used to feel, she thought. Did he feel the same?

After a little time he murmured, 'Oh this is so right! Why did I leave it so long? Forgive me.'

Stephie felt as if she was back home, as if the intervening years had only shallowly buried something that would always be waiting to return. Once known, never forgotten. It was not just the physical presence of Costas or the old magically familiar pleasure she had always had from him, but also a gentle reshaping of her mind, a putting back of her spirit. She knew the contours of his mind as she knew the contours of his body, and nothing was a surprise.

'Oh you feel just the same, so soft and silky,' he said.

178

She traced his face with her hands and felt the tears on his cheeks, and kissed them.

Slowly, in the half-dark, with only a faint band of light from the almost closed door to the next room reminding them of the world beyond the bed, beyond themselves, they made love. Quietly at first, then more passionately, as if each had been a vessel for conserving the precious distillation that only the other could release into the atmosphere and turn into a different more powerful essence when the two mingled.

But their lovemaking had always been simple, joyful, and uncomplicated, and it was so now. Only it also bore the print of knowledge of time past and the sensation of rebalancing towards the future.

'I love you, Costas,' said Stephie, no longer reluctant to say what she felt and not caring to hold back anything of herself. She trusted him, had always trusted him, in spite of the long years they had been parted.

'Did you think I would never come back?' he asked. 'I was young – foolish not to tell you then – but, you see, I didn't know! Only later, when I met other women, and realised what I might have lost. Forgive me, Stephie, for leaving you. I could not write what I felt, but I put myself in for this London work so as to see you again. Now I know I do love you, Stephie – I love your body and I love your soul. Whatever happens we mustn't part from each other again.'

She made love to him again then, and remembered all his little ways that had not changed. Neither had she.

At half past eleven they had to get up, for Stephie had to go home that night. Costas repeated on the way to the Underground that he would be in London until October. Perhaps they might one day find a little place together, though it was as yet uncertain where they would send him next.

She said nothing to her parents the next day except that an American friend she had known in Oxford was visiting London and she had promised to show him round. They were incurious. She did not want to invite him to Edgware yet; perhaps one day in the next month or two if he wanted to.... In the meantime she would get on with her work, and with her novel, but would be there for Costas whenever he was free from his committees or lectures. It was lucky she had no job, like Jo, with fixed hours. She had worked hard to finish her thesis and was mistress of her own time until the end of summer.

Stephie slept soundly that night, waking at eight o'clock on Wednesday morning, with an immediate feeling of happiness before she realised what was causing her such joy.

Costas was to be at work all morning, but would have his afternoon free. They had arranged for him to come over to the library at half-past two so she might show him a little of her usual surroundings before they walked around Bloomsbury, perhaps browsed a little in Dillons before having tea in a little café in Museum Street.

The sun was out; the sky was an icy blue, but the snow had practically all melted. She decided to work hard until lunch-time, wanting to sort out the final draft of the last third of her thesis ready for typing. The first two thirds were already lying at home on a table in her bedroom in a bright-red file, having been efficiently typed by one of the many middle-aged women who offered their services to graduates on a notice board in the Senate House library.

Stephie's other writing still with its provisional title of *Anna Victrix* was now in thick, lined exercise books. Of these she allowed only the latest one to travel with her in her briefcase, terrified she might lose the rest on the tube or inadvertently have them cleared away by a cleaner. Curiously enough she had never worried lest the thesis might meet the same fate. Her novel she would type herself, considering that so long as it was clean and readable it need not conform to the rather fussy specifications the university required for a thesis.

She accomplished a good deal in three and a half hours before eating a vegetarian lunch at SOAS, the School of Oriental and African Studies. Jo had once suggested she eat her lunch there for she had used the cafeteria when she was following her studies at the Institute of Education. There would be only half an hour before Costas arrived, so Stephie spent the time reading the paper in the common room.

She saw him through the window that led on to the inner court-yard and was quickly by his side. He kissed her on the cheek.

'Can I see your "work station"?' he asked. 'I like to think of you sitting writing – and I shall want to read your collected works one day, you know!'

She took him up in the lift and he looked round the library with interest.

'I can show you one day what I have already had typed,' she whispered. It seemed quite natural for him to be with her in her place of work. As they went out, and walked along the corridor back to the lift they passed one of Stephie's tutors, Mrs Barnard, who smiled a half-greeting as she passed them.

'Where now?' asked Costas as they came out of the vast building.

'Well, I thought you might like to browse in my favourite book-shop.'

He laughed. 'One of my favourite places of pilgrimage,' he said.

It was agreeable to feel so easy with a man with whom not many hours before you had been in the most intimate conjunction. She could not remember ever having gone into a bookshop with him in Oxford. They had spent most of their time in his basement, usually in bed. Apart of course from the occasional lecture. But now Costas put his arm round her as they walked along, and she liked that.

They spent quite a long time in Dillons. He made his way to the new thrillers after looking at the political science at the back of the shop. Stephie was lingering at the fiction table.

'One day yours will be there,' he said encouragingly. 'And maybe your thesis will be bound under the university imprint too.'

'I shouldn't think so,' she said.

'Which do you care about most?'

'Guess!'

'Your novel?'

'Yes.'

He squeezed her hand, and he thought what a lot of time he had wasted away from her. It was so delightful just to be with Stephie, never mind making love to her.

'What about that tea?' he suggested.

They walked down Gower Street to Great Russell Street and stood for a moment looking at the great grey British Museum.

'I shall need a ticket for the Reading Room,' he said. 'I hope they will let me have one. I carry bona fide references with me.'

They crossed the road and turned down Coptic Street and looked in the old jewellery shop at Cameo Corner. He thought, I would love to give her a ring – perhaps a pearl ring – but I mustn't suggest it yet – she might think me a little mad.

Although they had now met in London only three times, it seemed like three months since they had found each other.

'We just have to go across to Museum Street now,' said Stephie. 'That's if you want your tea.'

They found the tiny tea-shop at the museum end of the street and stood for a moment gazing into its window. Next to it was a shop full of magic.

'Look,' said Costas excitedly. 'Things for conjurors and witches! Fancy it being so near the fount of real knowledge. London is an extraordinary place. I wonder what was here before they built the British Museum? Do you think it was a necromancer's?'

'I just love this part of London – and Drury Lane and the Seven Dials – they're not very far away – and the Courts off St Martin's Lane – so much was pulled down by the Edwardians to build Kingsway and the Aldwych,' replied Stephie. 'But there are already plans to pull more old Bloomsbury buildings down, even those in the squares. Of course they were bombed a good deal in the war.

And they must have already demolished quite a lot when they built the Senate House – as though *that* building wasn't bad enough! But what would the old pre-war inhabitants think about it.'

'Virginia Woolf?' asked Costas. 'She was a great feminist wasn't she? I think I am one too.'

Stephie laughed. 'Yes, she and her sister, and then her husband, lived in Gordon Square. She seems to be rather unfashionable at present. She was my favourite writer for years.'

They were staring at a cardboard 'transformation scene', part of a toy theatre in the window.

'I do hope they don't do anything to the museum Reading Room. I hate change,' said Stephie.

'They showed us round yesterday; I was just a tourist. I really must get that card. Are you ready for tea now?'

It was getting colder – she needed something to warm her up.

They went into the little tea-shop and the door pinged with a tiny tinkle like a fairy bell, perhaps left over from next door.

'Russian tea – my favourite,' she said.

'Mine too. I remember your telling me you had Russian blood, Stephie.'

'Yes, my father's mother was born in St Petersburg. They call it Leningrad now, as you know. Horrible name. But Granny was Jewish so I can't really lay claim to be Russian.'

'What was she called?'

'Lara. It's the pet form of Larissa. She was Larissa Bromberg before she married my Grandpa Fischer in Berlin.'

'Larissa – Lara – what a lovely name!'

He put his hand over hers as it lay on the table by her tall glass of golden tea.

'Stephanie,' he said. 'My darling.'

The tea warmed them up though their hearts did not need warming.

After this they walked down to the end of Great Russell Street and found Bloomsbury Square awaiting their return.

A few days later, on a Saturday afternoon, Jo, in Bloomsbury to meet a friend who was attending a course at RADA, passed University College and felt sure it was Stephie she had seen on the other side of the road, arm-in-arm with a young man. But she did not cross the road to greet her. They looked so doubly self-enclosed. Stephie would tell her in her own good time. If there was anything to be told.

For the rest of the month of January and for the first half of February Stephie and Costas spent as much time as possible with each other in the afternoons or evenings. If Mrs Fischer wondered why her daughter was out every evening she did not say anything. Stephie had always been independent and if she were to be away for a weekend she would always let her know.

They would both work in the morning, Costas at one of his various 'think-tanks' or in the British Museum Reading Room, where he was now pursuing some historical research into ideas of European integration. Stephanie would be at her usual desk in the Senate House where she was putting the finishing touches to her thesis before giving it to Mrs Barnard for a second reading. Her other tutor had gone off on a sabbatical, and Helen Barnard, who had read the first two-thirds, very much wanted her to finish before the beginning of the summer term as she herself would then be overworked, reading and marking degree-exam papers.

Naturally, Stephie spent a good deal of time at the flatlet in Bloomsbury Square, but the couple also took the 24 bus north and walked on a cold wintry Hampstead Heath; went to the Academy Cinema to see French films; visited restaurants Stephie had never visited before, and generally explored London.

Stephie knew she would have to ask Costas if he would like to meet her parents, or rather her mother, as her father was away once again, but hesitated lest he might feel she was treating him like a fiancé. She would not think about the future until Costas mentioned if himself. What was the use, when he had to return to the States in October?

Then Costas said, one February afternoon, 'Could we go away next weekend? What about having a night in Oxford? We could see our old haunts and I might visit my old college.'

It seemed a century since she had been there, yet whenever she was with Costas the years dropped away and she could even imagine that when they woke together she would be back in the old room with him.

'I'd love to. I don't know whether my old tutor would want to see me, but it would be nice to walk round the old place. If only it were summer ...'

'Summer will come,' said Costas.

'And then you must come and see my suburb,' she suggested. 'I mean if you would like to. It's not very interesting.'

'I would like to meet your parents,' he said simply.

She blushed. 'They have met some of my women friends, but I don't think I have ever taken a man home!'

'About time then! And we must have a party in summer when I can meet your other friends. I have been very selfish during the last few weeks.'

Stephie knew that some subtle rearrangement was going on in his mind. Perhaps they had made so much love that he felt they needed a little fresh air. She said something of the sort to him.

'No, indeed! If I had my way I'd be even more selfish – for years and years and years! But I know I should help you fit your life together. It is different for me. I don't know where I shall be after October – all I know is that I shall want to be with you.'

His words filled her with happiness and yet she did not want to spoil them by assuming he meant anything formal. Love was enough for the time being.

She replied: 'Let's go to Oxford this weekend – and then next weekend, or the weekend after. Father may perhaps have returned from his travels and I'll invite you to tea!'

TEN

She had thought he would want to stay in some bed-and-breakfast place near Walton Street, though Oxford was not over-endowed with such places, but he did not. They were to stay at the Randolph.

'It's no good pretending I'm poverty-stricken,' he said. 'I want us to have a luxurious stay. Would you enjoy that?'

'Of course. I love luxury – haven't had much.'

But he knew that it would not really have mattered if he had taken her to some decrepit lodging in Jericho or Cowley; all that mattered was for them to be together.

As the train trundled into Oxford station from Reading she realised she had not been back since that summer afternoon when she and Jo and Susie Swift had taken their seats in the train that was to lead them towards the future. Nearly five years ago now. They hadn't seen Susie for ages, and she really must contact Jo again soon. She had been curiously reluctant to do so whilst she was with Costas. Jo had been back to her Alma Mater the previous summer to be given her MA degree. Stephanie had not bothered, knowing that an Oxford MA would not be necessary for the novelist she wished to be. Jo had been puzzled, still having the notion that her friend was really an academic with a certain yen to write fiction. She had tried to persuade her to go with her to the ceremony, which Adam was also to grace. Her school liked its staff to possess the MA Oxon.

186

Stephanie went back in her mind to that journey to London. What had she been thinking of that summer afternoon? Certainly the memory of Costas Mitsoukopolis had been somewhere in her thoughts but she had not heard from him since the May when he had written to wish her well for her Schools.

Now here they were together again and it was most curious, as if time had made a loop back or there was a parallel universe in which they had never left the place.

It was the damp and misty weather they were both used to in Oxford. They unpacked their two small cases, mostly full of books and papers, and then sat at the window seat and looked down on Beaumont Street.

'It's weather for toast!' she said.

'You are right.' He smiled and rang the bell and when the uniformed flunky arrived – a less spotty version than the boy at the Bloomsbury Square hotel, he said: 'May we please have a pot of tea for two and some toast and honey?'

'With pleasure, sir.'

'You used to smell of toast, you know,' said Stephie dreamily, thinking also of H.G. Wells and the honey.

'We never had enough cash to indulge ourselves with honey as far as I remember,' he said.

When the tea came on a little trolley and the dusk had begun to gather, he said, 'Right! Tomorrow I am going over to my college and I hope you'll come with me. Then we could have a walk, if it's not raining. And I insist on your taking me to your college. Men were only allowed in before seven o'clock, do you remember?'

'I expect that hasn't changed,' said Stephie. 'No revolution there yet – if ever. If I were Josephine, I'd go and see Katie Drines – she just loved that tutor of hers – but my principal tutor – she's quite old – has gone to America. I suppose there's more money there for historians.'

Then she thought, Oh dear, Costas will think I am referring to him too as a money-grubber.

187

But he laughed. 'Certainly there is, but she'll be back. Most of the English go back home when they're sixty-seven!'

'It's a pity Blackwells doesn't open on a Sunday,' said Stephanie, munching toast. They had not drawn the curtains and the sky outside was now a delicious pale lemony grey, a few pigeons cooing in the eaves above.

'Before we walk out again,' said Costas, 'and when we have finished our tea, I think we might lie down, before a bath?'

The bathroom was adjoining, a large room with palatial taps.

' "Lying down" is my favourite euphemism,' said Stephanie, placing herself on his knee. He rubbed his face in her neck. 'It's true – now you *do* smell of toast. Shall we eat here this evening?'

'I thought we might try a new restaurant. Do you remember – was it the Queen Elizabeth? Well, I'm told it's changed and been improved. We could go there, it would give our legs a stretch. It's down off the Turl.'

'It's like coming home,' said Stephie. But she thought, if I were alone here I know I wouldn't feel the same.

Later, both deliciously relaxed from their 'lying down', followed by a short sleep in each other's arms, and after another sensual abandonment – a hot bath – they ventured out.

The rain had held off but there was that indefinable misty scent in the air that spoke more of the Michaelmas term than the Hilary.

'They say Oxford is in the South Midlands,' said Stephie. 'So "sodden and unkind". I wonder if we hadn't studied here what we would think of the place?'

'Or of each other,' he replied.

They passed the queues outside the cinema opposite St Mary Maggers, and were then part of the usual Saturday-night crowd in the Corn.

'It might be nice to go to church tomorrow,' she said suddenly.

'We never talked about religion, about belief,' he said, looking at her.

'No, but I expect you were christened. Orthodox? I wasn't, since

188

Father is Jewish, but Mother used to like singing hymns. I think her mother – my grandmother – had been a Methodist in Cornwall – they had such splendid hymns.'

'I used to go to the House or to New College sometimes,' he confessed, 'just to hear the choir sing. But there's so much to do tomorrow, two colleges and a walk.'

'Both of us on the same pilgrimages,' she said.

The meal at the refurbished French restaurant was unlike any other Stephanie had ever eaten in Oxford, but as usual the wine was better than the food.,

'I should like to learn to cook,' she said.

'I could teach you. I like cooking. When I was a child we ate eastern Mediterranean food, but in New York I favour Italian.'

'My father likes experimenting with recipes. I suppose he misses the chicken soup with noodles his mother fed him with. Mother isn't much of a cook.'

She asked him about his early childhood in Athens, about the war when he was only a youth, about his relatives in Greek Macedonia, and the flight to Alexandria at the end of the war.

'The family dispersed in 1946. My parents went back to Athens but they both died before I came to Oxford. My cousins went to Macedonia; myself and an uncle to the West. My Uncle Peter went to Paris and then to the States. He's a businessman.'

She had known his mother and father were dead, though he had said little about them when she knew him first, except that his father had been a professor of archaeology.

'I wish I had met some of them,' said Stephanie. Before, she had never really wanted to meet people's families. She must be growing middle-aged.

'Oh well, you know large extended families – some of the members are nice, others you have nothing in common with. When I first came to England I just never thought about my family very much. Young men can be quite callous, can't they? But it was a shock when my father died of a heart attack. Then Mother just

189

seemed to fade away. I did go over to Athens at the end of my first year, do you remember my telling you? That was for her funeral.'

Stephanie remembered vaguely his telling her he had spent his first long vacation abroad. But in those days she had been centred on their times together. They had lived in the present. Now she thought how heartless she might have been. How long it took to grow up.

'I feel "family minded" tonight,' she said when they finally returned, a little tipsy, and went to bed, savouring the freshly turned-down sheets. It seemed that a maid had been in their room once more since they had left it.

'There's only Uncle Peter,' he said. 'I haven't much in common with him. He's quite successful, if making money is a badge of success. He has a son, Michael, but I've only met him once. I'd like to meet your mother though. Is she at all like you to look at? Or in character?'

'I look more like Father's sister, I think, and *she* doesn't look very Jewish. I think I'm more like my Grandpa Lorrian in the way I look at the world, except I'm not as artistic. You must meet my grandfather. We might go to his little place in rural Essex if there's time. He's my favourite member of the family.'

Thus murmuring they both fell asleep but woke a few hours later to make swift love.

Sunday morning and they were woken by bells, then came the slow minor tones, sounding the hour, of the Merton chimes that Stephanie remembered so well from the days in the Examination Schools when the chimes had been part of all their lives for two weeks.

When they drew the curtains they saw that the sun had even ventured out. After a quick breakfast they would visit Costas's college, and if there were time, her own. Costas had been at one of the smaller colleges near the Radcliffe Camera and they stopped to admire the Camera and the Sheldonian. Nothing seemed to have changed.

Costas looked doubtful. 'There probably won't be anyone around who knew me,' he said, as they entered by the gate next to the lodge.

But an enquiry there did not draw a blank. The porter recognized Mr Mitsoukopoulos and assured them that Mr Horsgall was indeed 'In' and often came back to his rooms after college chapel.

All the lives here appeared so ordered, so unchangeable, thought Stephanie. But perhaps she'd go to church herself if she lived in such a place.

'Horsgall wasn't my main tutor, but I think he'll remember me,' said Costas.

He scribbled a little note which he handed to the porter, asking him to deliver it to the rooms before lunch.

'We can go and have a drink at the King's Arms or the Turf,' he suggested, 'and come back here before lunch.'

'There may not be time to go to my college,' said Stephanie. 'It's a bit out of the way.'

'We could go after lunch. I'd thought of getting the six o'clock train back. Would that be OK?'

She agreed. It would be simple to collect their bags from the hotel after lunch as it was on the way to her college. How pleasant it was to be in a place where everything was within walking distance. They had not appreciated it enough when they were up at Oxford. London, with its miles of streets and tube-routes and tedious bus journeys, seemed a world away.

They each drank half a pint of beer in the cosy little Turf and then walked back to Costas's old haunts.

The porter greeted them again.

'Go up. He'll be pleased to see you – and the young lady too.'

Ernest Horsgall was an untidy-looking middle-aged man in an ancient tweed jacket which he must also have worn in church; the college chapel obviously did not demand sartorial perfection.

'Well, Constantine, this is good of you,' he began.

191

Costas introduced Stephanie, murmuring, that she'd been up the year after him and had also read history.

'Indeed. And how is life treating you both?'

He seemed to have sensed that they might be an 'engaged couple' for Costas Mitsoukopoulos would not have turned up with some minor light of love.

They were offered the inevitable sherry, everything in Oxford being lubricated by it.

Costas gave a rapid resumé of his career to date.

'You must let the editor of our *College Supplement* know all your news – so many men don't bother and then we hear twenty or thirty years later that a man has carved a name for himself. It must be tiring yet interesting, your work, and need a good deal of tact.'

Stephanie thought the don might be shrewder than he looked. They were a funny old race, these dons. Something about the life suited certain men, but she would not be tempted herself. She remembered Jo saying that it was ideal, all your meals were cooked for you, you had a library to work in and your friends were there whenever you needed them.

Mr Horsgall turned to her. 'And are you also working in the field?' he asked.

'Er ... no. I am just finishing a Ph.D. at London University,' she explained.

Oxford was often reputed not to consider other universities' Ph.D's as having the same value as an Oxford D.Phil. She told him a little about her research as they sipped their sherry, and he listened politely, although it was not his period.

'I would ask you in to lunch except we have no visitors on Sundays – gives the scouts a rest. Next time you must let me know in good time and then I can entertain you here.' It was obviously time for them to go. After a little more small talk they stood and thanked him and made their goodbyes.

'He hasn't changed a bit,' said Costas as they walked back to the hotel to have a quick bite of lunch and collect their bags. 'Still as polite as ever, but basically remote. They make an effort, and Horsgall did remember me, but you can tell his mind is on the eleventh century.'

The sun had gone in now and there was a sharp little breeze.

Stephanie found herself wishing that just for half an hour she might be twenty again, going to meet her lover on Walton Street.

After their quick snack lunch, she said, 'We can walk back from my college along Walton Street, can't we? I'd like to see your old digs.'

'We can walk back to the station that way too, and perhaps call in at Worcester if there's time, and look at the lake. We haven't much to carry.'

He remembered it all so well, she thought. I wonder what impression he had of England when he first arrived.

They walked along the Woodstock Road, each building and each shop so well remembered. Not much had altered. The entrance to her college was just the same. There were young women coming in and going out, often accompanied by young men; hordes of bicycles parked by their owners; a gaggle of notices on the boards in the entrance hall; the cedar tree still guarding the lawns.

'I hardly ever came here, did I?' he said.

'No. You were my secret. I didn't want to share you with a hundred other nosy women.'

'Does it make you wish you were back?' he asked, after she had pointed out the two buildings in which she had had her rooms.

'Not a bit, though I'm glad I came with you this time. It some-how makes a complete circle. We met here in Oxford and we still belong, a little, but now we're grown up!'

'Are you going to look for your tutor – the one who didn't go to America?'

'No. It's Sunday, and she'll be with her family.'

'So some of the women dons are married.'

'Oh, not many, but there are a few. Let's walk back now. We can come again another time perhaps, and see your other tutor as well as mine.' It would be dark and the evening wind was stiffer and colder than the morning breeze.

They went out of the college by the back door in the high wall that led to Walton Street, passing the little corner-shop where Stephanie used to buy paper and ribbons for her typewriter. Even when she was an undergraduate she had, unbeknownst to Jo or any of her other friends, even Costas, been writing stories. On the opposite side of the street was the pub where the strains of singing by townsmen from the Jericho quarter beyond it, behind the Oxford University Press building, had sometimes been borne along the summer air.

All that seemed a long time ago but when they paused a little further on, on the left-hand side of the street, and looked at the late Victorian house, one of a rather ramshackle terrace in a liver-coloured brick, where Costas had lived in his basement room, Stephanie felt it just as distant.

Had they been the same people then that they were now? She remembered his saying it took seven years for all your body cells to change. But their essential selves must have been there in Oxford, or how had they come together again so easily?

'Do you want to knock and see if we can go in to have a look?'

'Do you?'

'No, I don't think so. I think I'd rather remember it as it was. There'll be someone else there now.'

'There was another tenant, a graduate, the term after you left,' she said. 'A philologist with a ginger beard. But he'll have gone too now, surely, unless he's one of those who stay on year after year writing their theses.'

'Didn't you ever think of doing yours here?'

'Yes, I considered it,' she replied as they walked on. 'But I decided I'd rather have Oxford as the place for being an under-graduate, and make an effort to grow up a bit in London.'

'Oh you were always grown up, my Stephie!' he said. He was carrying both their bags and he stopped for a moment to change them round, taking the opportunity to kiss her cheek before they continued their walk. 'It makes you realise how quickly people's time here is over, yet didn't it seem to you that each term was an eternity?'

'In a way, but the terms were never long enough for me. I stayed up whenever I could. I know you had to, not having a home to go to. Do you remember the Christmas of your last year in Oxford in the middle of my second year? It snowed, and we were frozen.' She remembered that they had kept each other warm in bed.

He smiled, so she knew he remembered too.

'I went with Jo to hear the Christmas carol-service in Magdalen that year,' she said.

They walked on past Worcester. It was too dark now to go in and walk over to appreciate the lake. Also, they both felt like a cup of British Rail tea at the station.

In the train they were both quiet, thinking their own thoughts. Each of them always seemed to know when the other needed to retire a little into him or herself, and neither was possessive of the other's need to be mentally alone for a time to follow separate thoughts.

After a little time, however, Costas said, 'I expect when we visit next time, Oxford too will have changed. Nothing ever really says the same for long. I have the feeling things will change over the next ten years.'

'Get more like America, you mean?'

'I hope not, but I heard some rumour that my college is planning new buildings. I suppose that in future graduates will want better facilities than those to be found in a Walton Street basement.'

'People always say that *things* – buildings – books – places – stay the same whilst people grow and change, but it's not true, is it?'

'Well, I suppose the books in the Bodleian stay the same and buildings do if they don't fall down, but then they seem always to be in need of repair.'

He was sitting opposite her, a table between them, and there was nobody else near. He leaned across the table and took the long fingers of one of her hands in his, and repeated, 'It's not true that people change. I shall always love you, Stephie.'

She put her other hand over his, and stroked his wrist, and said, 'I love you, Costas.'

And they looked into each other's eyes, each seeing in the other a deep well of affection and friendship, as well as desire and passion.

Stephie stayed over in his rooms in Bloomsbury that night, having prepared her mother by saying she would be going straight to work from Oxford. It was blissful not having to get up and dress and enter the bowels of the earth, and they slept all night entwined in each other's arms.

In March Stephie invited Costas to come over one Saturday afternoon to Edgware to meet Sam and Lamorna Fischer. She didn't want to introduce him as a serious boy friend, not having much time for such a concept, but couldn't help feeling they ought to meet him. He was still planning to be in England until October except for his visit to Rome at the end of the month, so there was plenty of time for them to get used to the idea of a strange man being in love with their daughter, and of their daughter being obviously in love with him.

The difficulty was that she had very rarely invited friends to meet her parents, except when she was a teenager and had at one time gone around in a little group of boys and girls to concerts or the theatre. It might appear odd that Costas, of whom they had only had a vague description – 'an old friend from Oxford', should suddenly be invited. Of course they knew Jo from the summer when they had both left Oxford, and so she hit upon the idea of asking Jo to come along too. It was about time she told Jo about him in any case. Jo would cover any awkward moments. Not that Costas was at all socially awkward – she knew he would behave impeccably – but she had recently had an odd dream about him, in which he had suddenly appeared to lose his head completely, got down on his knees to her father and asked his permission to be betrothed to his daughter. Perhaps that was the way her subconscious imagined the procedure was in Macedonia or Greece.

Stephie had not seen Jo since the New Year, when she had seemed a little depressed after a long weekend in Paris with her sister Annette. Adam had been mentioned then only in the context of family Christmases, which he did not like. Jo and Annette had spent their Christmas at home and Jo had wished Adam had been there.

'But he wouldn't enjoy a family Christmas, even if he were married to me,' she'd said.

Stephie thought she was right. Adam was a conscious iconoclast.

Since then Jo had been busy working, and she herself had spent all her free time with Costas. She telephoned Jo on a Saturday morning.

Her friend sounded organized and brisk; she always made the most of Adam's sorties back to Hermione, which lasted from after work on Friday afternoon until he left for work on Monday morning, thus giving Hermione three nights and Jo four.

'Would you like to come over for tea next Saturday afternoon? I'd like you to meet a man I used to know in Oxford. Dad will be there and I don't want anything heavy afterwards. You know what parents tend to say: "Are you serious about him?" '

'Your parents aren't a bit like that!' objected Josephine. 'And why should they think any man you invite for tea is a candidate for your hand?'

There was a silence.

'You mean – he *is*? exclaimed Jo.

'Well, I don't take "boyfriends" home, do I? So they're bound to guess!'

She did not say exactly if their surmise would be on the right lines.

'Oh, Stephie, is he that mysterious foreigner we used to tease you about?'

You couldn't fool Jo, who had often wondered about the man whose existence Stephie had once vaguely referred to in her second year at college. Then Stephie had said no more and Jo had assumed that it – whatever 'it' was – was over.

'Yes, I knew him in Oxford,' Stephie confessed. 'And I believe you met him once or twice. He seems to remember you. But I don't want to say any more now. I'd be pleased for you to meet him. You may even have seen me with him recently, I don't know. We saw *you* in Dillons week or two ago.'

He must be the man whom Jo had seen walking with her friend in Bloomsbury.

'Oh, Stephie I'd love to come. It's ages since we've had a good talk,' she said, in case it sounded as though she thought Stephie had been avoiding her, or that she intended to embarrass her friend over the teacups. 'You must come round to my flat soon anyway. You want your parents to meet him? What's his name?'

'He is called Costas Mitsoukopoulos,' said Stephie and felt a slight shiver go down from the nape of her neck to her back.

'Sounds interesting,' said Jo. 'Well, I'd love to come.'

'How's Adam?' asked Stephie politely.

'Busy, as usual.'

How could she tell Stephie on the telephone that she had just had an abortion? She was trying not to think about it, and indeed was succeeding most of the time.

The tea party was a success. If Lamorna and her husband wondered why they were suddenly hosting a male friend of their daughter's, they acted discreetly. Mr Mitsoukopoulos, whom their daughter asked them to call Costas, was a delightful man. They were vague about how long the couple had known each other. Costas was amusing about his work in New York, though, as Sam said, it could not be much of a picnic working for 'that UN'.

Lamorna thought Josephine looked peaky and thin, remembering the time she had stayed with them that week after coming down from Oxford. She had looked healthier then. Perhaps it was just that she was older. London did tend to wear people down, and from what Jo was telling them about teaching in the East End she was glad her daughter Stephie had never wanted to enter that profession. They chatted about Jo's pupils, and about the trip to Oxford, and about Stephie's thesis, though not about her writing, about which her parents knew nothing.

At half past six the three young people thanked Mr and Mrs Fischer for the tea and went off to the theatre. Costas was getting on well with Jo, was interested in her views on education.

'Do you think Stephie's in love with him?' asked Lamorna of her husband when the young people had safely departed. He looked up in surprise from his evening paper. It was rare for Lamorna to want to discuss anything personal.

'If she's not, I'll eat my spinach,' he replied. He was apt to come out with inappropriate metaphors, translated, he always said, from Yiddish.

Stephie thought the meeting had gone very well.

The following Tuesday Jo met Stephie by arrangement after work outside Russell Square tube. They decided to go for a snack and a coffee in Sicilian Avenue, rather than go all the way up to Belsize Park. Costas had a meeting and Stephie was quite glad to have a girlish gossip. Jo might be full of curiosity but she was always honest, and Stephie really did want to know what Jo thought of Costas.

'He's lovely!' said Jo. 'Aren't you lucky! He *adores* you. I could see that, and you obviously love him. What did your mother say?'

'She hasn't pronounced – you know my mother. I think she liked him. But Jo, there's nothing formal yet.'

'Go on! You'd settle down with him if you could.'

'Oh, I would, but he's in New York and here am I in London and God knows where he'll be next. Anyway, when I've finished my thesis I'm going to get on with my novel. I did tell you about that, didn't I? How's your own work going – I mean your writing, not your prison sentence?'

'Too exhausted to do much at present. I read a lot at the weekends when Adam's at home with Hermione, and then Monday comes round again and I'm walking through treacle at school trying to keep up with everything.'

She did not mention the abortion until Stephie said, 'I have the strangest feeling – that I might be pregnant. Of course I don't *know*, it's only since we stayed in Oxford a week or two ago that I've felt like that.'

'Why? Do you feel queasy?'

'No, nothing like that, I'll just have to wait and see. I've no proof.'

'Stephie! Would you really want to have a baby?'

'If I found I was going to have Costas's baby? Yes! I sort of feel you have to let nature take its course. Even if it isn't the ideal time ...'

'Would he be pleased?'

'Yes, I think he would. I believe he's rather family-minded. But I shan't say anything to him yet. I'd rather be sure.'

Stephie felt superstitious about it. She wanted Costas to tell her what he wanted her to do, what he thought they both ought to do, without the additional complication of a possible baby. It was an accident, shouldn't have happened; they needed a year or two together first. Yet in spite of everything she wouldn't be able to help feeling glad if it were true. She was surprised at herself, never having seen herself as a maternal sort of woman.

'Well then, I hope you are,' said Jo. 'But even if he weren't keen, you'd go ahead and have it?'

''Yes. But I feel sure he would be glad, Jo. It wouldn't matter to me if we weren't officially married.'

Jo was thinking: Stephie knew this Costas years ago, so it must mean something that they've found each other again.

After a pause, she said, 'I was pregnant, you know. I found out after Christmas.'

There was a silence. Stephie wanted to hear more.

'It was only seven weeks. I had an abortion – a few weeks ago.'

'Oh Jo. I'm sorry. How unpleasant.'

Jo was glad she didn't say: Isn't it illegal? or castigate her morals. They were just different kinds of people, but Stephie wasn't censorious.

'What else could I do?' Joe went on rebelliously. 'Can you imagine me with a baby and Adam scurrying from me to his other children? I had to decide quickly. I just had to brace myself. It isn't as if I could disappear and have a mysterious baby at home, is it? My parents – unlike yours – would die of shame. Adam was relieved, I could tell that. Of course he left the decision to me, wouldn't say one way or another, couldn't have stopped me, but he wouldn't have relished confronting my mother. I wished I could have gone abroad, disappeared for a year, but how could I? I suppose I'm a moral coward.'

'You've never been against abortion though, have you?'

'No, I always saw it as something women should be able to have by right: "Every child a wanted child" ...'

Stephie guessed that if the circumstances had been other, if Adam Angelwine had been a different kind of man, or free to commit himself, Jo would have loved to have a baby.

Jo went on, 'In the last week or two I've been thinking. If I've "disposed" of one pregnancy, what would I do if it happened again? It means that there's no real future for me with him, doesn't it? Well, no future as his wife, or as mother of his children. Yet how can I leave him? It'll be five years this summer since we were together. He needs me so ...' she switched tack, 'you know Julia, well she must have had at least three abortions – pregnant by different men though. I really do want a baby one day, Stephie.' She was thinking, whose baby though? Just mine?

'Well, *I* may just be being silly. It's an odd premonition. I'll have to wait and see,' said Stephie.

The following afternoon Costas came round to the Senate House library for Stephie and they went off to the Academy Cinema to see a French film.

'We should have asked Jo,' said Stephanie. 'Her favourite actress is the heroine in this film. She waited outside the dressing-room last year when the actress was in Phèdre, and gave her a bunch of lilies!'

'She's a romantic, your friend, isn't she? But I like her, though she's very different from you.'

'You mean I'm not romantic?' enquired Stephie, laughing.

'Well you don't need to be, my darling!'

Stephie pondered this as they waited in a small queue outside the cinema in Oxford Street.

A touting photographer came up, and instead of waving him away, Costas said, 'Let's have our picture taken!'

They stood side by side as the man made great play with his camera. They paid him and he took the address of the flats where Costas was staying.

'I don't suppose we'll ever see the photo,' said Stephie.

'Don't be cynical, darling!'

Costas was to be proved right, for they were to receive quite a good photograph; Stephie in her long mac looking at Costas, and Costas looking directly at the photographer.

As they went into the cinema Costas reverted to their former discussion.

'Jo needs something to anchor her, doesn't she?'

'Oh Costas, how very old-fashioned of you!' But she was laughing. 'Jo thinks she can look after herself.'

'What's her man like?'

'Oh, he's married. It's all rather a mess. He's a "romantic" too. But it's easier for men to be romantic, isn't it? He can run two families and fall in love every five years or so. He doesn't neglect his old loves, just goes on to the next with impunity.'

'I should have thought that children would make that impossible – if he stuck by them of course. Many men don't, do they? Many men – especially where I come from, run a family and a mistress but they're not "romantic" about either. Myself, I've never found the prospect of a harem at all appealing. Also, I am too lazy!' He put his arm round Stephie, and said, 'You will always be quite enough for me – I'm sure of that. So long as you will go on loving me..' She pressed his hand and leaned her head on his shoulder.

Now might be the time to mention the strange certainty she had that she was pregnant, but she found she could not. It would seem unfair when she wasn't sure. Would she be raising his hopes or worrying him? She had been sure when she spoke to Jo that Costas would be delighted, would take it all in his stride, but what if he didn't? He loved *her*, might not want his love interrupted by a child, however much he loved her, and would eventually love their child.

They watched the adverts and then a trailer for another Continental film. When the lights went up for the interval and the ice-cream girl came round, Stephie said:

'I am writing a romantic novel, you know.'

'I imagined you were. Do you think it's easier to write that sort of tale if you set it in the past?'

'That's what I thought,' she replied.

The main film was also concerned with romantic love and Stephie found herself thinking how much Jo would enjoy it. Was the trouble with Jo that she was not in truth romantic about Adam, the one man in the world who loved her? Could Jo perhaps be in love only with a man who did not fully requite her own love? Adam had certainly been romantically in love with her, perhaps too much so.

Might others say the same of herself and Costas? But her feelings for him were not romantic. They had grown out of sex, and were therefore grounded in a mutuality that had existed, lasted, and been resurrected. Stephie, always aware of the other side of the question, wondered if you could say you loved *anyone* with whom you were happily passionate? The truth was though that she had never had, and could not imagine ever having that sort of spontaneous feeling for anyone but Costas. He might have had, though it did not seem so, and there might be other reasons for his preferring her, but love was not a rational emotion.

After this she concentrated upon Edwige Feuillère whose beautiful voice was modulating the words of Racine on the screen.

ELEVEN

That year spring had come in more like a lamb than a lion. Stephie hoped it had really arrived and that there would be no sudden reversal of weather before the late Easter. First there had been the snowdrops and crocuses in Russell Square and then the daffodils in swollen bud, followed by tulips. She was still waiting for confirmation that she was pregnant but it had not yet arrived. One part of her wanted to tell Costas; another part of her mind said: leave it until you have been to the doctor and got it checked.

Lots of women missed one month of the 'curse'. She did not feel sick, indeed she felt extremely well. She would tell Costas when he returned from his short trip to Italy before Easter. In the meantime she found his love-making was revealing to her ever-new dimensions of feeling, reaching deeper, more secret parts of her body. Costas too looked relaxed, happy. He was a passionate man but he never took her for granted. Love was a natural part of life; at present it appeared sometimes to be the whole of life but there were also long hours spent together eating or shopping, or discussing politics or history. They talked little about their own feelings, for they both took them for granted.

Some days after their visit to the cinema, she said, 'I don't mind if you take me for granted, Costas, I'm always here for you and I shall always want you.'

It was as if a joy was always sleeping in her like a second self.

On Monday 15 April Costas was to fly to Italy as an observer on behalf of the UN. The signing of the Treaty of Rome had just taken place in Rome and several of the signatories and their advisers were still there. This treaty, a new arrangement for the economic coming together of The Six, all of them countries in Western Europe, had been intended to inaugurate not only a common market but eventually a political alliance.

Stephie and Costas had not been apart for more than a day or two since that evening in January when Costas, having arrived from New York a day or two earlier, had come to find her. They were not usually together all night, but saw each other every afternoon or evening, sometimes both, and Stephie wondered how much she would miss him during the three days of his absence in Italy. He had suggested she might accompany him but it was still term-time and she thought his absence might give her an opportunity to tidy up her own work before Easter. At Easter they had promised themselves a weekend in the Cotswolds, or perhaps Costas might hire a car and they could visit the cathedrals of Hereford and Worcester, or Exeter and Wells. Or they might go on a visit to her grandfather Lorrian in East Anglia.

She saw him off on the airport bus at the Gloucester Road terminus, on his way to London Airport. He was with two other officials so they did not linger in long farewells. The previous night they had made love over and over again, 'to make up for missing you for three days!' he said.

She went back to work, determined to have the last part of her thesis ready for fair-copy typing before he returned.

During the afternoon of his return from Italy on the Thursday Costas did some shopping before meeting his two colleagues at a cafe, and taking the coach back to the airport. It had been quite an interesting three days, more for his observation of national characteristics than of anything momentously political.

He had missed Stephie, and had sent her a postcard, though he knew that the Italian post being what it was it would probably take weeks to arrive. How he looked forward to seeing her again.

At four o'clock he went to an expensive leather-goods shop and bought her a bag big enough to put her notebooks and even her thesis in.

It was a muggy day, neither cold nor warm, just a little misty. He was waiting to cross the road to the café meeting-place, which he could see across the wide street, and had just begun to cross at the pedestrian crossing when a car jumped the lights and with a screech of brakes crashed directly into him. His purchases went flying along with his bag and he lay there whilst the traffic swirled around him. One of his colleagues who had seen him on the other side of the road and who had remarked. 'There's Costas – we can all go now,' saw what happened.

He got up from his table, and, holding up both arms to the traffic, ran across to the middle of the road, followed by his colleague.

The traffic was eventually stopped, not without much altercation. The car that had jumped the lights was long gone; a traffic policeman came panting up, blowing his whistle.

But it was too late for Costas Mitsoukopoulos. He was transported to the Ospedale Centrale where he died at half past five.

His belongings were picked up by the traffic police and brought to the hospital where they were given to the two Americans. They delayed their flight, staying on to give details to the police and the embassy.

The news was telegraphed to New York and London. It was only the next day – Good Friday – when Stephie, anxious because Costas had not telephoned as he had promised he would, read in the first edition of the *Evening Standard* that her lover was dead.

With a sense of complete disbelief, and yet shivering from fear, Stephie walked to the Bloomsbury hotel holding the newspaper.

She must speak urgently to the manager. When he came down to the little foyer she asked him if he had been informed that one of his temporary tenants had been killed.

'His boss, Mr Hirsch, came in just now. They're still there in his room. Do you want to speak to them?'

The man obviously remembered her from her many visits for he looked ill at ease. What could she say? Shock had made her reckless. Well, Costas would not mind – she corrected that in her head to 'would not have minded'.

She said, 'I am his fiancée.' Now why did she say that. 'There are things of mine in his room?' She must find out more of what had happened.

'I shall telephone Mr Hirsch,' said the manager. 'He is up there in the flat at present.'

'I will wait,' she said. 'Will you please tell him I am here.'

Where was the body of her beloved Costas? Where were the men who had accompanied him to Italy? When would they get back? Would they bring him with them?

A man was getting out of the ancient lift. She stood up as he came towards her. He was a tall American with a buttoned-down collar. She must certainly speak to him.

She went up to him. She said stiltedly, 'I am Mr Mitsoukopoulos's – Costas's fiancée – I have known him for many years. Please tell me what has happened. I have only just seen the news.'

'Joseph Hirsch,' he said. 'I am so very sorry – we are devastated – these bloody Eyetie drivers ... the men who were with him will be back tonight with the....'

She knew he was going to say body but he did not finish his sentence.

She thought she could not bear to go to his room and yet perhaps she should. But no; the man said,

'They have cleared his things. They will bring his other belongings back to London.'

'Will you tell me please when the funeral will be?'

How could she speak so calmly?

'We don't know yet. His uncle is flying over from the States.'

That would be Uncle Peter.

'Keep in touch with the embassy, Miss – er –?'

'Fischer.'

'Well, Miss Fischer I can't say how sorry I am – we have lost a fine colleague.' He cleared his throat. 'The embassy will tell you about the funeral as soon as they know.'

He handed her a card with his name on it. She did not remember Costas mentioning a Mr Hirsch. Perhaps he was the 'Joe' who had been a GI.

She had no status, was not married to Costas. The officials probably thought it was just a light love-affair between them.

Before she went home she telephoned the embassy with her home number and then in a nightmare of anguish took the tube to Edgware. But on her way home she knew absolutely, as though Costas himself was telling her, that she was going to bear his child.

All she could do when her mother opened the door to her in surprise – she was not usually home in the afternoon – was to point to the paragraph in the paper and then, at last, sit down. She could not yet even weep.

The body of Costas Mitsoukopoulos was cremated a few days later, after Easter, at Golders Green. His Uncle Peter, who was married to his mother's sister, and his son Michael were there, and Stephie's parents, and Jo, and all the Americans from Rome and those at the hotel, and all who had known him through his work.

Mr Hirsch handed her an envelope. 'It was in his pocket,' he said.

It was the photograph taken in Oxford Street.

Stephie spoke rationally to his relatives and they took each other's addresses but she could see that she and they had little in common.

She had wept enough by this time not to weep at the ceremony. She did not want to acknowledge that Costas was dead to anyone now but herself. He had been hers; he would always be with her, though there was nothing more to be done, ever.

A few days later a postcard arrived from Italy, from Rome, with Costas's love, looking forward to seeing her again very soon.

Her pregnancy was officially confirmed two weeks later.

In August her thesis was accepted.

At first she was living in a half world, or rather, she sometimes thought, a double world. Costas was dead; that was the dark half of the globe in her head, a place she thought would never leave her. She talked to him in this place every night before she slept, told him that his child would live on in the real world. Yet how could she bear to live in it without him? Mingled with her unfathomable grief which was with her when she woke and with her as she worked, was the knowledge of the other side of this globe, a place lit with hopes and fears, full of obligations, duties, preparations, plans. If she were to be true to him she must live in this part of herself too.

Her parents were kind, accepting that the cruelly killed Costas had been the love of her life, and also accepting that she was to bear his child. But they found it hard to express strong emotion. It was only Stephie's grandfather, Lionel Lorrian, who came over in June and took her away to his house in North-east Essex on a bird-haunted estuary, who knew what to do. Now that her academic work was accomplished for the time being, she must make a new life for herself. A different kind of work awaited her.

On the third evening of her visit they were sitting together after supper – he was a good cook – in the shabby old morning room, which was crammed with portraits and water colours and mementoes of Cornwall, and untidy heaps of books.

Stephie said, 'I wanted Costas to meet you. I told him about you; I hoped we might visit you this summer. Or we'd planned a little holiday looking at cathedrals ... ' Her voice broke. She had not yet wept in front of anyone, even Jo.

He put his long lean hand over hers and said, 'I wish I had met him, Stephie. Anyone you loved who loved you would meet with my approval; It's all a bloody, bloody mess and there's nothing you can do about it. Except – you are lucky in one way, I think, though I suppose you may not.'

'Lucky with the baby?'

'Yes.'

'I think so too. I wish I had told him, but I wasn't sure. You see, if I can have the baby, and then do what he wanted me to do, which was to write the books I told him about, that is the only thing that will save me. I know I shan't be able to do much at first. I've no illusions about infants, but I must write, and he wanted me to. And I wanted his baby and I shall have it....'

'Stephie, I have been thinking. You can drive, can't you? You could live here, you know. There's the little cottage down the drive that's empty. When I die I could leave you the house as well, to do what you wanted with. It's a lovely spot to bring a child up – better than Edgware. And you wouldn't be lonely. There's a young family at the farm and lots of visitors who've been coming for years to sail.'

She smiled. Her facial muscles felt stiff, it was so long since she had smiled.

'But how should I manage for money?'

'Don't worry about that. I have enough, and I don't expect your needs are very great. Anyway, you'll make money with your books; I feel it in my bones. You could wait till the baby is six months or so and then decide....' He did not say that he thought she would marry one day. Not yet. Not perhaps for a good many years.

But this place could be a haven for her, even when he had gone.

She had always been his favourite and, unlike many men, he adored babies.

Stephie had booked in at University College Hospital as it was so near her work. She intended to go on with her writing until the autumn. She acknowledged too that it was where Costas would have looked for her if he suddenly came back from the dead. She still dreamed occasionally that his death had been an error and that he returned to her. Waking on those mornings was the hardest thing to bear.

The baby was expected some time in the first half of November. She had visited the hospital clinic regularly, amassed the basic necessities, and read a book proffered to her by Jo all about some Frenchman's revolutionary attitude to childbirth.

Jo was very caught up in her friend's pregnancy and Stephie realized that if Jo had not had the abortion she might have expected her own baby not long before Stephie's. Jo never told her she envied her, but Stephie knew what she was feeling. Jo was fascinated by the whole process, and wanted to be of use. The two friends grew closer at this time.

Adam said little when Jo told him Stephie's lover had been killed, but that she was going to bear his child. Perhaps he looked a little ashamed. But Jo could see that he thought Stephie slightly deranged. He was politely benign towards her when she visited them in the flat, but took small interest in the whole endeavour.

Oh well, thought Jo, he's had children already – or at least his wives have. He never appears to regret our baby.

She went out to Edgware and inspected the various items which were apparently necessary for the nurture of a new infant: a little chest on wheels which Stephie calmly demonstrated, nappies in the drawers and a changing-mat on top, many Viyella nighties and Terry squares, several bonnets and woolly matinée coats provided by aunts and cousins who didn't seem to mind Stephie having an illegitimate child. How different her own situation would have

been. The fact was that Stephie's family was sufficiently unconventional to take it in their stride. If only her own respectable
parents had been the same....

She was not getting on too well with Adam that summer. She
knew that his real criticism of her was that she could not accept
that their life would go on together for ever; yet she could not see
how she might end it. When she was sad she did mention having
child, which disconcerted him. No bargain had been struck, but
she must have known it was impossible.

Jo asked Stephie which she wanted: a boy or a girl, but Stephie
would not commit herself. Jo thought she must want a boy like
Costas. She felt sure her own aborted 'tadpole' had been a girl;
why, she did not know, she just felt sure it had.

Stephie had the viva for her thesis. Her gown covered any
unseemly stoutness and probably most of the tutors and the visiting professor had no idea she was pregnant. She had not suffered
from morning sickness nor had she nurtured any wild desires to
eat coal. As she was tall she carried everything well.

Her tutor, Mrs Barnard, *had* noticed though. She had wanted
her to apply for a job at University College, but when Stephie officially broke the news of her pregnancy, she was silent for a time.

Then she said: 'Is it just that you are pregnant and would need
someone to look after the baby? Perhaps you could leave an
application till next year and then begin to look for a post next
year rather than this. I know there are no allowances for maternity
other than a few shillings – and you haven't started your career so
wouldn't even get that.'

'I shall be able to work out something with my family, and I
wanted to tell you this before but hadn't the courage – I'd already
decided in any case to write, not be an academic. I'd always
planned to write historical novels.'

Mrs Barnard thought for a moment. This was not the usual case
of a girl doing research so as to put off the finding of a job, or
getting herself pregnant to get married.

At last she said: 'Well, you could do worse than write, provided you can get yourself published! You have the talent, I'm sure. But if I were you I'd get a book finished before declining a job!'

'Yes, I have nearly finished it,' said Stephie. 'I've been writing in the evenings and sometimes, I must confess, in the library. I've sent a synopsis and the three sample chapters they ask for to an agent.'

'Well, my dear – you are very organized!' She did not add: but your organization has fallen down over getting yourself pregnant.

Stephie was so grateful for this that she said: 'I'm *glad* about the baby. You must not feel sorry for me about that, but – its father was killed, you see.'

She burst into tears, shocking herself more than her tutor. The story had in fact gone round a few of the staff and students but had been garbled in the telling.

Stephie told her a little about Costas then and when she had gone Mrs Barnard remained thoughtful. She was an Oxford graduate herself and Stephanie Fischer was one of her best students ... but perhaps the ways of nature were best. Under her firm manner she was a soft-hearted woman who would very much have liked to have had children, but they had not arrived, and she had been able to pursue her own work with no conflict of interest. Stephanie would find it hard. Writing novels was a hard slog, though could perhaps be better fitted in eventually to looking after a child than to pursuing a career outside the home. Bearing an illegitimate baby was not an event much rejoiced over in society, but Stephanie would not care about that. Neither did she, but was of the firm opinion that if you had a child it was your responsibility to stay at home, at least until it went to school. She felt optimistic that the girl's writing would find a publisher – her thesis was excellent. Stephanie Fischer was lucky in her family too; she need not worry about her.

In the late October of 1957 Stephanie gave birth three weeks early, at four o'clock in the afternoon, after a labour of only eleven hours to a baby daughter who weighed almost seven pounds.

She was to remember every hour of the birth, even the painful parts, which she had consciously offered up to Costas. Was a new person in the world, a person created by Costas and herself, not worth a few hours' agony?

They told her afterwards that she had had an easy time of it. For the hospital's sake rather than her own they called her Mrs Fischer, though she had explained that the child's father had died. But they were very kind.

One nurse explained that they appreciated people like herself who did not make a fuss. Another woman had been screaming for what seemed hours in the last hour before Stephie's own baby was born and Stephie had found herself irritated.

They showed her how to put the nappies on, would reveal in a day or two how to bathe the infant. Three days after the birth the milk would come in, they said. They would help her. They would wheel the tiny scrap into the adjoining nursery if Stephie wanted a rest and the child would be weighed every day for the week she was there.

Stephie had already instinctively fed her baby – which she found easy and pleasant.

'A natural mother,' the ward sister called Stephie.

Stephie enjoyed the comparative luxury of lying in bed and having her meals brought to her, even if the food was either bland or stodgy. She gave the National Health Service full marks. The nurses even arranged flowers on the table at the end of each bed and often sat down for a chat.

There were only five women in her ward at the top of the old building, and the only annoyance was the endless chatter of two of the other mothers who seemed heartily to dislike men. They were both older than Stephie so she presumed they had other children at home. The other two were about nineteen and appeared heavily sedated at first. Visitors were allowed in for an hour each evening which she did find rather tiring. Her mother and father visited her when the baby was only a few hours old and the next evening there came Jo bearing a great bunch of flowers. She sounded very excited.

'Can I see her? Who does she look like? Have you decided on a name?'

'Yes, but I think she's asleep at present. They wheel the babies in their little cots into the next room. You can see them behind the glass. They don't allow visitors in there, but I can hold her up to you behind the glass when she wakes. I don't know who she looks like, Jo. To me she just looks like a baby.'

'I don't want to give you any bother – I came to see *you* anyway. How was it? Did you do the breathing?'

Stephie laughed. 'I did as your book instructed – I didn't have any pethidine or gas and air, and they said it was fine. They've put a little tag on the cot that says "normal birth".'

Jo gave the flowers to the nurse who came up all smiles. Everyone around Stephie appeared to be smiling. One of the older women had a large husband sitting on the chair by her bed with his shirtsleeves rolled up, in total silence, and one of the nineteen-year-olds had her mother with her.

'There's enough copy here for a novel,' whispered Stephanie. 'It's quite pleasant and they spoil me, but I'll be glad to get home and sort it all out for myself.'

Neither woman had yet mentioned Costas. Then Jo asked again: '*Have* you decided on a name?'

Jo was known to be fanatical over names, collected books on the subject and produced what she called a short list from her handbag.

'Let me see ...' Stephie studied the names: Jane and Felicity and Isabel and Catherine, and Amaryllis.

Then she said: 'Dad's mother was called Larissa – Russian, you know – Lara for short – and I remember mentioning it to – to Costas. It's sufficiently unusual, isn't it? I want something vaguely un-English.'

'Do you know,' said Jo excitedly, 'I was reading somewhere about Pasternak – you know – the Russian poet. He's published a book in Italy – well, an Italian translation, I suppose, and I think I remember the heroine was called Lara. It's a lovely name. I know Amaryllis is a bit much,' she added. They both giggled.

'I shall get up now, and show you my baby,' said Stephie, putting on a long cotton dressing-gown. 'I still look pregnant.'

Jo was thinking, I can be Aunt Josephine.

The baby was lying there, eyes open but not crying. The cot had a pink ribbon tied to it, along with the 'normal birth' notice.

Jo stayed behind the glass wall and Stephie took the small bundle in its hospital blanket and held her up against her shoulder. Squashy nose, tiny hands emerging from hospital sleeves. Jo felt a lump in her throat. Not only for the dead Costas, or for the miracle of birth, but for her own botched life.

She must stop thinking about herself.

'Time to feed at ten,' said Stephie. 'They keep more or less to every four hours though most of the babies cry every three – and some all the time!' One large baby was already bawling his head off.

Stephie put little Lara down on her side, tucked a blanket round her and came out to say goodbye.

Jo thought, she looks as if she's been doing this all her life. Incredible. I wouldn't know where to begin. What does she really feel?

'Soon they will have to be washed and changed and weighed and then put down again,' Stephie explained. 'Once I'm home I shall just play it by ear.'

'I brought you Doctor Spock,' Jo said when Stephie came back into the ward and Jo had helped get her comfortable sitting up in bed with a big pillow behind her. 'They said at Dillons it was the one everybody bought.'

'Oh, thank you – and for the lovely flowers.'

'When will you be out?'

'On Saturday,' said Stephie. 'Then I can dress Lara in the clothes I've brought for her, and take her home. I haven't given her a bath by myself yet. Such a lot to learn.'

And then you'll be on your own, thought her friend.

'Don't be sorry for me, Jo,' Stephie said quietly as Jo kissed her goodbye.

As she went out, the ward sister was coming in. She said to Jo, 'So did you see the little one?'

'Oh yes. Isn't she lovely!' breathed Jo, unable to sound matter-of-fact.

'She's doing fine – lost hardly any of her birth-weight,' said the expert, taking out a watch from her clean blue short-sleeved shirt that was half-covered by a starched white apron top. She looked so organized! Perhaps it was more interesting being a nurse than teaching adolescent girls.

Later, in the night, Jo woke and thought of course I don't feel sorry for her! Except about her lovely Costas. Stephie has *almost* everything. She has lost Costas, but she has her future laid out for her. Many people might not want that, might resent the fate that had overtaken them, but in a strange way Jo found it comforting, and considered that Stephie might also feel the same. Stephie could now confront the rest of her life: her work, and the future of that little daughter.

Jo was self-aware enough to understand that her own situation had left her adrift. It was a sensation she did not like. She even wished she could have swapped places with her friend; then she would not have had to make a choice. Stephie had made a choice, of course she had, but to Jo there had never been any question about what Stephie would choose. Unlike her own choice.

In the morning she found her depression slightly modified but still one which she had good reason to feel. There was nobody to talk to about it. Adam was away and would not be sympathetic, thinking she was getting at him, and she did not want to confess her feelings to Clare or Susie. So she confined them to her diary.

*

Lara put on weight rapidly. All in all she seemed a remarkably good baby to have arrived out of such a traumatic nine months. Stephie and Lara were taken home in Mr Fischer's car, and it was only when she was back in the old familiar place that Stephie realized that Lara was not only a person who would never know her own father, but was a new unknown person in herself.

Would she suffer from the lack of a father?

Stephie was prepared to suffer herself but determined to do all she could to give her daughter a happy childhood. Later, Lara might understand that one person had not been there, but for the present her life would have nothing missing from it.

TWELVE

Stephie was at home in Edgware waiting until everything should be ready for her and the baby at Grandpa Lorrian's. Jo visited the two of them every week, fascinated by the rapid development of the little girl.

'I know I don't see the underside, like having to get up in the night, and worrying about sniffles, and weight, and never having a minute to yourself,' she confessed.

Stephie said it was not too bad; she enjoyed breast-feeding and Larissa, who was always called Lara, was a fairly good baby, though she had her moments.

Jo did not exactly envy her friend's new way of life, at least not for the present, but felt she would one day want to do it herself. For a woman, having a baby, she thought, was like going into battle for a man. She admonished herself for being so old fashioned. Nobody was obliged to have a baby, but she did feel that to duck the whole thing was a form of cowardice. She wanted a child one day, not just 'a baby' but a live human being. If you thought the human race was worth carrying on – and Jo felt it was just about worth it – then you would help to carry it on after yourself.

If only a child did not change you for ever, change your way of life so that you were never free again.

Jo's mother had often spoken on these lines but, when chal-
lenged, had denied any resentment. Indeed, she had said the
happiest times of her life were when her children were small.

'That's because they can't answer back then,' Annette had
remarked with her usual asperity.

Most women seemed to express ambivalent feelings about the
whole business of being a mother. On the one hand they did not
want you to escape what they had been through: 'indescribably
awful'; on the other they wanted to say how wonderful it all was.
Jo had no illusions, though Stephie's happiness might make her
wonder whether women varied in this as both men and women
did in everything else.

For the present, though, as she watched the young woman from
down the road totter to the shops, pushing a large, high-wheeled
perambulator with two infants inside, her thin legs and pale face
making her look like a martyr, Jo was glad she had no such
responsibilities. She must make the most of her freedom whilst
she had it.

Yet, even so, she felt constrained and impatient, with Adam
tugging at her on the one side and her own inner life tugging at the
other. If she ever wanted to change her way of life; indeed,
become a mother, Adam could not be there, could he? The abortion had put paid to that. Every day, every month, every year was
in this sense a wasted year. It would have been different if she had
been the sort of woman who had never wanted children, content
to enjoy life from moment to moment.

On the other hand, when she felt this, was she being unfair to a
man who after all had loved her passionately? He had always said
he knew her through and through, which was not the case. She
reflected that he should have known she was more conventional
than she looked; or that she was growing up, and twenty-seven was
no longer twenty-one. Maybe the abortion had made her want a
child one day more than she had ever wanted one before. Not that
she yearned for a baby; no, she just felt that she had been lucky in

one way but cheated in another and that one day she must put matters right.

In the early summer of 1958, when baby Larissa was eight months old, Jo's school planned another visit abroad. They could not have considered that she had handled the Paris fiasco too badly or they would not have asked her again.

To be in charge of twenty-four girls was quite a tall order when you were only twenty-seven yourself and responsible for getting them all to Baden Württemberg via Ostend. The German exchange pupils had already stayed in London and Jo was to stay with the most intelligent of them, a girl who was about to leave the *Gymnasium*.

Jo felt she had done her bit for three years in the East End and needed a change. She had decided to leave the school at the end of the summer term, so the holiday would be in the nature of a farewell. To her satisfaction she had been offered a post in a much more academic establishment.

She also wanted to get away from Adam for a month, to think about her future, and there was also the possibility of spending the last two weeks of the summer term in Paris once again.

This time the embarrassment was more social. The German school was very middle-class; they had never heard of working-class girls attending grammar schools, and the conduct of the English girls amazed them. The girls wandered round the town after curfew looking for fish and chips, they refused the lovely food prepared for them; a group of them misbehaved at the youth hostel in the Black Forest where a few of them were staying, and they hung around the American Air Force base:

'They speak English, Miss.'

The school was in the American Zone, and the worst experience was to be the visit by Herr von Brentano, the Minister of Transport at that time for the district, who was to open a new road the Americans had helped to build. Jo had not been there that Saturday afternoon and thanked her lucky stars she had not.

The politician was introduced to Our English Friends from London.

'And what are your hobbies, my dear?' he asked one Valerie who was sitting on a table with crossed legs. She was a girl with a rich docker father, who had brought several trunks of clothes.

'Oh, I'm only interested in men,' said the wretched girl.

The poor politician, a bachelor, blushed beetroot. Would he remember this girl when he became Foreign Minster? Would he have learned by then not to ask English adolescents awkward questions?

The incident was reported the same evening to Jo, who was called in to the school by the *Direktorin*.

'We do not expect your girls to be as well behaved as ours,' said the German headmistress in English, though she knew perfectly well that Jo spoke German. 'But we do draw the line at girls meeting' – a pause – '*woodcutters* in the forest.'

At the end of the month, Jo was thankful only that she did not have to return with any pregnant girls. Let them spend the night in the train curling their hair; let them revert to their tribal habits whenever they wished, so long as they had not slept with any Americans. They had not.

'We're good girls, Miss,' they said, and it was true; they probably were, knew how to look after themselves.

Unlike herself, apparently.

She was right: the school asked her to visit Montmartre again in the first half of July. This time it was easier. She only had to teach English to the older girls, with the help of the *surveillantes* who were in charge of discipline and collecting homework and everything English teachers were expected to do as well as teach. No girls to supervise.

On one of her free afternoons there was a demonstration starting from the Bastille in favour of leaving Algeria to the Algerians. Jo joined the procession, which was headed by Sartre and Simone de Beauvoir and other luminaries. A few *pieds-noirs* stood by shouting their disapproval, chanting: '*Algérie Française! Algérie Française!*'

A man came up to her in the crowd after the procession had dispersed and began to importune her. Jo let out a stream of English swear-words she had hardly known she knew. He turned tail and vanished in the crowd. A few people standing nearby actually clapped. She must be growing a harder shell.

She also met Will Morgan, now working in Paris. He took her to a little *boîte de nuit* on the Champs Elysées. After six years she still found it heaven to dance with Will, but in spite of the warmth and familiarity she found with him, feelings that left her comfortable and peaceful, she sensed he was just as elusive as ever.

Back in England, during this late summer of 1958, things were reaching an impasse between herself and Adam. The previous year she had threatened to leave him, but he had talked her round. Now it appeared that she had tried his patience, or that he had realized that things would never be – or could never be – any better than they were. Jo felt it was not fair.

A new atmosphere of constraint had built up, for which she could not at first account. She had done her best for a year not to grumble, to accept the situation, not to go on about babies. She kept her unhappiness for her diary, which she suspected he read.

Yet it was now Adam who threatened to leave.

'What are we to do?' he kept repeating, and then, in answer, made love to her in a despairing fashion.

Jo bought the new Elizabeth David cookery book so that she could try to improve her cooking for him. Adam was a good if rather slow and perfectionist type of cook. Jo loathed slaving over cooking but she loved good food, so she decided that a diet of olives and butter and Mediterranean dishes would be nice, though the ingredients were not always easy to find in London shops, even in Soho. Adam saw she was making an effort. She had realized he did not like too much garlic, and did not like *paella*, the one dish she really liked to cook, as much as she did.

If Adam had decided to leave her, pondered Jo, how could he contrive to carry this out? *Contrive* was a very Adam kind of word; all her vocabulary seemed to have been taken over long ago by him. How would she survive without him? Would she go back to her real self? Often she decided that Adam had taken his colouring – his vocabulary, his opinions, his taste in clothes – from Hermione in exactly the same way as she had taken hers at an impressionable age from him.

It was now late August. One evening he announced that in two weeks he was going to spend a few days in Paris with his research assistant, one Rebecca Lawrence. Jo was surprised, but did not attach too much importance to the trip. After all, she had been to Paris without him that very summer.

The week before he was to go to France, Hermione asked Jo if she would come over to their new, or rather, old house to child-sit whilst she went away for the weekend. The younger girl was now nine and only needed a general overlooker of her bedtime. Hermione knew how to enjoy herself, had plenty of friends and many invitations, and Jo was pleased to oblige her. Nobody would believe how well they got on together. For some years now she had kept in touch with Adam's other home. Hermione appeared to have accepted both Jo and the situation but had said one day when Jo was staying with her and the children – Adam was away at a conference – that *for her own sake* Jo ought to find a younger man. It was after Jo had confessed, while doing the ironing, to her abortion of the year before. Hermione had been upset, even aghast, sorry for her.

'I knew nothing about it,' she said.

There had been so many ups and downs with Adam that Jo had

quite lost count, but on the whole things appeared to be beginning to slide. Like an avalanche that is at first just a tiny heap of snow and ice moving slowly downward and which then quickly engulfs a whole village and its inhabitants, the disintegration of their life together had begun.

Hermione had gone to Gloucestershire. Little Phoebe was already asleep in bed when Jo heard the door open and the murmur of voices. One of them was Adam's.

Adam and Rebecca Lawrence came into the sitting-room where Jo was reading by the window. She had met the young woman once or twice before. Not her type, but pleasant enough, and clearly besotted with Adam.

'Were you staying until Monday morning?' Adam asked politely as if she were the nanny devoted to guarding his residence and his daughter. He had known she was to be there but not any of the details.

'Hermione said she'd be back late Sunday night or early Monday morning, so I said I'd stay over till Monday,' Jo explained. 'She thought you wouldn't be back from your meeting till very late tonight so would go back to the flat, not come here.'

Rebecca went out and was seen a few minutes later to be carrying a suitcase upstairs. Adam was taking it all in his stride.

Jo thought. he's pleased. He's got two women here in the house of another one....

'You needn't stay tomorrow,' he said. 'I'll be here.'

He did not say who else might be there and Jo did not feel it was the right time to ask, but understood very well.

She had her own little bed in a small room under the eaves with a window opening on to a sloping roof. Hermione had said: 'When you come to stay you must have this room.' It had been the day Hermione had asked Jo: 'Why are you always so nice to me? Is it female solidarity?'

Jo had not known what to say. She liked Hermione.

Now she said: 'Well, I'm going up to bed. Phoebe is asleep. I shall go home after breakfast.'

This is what she did.

On the Monday at about six o'clock in the evening Jo had just got back from shopping when the telephone rang in the flat. It was Hermione, and she was furious. Not with Jo but with Adam.

'We are all used to you – the people in the village and the children – and myself – but I can't, won't have him bringing another woman here! Who is she? What's happening? I got back on Monday and there they both were.'

'I left you a note on your dressing-table,' said Jo.

'Yes. Thank you. I can quite see you had to go – there was nothing else you could do. But I'd like to know what's going on!'

'I wish I knew,' said Jo.

On his return to the flat an hour later, Adam at first made no reference to Rebecca until finally Jo said:

'Are you sleeping with her?'

'Since you're not too keen to sleep with me, yes.'

'But I do sleep with you!' said Jo.

'Sorry, darling, but you know how things are!'

Was he planning a new life, or trying to see if he could hurt her – or had he fallen in love again? Was this to be how their affair would end? Adam falling in love with a new woman? Did he just want to see if she were jealous? Yet she knew he still loved her. The rift was half her own fault.

She decided to mention Hermione. 'By the way, Hermione rang. She wanted to know what was happening. She didn't like your – Rebecca – staying in her house.'

'Bloody woman,' he said. 'She's no business to interfere.'

Jo and Adam rarely had real rows, but Jo knew this could blow up into a full-scale one if she let it, so she said nothing. It could all come out after he had been to Paris. In the meantime....

The weekend arrived and Adam went straight off from work on

the Friday night with Rebecca.

On his return Jo was still on holiday from her work, though she had to start at the new school in mid-September. Even then he did not like to say exactly what had happened but approached the matter sideways. They had endless repetitive conversations.

Yes, he was soon going to leave her.

Yes, she could stay in the flat until she found a place of her own.

Yes, Rebecca appeared to find him a very satisfactory companion (he meant lover).

Yes, he was going to take Rebecca to *Tristan and Isolde* next week at the Garden.

Yes, he had seen that the letter on the hall table was for him. (Jo knew very well who had written it, having steamed it open and discovered her rival could not spell.)

It was a few days later that he confessed that he was buying another flat along with Rebecca Lawrence, in Battersea as a matter of fact, as far away as possible from this one.

When he said that he was leaving her for Rebecca Lawrence, the fact that he had so quickly found a woman as a replacement for herself was what hurt her. But she found she was puzzled rather than angry. Later she was to realize that Adam would never have gone from something to nothing, would always plan to have some girl or woman waiting in the wings. Just as he had kept Patricia as a stop-gap for when he was in London all those years ago when he had fallen in love with Jo. At first, his apparently sudden decision to take on Rebecca Lawrence had amazed her. But she did not hate Rebecca, she was actually sorry for her. It was not worthy of Adam, using Rebecca to escape more easily from herself. What ought she to do? Or would matters soon be taken out of her hands?

One half of her did not want to lose domestic togetherness; the other half longed for a fresh start, even for a new love affair....

Jo allowed herself one evening of hysteria, writhing upon the floor, screaming, that he need not have treated her like this, that he had never really loved her, that she had loved him, still loved him, but it was not her fault that she needed more than a lover.

What could she do? At the bottom of her heart she knew that he was releasing her, that this was what he should have done long before, and that her hysteria and cynicism were misplaced. Indeed, she caught him occasionally looking at her with a strange expression on his face that was half regret, half longing. Even now, if she had said: 'Stay with me for ever – I will not ask for anything else – I love you – I don't want anyone else,' he would have stayed. But she could not.

It was in truth her leaving him, not Adam leaving her. He was just braver and more decisive. Also she did not believe he loved Rebecca. Jo asked herself if she was just one of Nature's solitaries.

Adam was a difficult man and whenever things went wrong he had wounded her with cutting criticisms. He was jealous, she could see that, and had had reason to be so once or twice, though never since they had begun to live together. She felt guilty that she did not appear to need sex with him as much as he seemed to with her, yet that was not it, for she could be lustful enough. That the relationship could never be publicly acknowledged had upset her. If it had been just an affair of sex and passion, as she had wanted it to be six years earlier, it would not have mattered, but living with someone who was like a husband meant one got the worst of both worlds. Then there had been the abortion, which she could not truly regret, but which she was coming to see as something inflicted upon her. It was not an issue of feminism but of freedom.

She went over and over these matters even after Adam had gone, which he did one rainy night, taking a taxi with the rest of his belongings to a mansion flat near Battersea Park.

Adam was now in the States.

When she woke in the night or sat reading, and looked up from her book, Jo knew without a doubt that she had been loved. Loved in the trim, well-restored, chi-chi streets of Rye, loved in trains, and out of cars lying in unknown fields miles away from anywhere and in forests and mountain huts. Adam had chained her to him and then six years later he had broken the chain. Jo had now and again tugged at the end of the chain that bound them, and cast out her own slender wires to trap some other who might release her from this burden of being loved, But Adam's chain she could not unlock till he cut it himself, wounding himself in the process and her too, a little. It had been a long, long love-affair, taking her from twenty-one to nearly twenty-eight.

Had he changed the whole course of her life?

Having had a longing to love before she was finally caught in the love of another, she had longed for a more secure emotional life. Adam had not needed security of this kind. What *she* had needed six years before was sexual experience. Now he had broken the chain because she had been too cowardly to do so.

Why could she not have loved Adam as much as he loved her? In spite of the abortion, in spite of the situation, in spite of her parents, of society, of her need, if not to marry, to be settled and get on with her life?

Only Rebecca Lawrence still made her uneasy. Was she wrong and had Adam really fallen in love again? He had not said so, and she still did not believe he had; he must be used to women appearing when he needed them, when he left a woman he had really loved – and perhaps still did....

She wanted a baby, eventually, but also an independent life. Were the two incompatible?

She must never use a man the way Adam had used her, but if she had some money from a little success in her own field, and perhaps eventually a child, she might never need family life.

If you could have children by parthenogenesis, or when you were fifty and had done other interesting things ... she wrote in her diary.

Or if she could have met a man who loved her like her imagined Kristin, she thought. Or one who was of her own generation. Adam said young men did not know how to love.

She wrote some verses to try and clarify what had gone wrong.
Was it her fault? Or his? Or just the situation? Or all these things?

Doggerel on a Situation

Why should we hurt one another
When you love me
And what I could ask of some other
You want to give me?

Why can we not live in the present
In its fire-ball thrall
Why wander all over the future
And seal it not at all?

Why can you not be what I dreamed of
Long ago, and even now
Why must I hurt *you* by saying so
Or kill *me* by letting it go?

Do I only ask too much
Of you or any live man
That he must be such and such
The things that he never can?

Am I too true, or too honest
In all my trailing thought?
Do I really love in a way that
To others would be all it ought?

Or are all my ideals that much higher
My longing to love past all bounds?
Can I never remain calm and faithful
Must run with both hare and hounds?

231

On one hand there lies perfection
Remembered, imagined bliss
Which may never again come to action
And certainly not in a kiss.

He had not tapped into her inner self, the self that was in dreams or in her reactions to poetry; that was the problem. Perhaps nobody could do that.

She had *wanted too much*.

It was not 'sex', or not being able to have a child, or get married that had been the trouble.

Next time she would ask for less.

THIRTEEN

A new job for Jo? Well, that was fixed up. A new life? A new man?

At first Jo met only the men she had known for years. Stephen Carnforth returned from abroad. All Jo's male friends had been obliged to undertake what she called their 'stint in Valparaiso' if they wanted on their return to earn their living in the literary world. Stephen seemed to want to share her flat with her for a time. Jo did not want to share living-space with anyone, but it was nice to be wanted, and the money would come in useful, although he would probably not remember to pay the rent. She enjoyed his lusts. She had not abjured sex. That was not the problem.

A week or two showed her she could not love him, though she liked him, and that he could never be in love with her. She was not sure if he liked her but thought he did. He had shown her she might still be capable of intimacy. They parted as friends.

Will Morgan then returned to England.

Jo seriously considered a future with him, hoping he did not notice her preoccupation. Now perhaps they might fall in love again. She was not unwilling to do so, surprising herself, in spite of her knowledge of his evasions. But it became clear, as it had been at the little night-club in Paris, that Will had no desire to resurrect past feelings. He had not changed; he vowed eternal friendship instead, which cheered her up a little.

She met new men: A 'concrete poet' whom she sat next to at a poetry convention in Hampstead town hall stared and stared at her. In the interval he turned to her and remarked:

'You look very like Claire Bloom!'

Untrue, but his remark did not make her unhappy. It transpired that for years he had been in love at a distance with the actress and spent all his time looking for women who resembled her. He came after a few days to the flat for a cup of tea and talked pleasantly, apologizing for his obsession. It was Jo's birthday and she felt emancipated.

A young Australian at a loose end stayed a few weeks with her. The sex was passable, but he was detached, said she was not his type. Women he fell for all had a certain *persona*. Should she apologize for not possessing this? Was she to be loved only by middle-aged academics?

Another former Oxford boyfriend visited, then another, about to be married, and several other acquaintances called. She did not lack company. Gradually, she felt more cheerful, realized she need not rush into a new life. She could lick her wounds slowly.

Adam was still in the States. He had turned her life around but now she felt relieved of a burden, free.

The trouble with a small baby, never mind trying to write a novel when that baby was asleep, was that you forgot that other people's lives were changing too.

Stephie telephoned Jo.

'Do come round after school – as we're so near you. What's it like then, the school?'

'It's wonderful. They actually want to learn!'

Stephie was preparing to go to the country before winter set in. Nobody could dissuade her, least of all her parents. She had delayed until Lionel Lorrian had very kindly had the small cottage in his grounds modernized for her, with electric rewiring, an immersion heater, new windows, the roof repaired, a lightning-conductor placed on the roof in case of storms and a separate telephone line put in.

With the rest of her savings Stephie was to buy a little Morris Minor, though there was always the taxi service provided by 'old Mr Gong', a fixture in the district who took children to school in his bus, brides to their weddings in his special white car, and old people, or the carless, to and from the shops.

Clare Jackson came to share the flat with her. Jo stayed on for eighteen months at Leyburn Court, where Adam let her remain until she found somewhere else. He felt guilty, she knew that.

She was enjoying her new teaching post in its beautiful green parkland, but she missed seeing Hermione and the girls. Letters came from Phoebe, who said she missed her too.

Jo worked hard, began again to enjoy life. Perhaps her Bohemian days would soon be over.

Jo's feelings after seeing little Lara that first time remained with her. When Stephie's first novel came out, its title having changed from *Anna Victrix* to *The Ladder of Time*, she felt again that Stephie had almost everything, herself nothing. But she scorned feeling envious and was determined to do something about it. She would never have Adam's baby but she would have a child one day, perhaps a son this time.

She might even get married; she would try harder with her free-lance journalism, and she might one day write about her teaching experiences.

Stephie had always appeared to steer on an even keel. If she had explained to friends that after she had Lara she had never wanted to marry, she supposed they would not have believed her. Jo believed her though. A daughter and the vocation of novelist was new life enough. Stephie would never have wanted anyone but Costas.

Also, thought Jo, if you don't fall in love you cause less misery to fewer people in the end.

Jo was to marry earlier than she had imagined. She made the acquaintance of Philip Ross in 1960, a man whom she had never met at the time she wrote her sad verses.

Like Adam Angelwine, Philip Ross was an academic, but of a very different kind, with a degree in social history. He loved his subject but held it at a slight distance, which gave him time to think about other aspects of life and eventually to synthesize these aspects and join them to his sense of the past. He also had to teach quite a few undergraduates, or students, as London University preferred to call them.

Jo found him a much easier person to adapt to than Adam. Philip actually appreciated that she had her own books to read, her own thoughts to think, as he had himself. It was a new life.

Clearing out the flat before she got married, she found some of Adam's anti-capitalist ravings, and wished she had had the guts to reply to them a few years before. He had appeared to think, because Jo had withdrawn spiritually 'from work at the Municipal Halls, not liking the reality of the world in which she was working, that she was a "spoilt-idealist".' He compared her with a rentier! Was he perhaps confusing her with Hermione, who had a private income? He had written in reply to some letter she had sent him about the values she wanted to espouse:

> So people like you would go on drawing your income – as though in a dream – but withdrawn 'spiritually' into a world of reality, a 'spiritual' world – where the difficulties (moral or other) to be reconciled in making a bourgeois livelihood, play no part; a world which because it is not material, can be perfect with absolute standards; a world in which the difficulties, which are life, do not exist.

Adam had been cruel. She saw a portrait of herself through his sarcasm. But she had been poor, had earned her living, and had been after all only twenty-two. With whom had he really been angry? His father? Himself? Hermione?

Jo and Philip bought a small house in Richmond, another 'green' suburb, unfortunately a little too far away for Jo to travel comfortably forwards and backwards to her school, though there did exist an old railway line that helped her to do so for a year. After the birth of their son, John Francis, she stayed at home for a time.

She was to have quite different feelings about her own little boy from those she had nursed for Lara. John Francis was a sort of unusual extra gift she need never agonize over. Although life with a baby was hard work, she still had energy over for writing when he was asleep, for Francis was a good baby and slept well at night. She had no intention just yet of returning to work in the big world outside; this domestic world suited her very well. One day she might go back, perhaps to a part-time job. But for the time being there was no division between her inner private life, and work. Stephie never seemed to have suffered from this kind of self-division, but then Stephie had never been self-conscious. Nor had she taught children from the East End.

Philip had his own work to be getting on with. Jo returned eventually for a time to part-time teaching in a small and slightly progressive establishment in the green suburb, but also continued her occasional journalism, and succeeded in publishing a 'literary-sociological' article.

Once John Francis appeared launched at primary school she began a column for the local paper. A few years later her column was taken up by a larger news syndicate which also owned a local radio station.

It was a truly new life, and Jo was surprisingly happy. Her only regret was that she had as yet no daughter. Sometimes she regarded this as a punishment from the gods for the abortion.

*

Until Lara was a year old her mother fed her. Once settled in the country by the estuary with her baby and her books, another life-time of research lay before Stephie who had already begun her second historical novel before *The Ladder of Time* came out, often writing after the child had woken at dawn, and before she woke again.

Lionel had insisted he help to pay the bills, saying, 'You might as well have my money now as later.'

Stephie found an agent who secured her a contract for three books. Her and the child's needs were not large, though still more than two books could pay for, so Stephie went on accepting that the electricity and rates and water-rate were paid for by her grandfather. She also coached farmers' sons and daughters in history and English for their O and A levels and made a little money this way too.

She enjoyed driving, so she occasionally went across to Chelmsford to the big library there, though there were plenty of books at Grandfather Lorrian's. Grandpa, or the tenant farmer's wife, would take the baby for a few hours and add her to her own brood. Once she had grown into a tall sturdy toddler, Lara accom-panied her mother to the village stores in the nearest village of Spire, and very occasionally Stephie would take her to Chelmsford.

Lionel Lorrian had chosen an unusually secluded spot for his retirement that was not really a retirement. A short drive down winding country roads led to a larger village than Spire, about five miles away. Eastminster, which was beginning to think of itself as a town, and was threatening 'development', had a railway station. There was a train twice an hour to Liverpool Street, with only one change, so that Lionel could be in London within an hour and a half. He chose not to go very often, instead inviting clients occa-sionally to come out to him and inspect the pictures he still acquired from old, or as yet unfashionable, artists. If they had come all that way – and it always seemed to visitors that Gateswick was further away from London than it actually was, so hidden and secret was its position – that they would feel they might as well buy something to make the journey worthwhile.

Gateswick was a paradise for ornithologists, for painters and especially for small-boat sailors. Storms could blow up in the estuary around the end of Eastsea Island, only half a mile away opposite the shore in front of Gateswick House. The cottage which Lionel had had improved and painted, repaired and prepared for his granddaughter and great-granddaughter, was only a few hundred yards away from the main house but set at an angle to it. It had a long grass meadow on the side that faced the sea, an orchard, and a decrepit barn that could be used for a garage. Trees guarded the whole place: great elms, and hedges of blackthorn. There were farms all around, with meadows and salt-marshes, for water had long ago flooded other fields nearer the estuary, and the sea wall was slowly being eroded.

Stephanie had always loved the place. When her grandfather had bought it after the war she had been an adolescent and had found it all so very peaceful and reposeful, if rather chilly. She had had some of her best ideas whilst staying at Gateswick.

In the war the Royal Navy had commandeered the house and land to practise D-Day landings. They had left a good deal of mess, but Lionel had seen it was all cleared and cleaned with a small reparations grant and a windfall from a painter who had unaccountably left him some money in his Will. He himself had survived his first winter there in 1947 and reckoned that if you could survive that you could survive anything. He had kept a fire alight with wood gathered in the autumn, for coal was scarce, and with the help of oil- and paraffin-stoves had managed to keep fairly warm. But he warned Stephie of the Gateswick winters. Even in the summer it was never very hot; cool even when London was stifling. Stephie said she did not mind the cold and

Lara could be kept snug, she was sure. Lionel had got the cottage's two chimneys swept and laid in a good stock of Coalite.

There was plenty to interest a child at Gateswick. The farmer, whose eighteenth-century house was in fact more beautiful and older than Lionel's, had two horses usually galloping or munching in one of his fields. Cows grazed in the fields nearer the salt-marshes and occasionally a bull could be glimpsed in another field behind the hedge bordering the lane that wound from Gateswick to the village of Spire. There were fields of barley and of wheat, spring-sown, and harvested in August, and round hay cocks were neatly stacked by the lane.

In the orchard the trees were so old that their fruit was unpredictable, but one summer an old apple-tree produced hundreds of apples. The pear-tree was less productive, but the greatest glories of the other orchard behind Lionel's house were the damsons and greengages, and the fruits of the mulberry-tree were like large ruby jewels. Every August the blackberries began to ripen and went on ripening for a month or so; many were the apple-and-blackberry-pies baked and eaten. Not every year, but when it had rained a good deal in the spring, a large patch of the grass by the sea wall became host to dozens of large pure white mushrooms. Lionel had tested them during his first summer there and pronounced them delicious and safe.

At night a fox could often be heard barking, though nobody was sure where was his den. Every evening in summer large rabbits came out for what Lara was to call Zinsel time. They would nibble at the succulent grass, disappearing at the slightest sound from a human. Many a time, from an early age, Lara would stand by the window watching them.

Stephie listened to the birds and tried to distinguish their songs at dawn when their chorus was loud and lengthy. There were goldfinches and greenfinches, linnets, yellowhammers, wood-pigeon and swifts. In the fields and on the salt-marshes there were skylarks, heron, mute swans; on the estuary, oyster-catchers and curlews. Swallows nested in an old barn and came every year to the same corner of it; house-martins slept under the eaves of the old house. There were countless other wading-birds whose names Stephie did not know. Lionel told her about the dunlin and cormorants he had seen, said he had counted in all sixty-eight species of birds in the place.

Gateswick was not an ideal site for flowers because of the salty air and soil, but common mallow grew in small pink clumps in all the fields, with germander speedwell, wild violets and vetch. A hibiscus planted years ago, even before the war, by whoever had lived at the cottage, had grown tall and was covered in blossom in spring.

There were many butterflies too, above all the beautiful peacock butterfly with its soft russet-brown wings edged with a slightly darker brown, and its four blue-black 'eyes', two large at the end of the top wing-tip that grew from the 'shoulders', and two slightly smaller at the end of panels of a lesser span, joined to the 'waist' like an underskirt.

Lara called all butterflies 'flutterbyes' and would not believe that this was not their real name. When Jo came on a summer weekend visit to Gateswick just before her marriage she had the strange conceit that if you looked at the butterfly upside down it resembled Adam, whose eyes were of an even more brilliant blue than the peacock's. Had he been a vain man? Not about his looks – though he was good-looking – but certainly about his intellect.

Even more beautiful than the butterflies was a 'visitation' to Gateswick given to Stephie after Jo had left.

She had woken in the middle of the night and gone to draw the curtains, so bright was the silver light coming into the room. Lara was asleep next door so she stood quietly and marvelled. The moon was the harvest moon and she had never in all her life seen such brightness. Silver rays made strangely beautiful every tree, every bush, and shone through the trees on to the old pond. The light was, as was natural, 'unearthly', of a silver beyond silver.

Stephie was entranced. One night Lara must see this, she thought. The moon itself was large and directly above, as big as the sun usually was, almost as if it were about to drop into the garden. She shivered. There was something a little frightening about it. She thought of Costas, which was her wont when any strong emotion took hold of her, and went back to bed to go on thinking of him, and of the two of them walking together under such a moon.

Gateswick was, Stephie discovered, exactly the kind of place with a past that suited her as a historian, and now as a novelist. Lionel had not been so interested in its past. He was a man who lived for the visual; everything of importance could be found in a painting of a place or a person. However old the place was, whatever its past had been, there would be the same atmosphere conveyed in colour and form.

When Stephie told him of some of her researches in the old library across the estuary, he was politely interested and then a little surprised.

'There was a Cluniac monastery here – right till the dissolution of the monasteries,' she told him. 'They were a branch of the Benedictines from St Germain, you know, and they say the old wall behind the farm is built from the original stone.'

'I believe there is a painting of the wall,' he said. 'It must be in the attic. It wasn't very good so I didn't try to sell it. You can have it if you like.'

Stephie was pleased. She hung the painting in her little sitting-room. Surely there must be other evidence of the past buried here.

A year or two later her intuition was proved correct. The farmer who farmed the fields on the other side of the lane was digging for a new petrol-pump, or his labourers were, when they suddenly unearthed bones. Being superstitious they stopped digging and went to inform Farmer Raven.

'Perhaps there was murder here,' said one.

'I suppose we'd better inform the police,' Raven replied reluctantly, having seen for himself that the bones they had found were ungraved and perfectly preserved, maybe on account of the salty soil.

Stephie was already out having a look. 'Dissolution of the monasteries?' she murmured to herself. 'They wouldn't have lasted so long, would they?'

The police came and took samples. They reported after a week: the bones were long, definitely of men. They were asking the police pathologist to find out if they were recent.

Stephie did not want Lara upset. The child knew about death, but bones were not a very good way for a five-year-old to learn more. She need not have worried. Lara had just started at the village school and seemed not to connect the bones with her missing father. Stephie suggested they sent a sample of the bones – there appeared to be more of them underneath in a large pile – to the local museum, which might have some record of a mass-burial. She would like to have taken them herself but they were not on her land and she was always busy with her work and the child.

A kind policeman took a vertebra and a thigh-bone to the museum for her. They had been cleaned up but had not been very dirty when they were found, which was unusual. In the meantime Raven was waiting to continue digging for his new petrol-pump.

The museum reported quite quickly, the same day as the police pathologist. Both said: Certainly not from this century. The museum added that they were all of grown men, and were probably from the sixteenth or early seventeenth centuries. But they knew no more than Stephie did of the actual circumstances of the local dissolution. Monks then?

A research assistant added, however, in a handwritten postscript, that there had been some interference that made it difficult to use carbon dating. Stephie realized immediately that the assistant meant that there might have been some soil contamination from the nuclear power-station, that unseen but brooding presence at the mouth of the estuary. If bones that had lain there for at least three centuries could have been affected, how much more could the milk from the farmers' cows, and the very air they breathed? She resolved to read up on the reactor which was of course presented as completely safe by its apologists, and by the government, which knew the place gave work to many in the area. Farming as usual was not doing very well.

She asked Jo to bring down a simple lichen-tester to test purity of the atmosphere next time she came to stay. It might not be the right test but it would be interesting to see how much pollution there was.

How could she ever know for certain whose bones they had been? The monastery, now discovered to have been called an abbey, had been abandoned long ago, and this could have been a later plague-pit, or the men could have been farmers or workers on the land. But the fact that there were no women or children seemed odd, and Stephie was now convinced that they were actually the bones of monks.

Underneath the land adjoining where the abbey had once stood there must still be the remains of a charnel house. This fact was a little spooky, but only what must be true of many places. Only two further houses had been built on what had originally been Gateswick Abbey land, after the farm was built in the eighteenth century, so the bones had lain undisturbed.

One summer morning when Lara was almost six Stephie had to go to Maldon. Lara was busy playing at the back of the big house and was reluctant to accompany her mother that day. Would she please bring her back some lemon-sherbet sweets. Stephie promised and left Lara in the charge of her grandfather.

Lara had seen Magda Harrison, one of the tenant farmer's daughters, playing on the beach in the distance. The tide was out, and beyond the strip of sand that edged Great-Pa's land there were miles of pebbles. She considered whether to call out to Magda and join her for a pebble hunt but then remembered that they had fallen out on Friday afternoon over some sweets that had disappeared from her satchel. She didn't think for a moment that Magda had taken them but Magda had said she was accusing her brother Patrick – which hadn't till then entered Lara's head. No, she wouldn't bother with Magda, she'd play by herself till Mother got back.

She walked across the lawns at the back of the Big House and came to a wicket-gate she had never seen before among some trees by an ivy-covered wall. She pushed it open – it was stiff and rusty – and then walked down a path that skirted the back vegetable-garden of the Ravens' farm. When the path turned she followed it and found herself on another path with an arch of trees on either side.

Looking ahead when she came to the end of the path she saw the estuary water again, and on the left, at the edge of a field full of weeds, a tumbledown hut. She walked over to the door, which was half-open. There was a pile of hay and there were two windows and a little ladder going up to one of the windows. This would be just the place to hide and have secrets from everybody. Perhaps she might one day let Magda see it.

She advanced further into the hut. There was a funny smell as if an animal had done its business there and nobody had cleared it up. Lara did not mind this. She would pretend to be ship-wrecked there, like in the story Miss Hankinson had told them at school.

Time passed as Lara made a hole in the hay for a bed. She felt rather pleased with the result, and sat in it. This hut would be lovely for hide-and-seek, a game Patrick and his friend Ian played. They always found her but she could never find them. Now she had a secret.

Then she heard Great-Pa call to her. 'Lara, Lara, where are you?'

She'd wait to see if he could find her, so she didn't reply.

It must have been a long time after this that she heard the voice of Magda's mother shouting: 'Lara, Lara! time for dinner! Come home!'

Then, 'No answer,' the voice said.

Lara waited and then she heard Mother's voice from down below on the shore.

'Are you sure you didn't see her? Could she have walked to the water?'

Lara didn't hear Magda's reply. She wondered whether she ought to come out of the hut now. Mother sounded worried. But she had better pretend she had not heard anybody. She didn't want anyone else to find her secret, so she mussed up the hay-bed and then came out of the hut and shut the door behind her.

Then she walked down the narrow lane between the trees, before turning and walking back towards the lawn and scrambling under a hedge.

She appeared on the lawn to Stephie as if by magic. Great-Pa was there too and Magda and Mrs Harrison, and they all shouted: 'There she is!' and Mother came running up to her. She had tears on her cheeks and Mrs Harrison said: 'We thought you was drowned – where have you been?'

'Didn't you hear us calling, Lara?' asked Great-Pa. He sounded very angry.

'No, I was playing down there.' She pointed vaguely in the direction of the weed-filled field but away from the hut.

'Oh, Lara.' Mummy scooped her up in her arms. 'Do you know what time it is? You must never ever stay away so long – we were very anxious.'

Lara, who had enough imagination to pretend she was Robinson Crusoe, had no imagination to understand that her mother would be terribly worried when she came back and found Lara had not come in for dinner.

'When did you get back?' she asked her. 'Is it dinner time?'

'It's two o'clock!'

'I must have fallen asleep,' said the child.

246

'Lara, do you understand – we thought you might be drowned,' said Great-Pa, and he was holding her mother's hand. 'You must say you are sorry,' he said.

She realized that she was a precious thing to them all.

'I'm sorry Mummy.'

Magda asked her on Monday where she had been hiding. 'I know you was hiding,' she stated.

'No, I was just having a walk to Spire,' lied Lara.

A day or two later she heard Mrs Harrison saying that Mr Lorrian was a bit deaf and anyway he let time go by without realizing so really next time Stephanie went to the shops and left her daughter it had better be playing with their Magda.

By this time she and Magda had made it up.

Lara really did love playing out at Gateswick. As she grew older she liked watching all the things they did on the farm.

It turned out that the simple 'litmus' test bought by Jo and brought the previous year to Gateswick had shown that the place was only a little polluted. Lichen grew there quite well. But she was amazed to discover that her own little green London suburb was a little less polluted than Gateswick! Stephie decided to keep an eye on things, follow the news and hope the nuclear power-station would soon be decommissioned.

Larissa Fischer was eight when the film of *Doctor Zhivago* arrived in England. The book had been translated into English a year after Lara's birth. Stephanie took her to see it in Chelmsford and the child was thrilled by it. Above all she loved 'Lara's tune'. But she was at a loss to understand why people in the film were so nasty to each other, and why her mother had tears in her eyes when they came out of the cinema. She knew the lady disappeared and the man died – but they had a daughter who could play that funny musical instrument – so there was what her mother called a 'happy ending'.

247

FOURTEEN

Lara grew from being a tall solid child into an adolescence that came early. She was still tall but not particularly fat, only muscular. She was not a difficult teenager, as the English now called young people, did not scream or sulk or wear outrageous clothes, but she was clearly not interested in her school work. What she loved was the land and the farms.

She had begun at the age of eleven to grow her own flowers and vegetables at the back of the cottage, and a few years later she added raspberries and strawberries and runner-beans. Stephanie was amazed. She wished she had met Costas's mother or father. Surely this child of hers must take her physical strength and solidity and her love for growing things from her father's family, though Costas himself had not been in any way interested, as far as she knew, in growing things, or in a rural way of life. Was it her own fault that Lara was not 'streetwise', had possibly limited horizons? Should she have moved back to London once she could afford it?

About this time the Costas's Uncle Peter and his son Michael, both businessmen, came on a visit. Stephie had kept in touch with the uncle, as time went on, only at Christmas or the New Year. One summer, when Lara was fifteen, Stephie received a letter to tell of their imminent arrival in London. The men could stay only a few days in England but would be pleased to meet mother and daughter. Then they were going on to France and Germany, better pastures at this time for their business plans. It was the early 1970s just before the oil embargo arrived and OPEC raised the price of petrol sky-high.

Great-Pa was still alive, now almost ninety, and Stephie asked his advice about inviting them to Gateswick or meeting them in London.

'Lara will show herself in a good light *chez elle*,' he said. So Stephie invited them to Gateswick.

They were driven over from London by a chauffeur after she had given them lengthy instructions how to get to Spire, which in the last ten years had begun to put out a few feelers in the matters of house-building and caravan-renting.

They had got an English tea ready with Lara's raspberries, and cream from the farm, and home-baked scones. The sound of a car was heard on the lane at three o'clock and the farm dog barked. Then a large limousine drew into the grassy space in front of the cottage, and stopped. Two men got out, and then the driver.

Stephie felt a little nervous but welcomed them all at her little white gate.

The chauffeur stated that he'd like a look round if she didn't mind, tea not being an item he really cared for. She left him to walk round the domain and he directed his steps towards the estuary strand.

She had almost forgotten what Uncle Peter looked like but as soon as the two men appeared she recognized the older one. So long ago now! How could she bridge the gap?

She need not have worried. As soon as Lara appeared, the uncle exclaimed in Greek.

Then he turned to Lara, saying, 'She is just like my dear wife and her sister Auntie Irina – Costas's mother! My goodness me – I would have recognized her anywhere!'

Perhaps, thought Stephie, he had formerly been a little unsure whether her child had truly been fathered by Costas.

Then he brought out a photograph. 'I have had an old family photograph copied for you,' he said. 'It is my nephew when he was about eight years old, and his parents just before the war.'

Lara stared at it intently. Stephie thought she would have a good look later with a magnifying glass.

Lara was taking it all in her stride, serving their tea and listening to Peter's tales of his wife's nephew, her own father, Costas. She was pleased, blushed a little, but her hand as she poured the tea was steady.

'I love your country,' said Uncle Peter. His son was more taciturn. 'You must come to see us in New York, my dear Larissa,' he said, before Stephie and Lara took them over to see Great-Pa. 'And you too, madame,' he added.

He appeared puzzled that Stephie had never married, and did not seem to take in that she earned good money writing.

Great-Pa obviously impressed them both and even spoke a few words of Greek. On their leaving he gave them a painting of an English scene.

It was the summer of 1976. Lara was nearly nineteen, and Lara wanted to get married. A local gentleman farmer, one Dominic Pearce, wanted to marry her. Stephie had nothing against Dominic who was a nice if rather taciturn young man of thirty.

She did not want Lara to marry so young, but what could she do? Perhaps her daughter was the sort of woman who would in any case have married young, though Stephie couldn't help believing that, never having known a father, the child felt the need of a strong silent man.

She had passed a two-year diploma in business studies at a local college but made it clear that she did not want to continue there, stating that she knew enough about typing and accounting to help Dominic run his farms, which were really more like businesses.

They had met only the year before at the village fête at Millingham, a pretty village a few miles away, and had met every Sunday since for a drink in the pub there. Dominic was always so busy, Sunday was the only day he could get away for a few hours.

Stephie couldn't help thinking he would be getting a good bargain, but after all Lara did want to work; it was just that she wanted to work at home for a husband. Had she also missed her mother's not having a husband?

Just before her twentieth birthday Lara Fischer married Dominic Pearce in the village church at Millingham, a prettier and much older church than the one at Spire, which in any case Stephie would have felt a bit of a fraud for using, since she never went there. It was a lovely wedding. Lara had many friends from all around the place: friends from school, from college, friends she had met with Dominic. She looked soberly happy in a straight-skirted satin dress, and carrying a sheaf of lilies. Stephie could scarcely believe it was her daughter.

Jo had stayed married and continued her suburban family life with John Francis and Philip, doing occasional lecturing as well as continuing her journalism. And Jo had had a late baby – a daughter!

After her marriage she had changed in many ways. Still hard-working, she was more down to earth. Was she even the same person as the girl who had once drunk too much, smoked too much, flirted too much and fallen in love too often? Her toes curled with embarrassment when she thought of how she had behaved when she was young. But Adam had got away with it, and was still getting away with the same sort of thing, and he had never appeared ashamed. It must be her own puritan upbringing? Or was it that men were able to enjoy themselves with no anxieties, no self-consciousness? Jo might still grow hot under the collar over past social gaffes, but Adam, who had behaved much more outrageously, had never appeared embarrassed. Jo and her husband and children were there at Lara's wedding.

Jo's feelings on seeing the baby Lara that first time had never left her, even when she had a child of her own. She was Lara's honorary godmother and had observed her growing up with interest and love, and she felt the wedding was a triumph. Not the kind of wedding she would ever have wanted for herself, but just right for her strong sensible goddaughter. It was Stephie who should be congratulated, Stephie who had never tried to mould her daughter into the image of herself or of her dear lost lover.

Stephie's mother and father were resplendent in morning-coat and silk designer-dress and coat, and Lara was given away by her maternal grandfather since Great-Pa was now too frail. He was there, of course, keenly watching the proceedings.

He even managed a short speech after Stephie's father and the best man, Dominic's brother Toby, had done their bit. At the top table, at the reception in the hotel over the estuary where they had all repaired after the service, Lamorna and Jacob Fischer were getting on like a house on fire with the Pearces, and, sitting near them, Jo and Philip Ross and John Francis along with their four-year-old Dorothea. What a surprise addition to their family she had been! Jo was amused to listen to Great-Pa who was decribing the paintings he had given his great granddaughter.

Nobody wanted to leave but when the bridal pair finally made a move – they were to be away for only a week – the older staider couples stayed to chat over their coffee and the younger ones to dance in another room to their kind of music.

In a rapidly changing world that they sometimes scarcely recognized for their world, the older guests felt that the marriage and the wedding had been very satisfactory. It had quite cheered them up.

Lara and Dominic's daughter Helena was born in 1978 exactly a year after their marriage. A son, Harry, followed two years later.

Right from the start, Helena resembled neither her mother,

Lara, nor her grandmother, Stephie, nor her father's family, the Pearces, who were of a fair-haired, solidly built, Essex yeoman stock. Maybe her nose had a look of Stephie's, but more than anyone she looked like her dead grandfather Costas Mitsou-kopoulos.

Jo thought she was the first to notice it. She had met Costas only once, but she had studied the Oxford Street photograph, which Stephie had kept, and the old family photograph of Costas when he was a child with his parents that Uncle Peter had given Lara.

She waited for her friend to say something, but Stephie had said nothing whilst Helena was a baby. However, by the time she had grown into a lively six-year-old, her maternal grandmother came out with it. Jo could still not envisage Stephie as a grandmother. For one thing, although her own son John Francis was eighteen it did not appear at all likely that he would be the type to marry early, and his sister Dorothea was only ten.

They were sitting in the old morning-room at Gateswick. When Great-Pa had died and left the house to Stephie and her descendants she had taken some time to decide whether to live there, and perhaps let the cottage to Jo and Philip and other friends on a 'time-share' basis. She had been lazy about making a decision. There were still all the canvases to bring down the twisty attic stairs, a job she was not looking forward to. Then there would be the valuers and the dealers to pick them over.

In the meantime, she often came over to check that all was well in the house whilst it waited for her to decide and arrange things. In any case she would have to install central heating in the Big House as well as the cottage, and improve the kitchen and bath-rooms in both houses.

Stephie was discovering as she became older that she enjoyed her creature-comforts, and as she had made a reasonable amount of money from her novels, she could afford to be comfortable now in her early fifties.

'She is the image of him,' she said suddenly, as they sipped their coffee.

Jo knew she was talking about Helena.

'I feel sure it will not only be in looks,' added Stephie. 'Helena is quick – and yet she is reserved.'

'I think she is charming,' said Jo.

Their own John Francis had always been a quiet child who amused himself drawing maps and reading and making up silly stories about his sister, which he then read to her. Now he was busy studying for his A Levels and wanted to go to Cambridge.

Today, Dorothea had gone on a walk with her father. She wanted to cross the estuary at low tide over the causeway that crossed over to 'the other island', not 'their' island which they saw whenever they looked out of the windows over the lawn. Dot was jolly and more extrovert than her brother, and also noisier.

Stephie was saying: 'It's the way Helena puts her head on one side, and the way her eyes are set, and the way she holds your hand. Can such things be inherited?'

'If they can, then they bypassed Lara completely,' said Jo.

'I never thought she was in any way like her father,' Stephie agreed. 'Uncle Peter said she was like his wife and his sister-in-law Irene – Costas's mother. But, you know, she can paint rather well! How could I not have realized that earlier?'

'Still waters run deep,' said Jo.

'If she needs a break from the children or from office-work for her husband she goes out sketching around here for a few hours and bases water-colour painting on them. She says she doesn't need to go any further than the few square miles round here – apparently it's got a wonderful light for painting. But she never showed any particular talent at school. It must come from Great-Pa's father. I shall hand over all the canvases he left here to her and Dominic and they can dispose of them as they wish. She'll know what's worth selling or keeping.'

'It's wonderful to have a talent for painting or for music. I must see her paintings,' said Jo. 'Does Helena show any particular talent? I know grandmas are rather partial.'

'Do you think you can tell at seven if someone is highly intelligent?'

'Yes, I'm sure you can. I was going to say that I think your little Helena is a very clever girl. There are so many ways of being intelligent, aren't there? I was brought up to think I was clever, and sometimes I wish I'd been thought stupid. It might have done me good to have intelligence measured by one's ability to sew or mend fuses or ride a horse or swim. I bet Helena will do all those things as well as win the maths prize, not that they believe in prizes now, in many schools.'

'No, you never know how intelligence will operate. But I agree with you about her. I didn't want to swank! She loves school,' said Stephie. 'I do hope Lara and Dominic will send her to a good one when she's a bit older.'

Jo put on her schoolmistressy look. She still took a partisan interest in education.

'There is an excellent academic day-school reachable from here that wouldn't cost you a penny. I feel sure she'd be happy there.'

'My own mother wasn't too bothered about my brains,' said Stephie, 'but Father wanted me to have the best education that was going.'

Mr Fischer had died three years earlier. Lamorna was still alive. She had a touch of arthritis but still played bridge and regularly met her friends in the suburb. Stephie had offered her a home at Gateswick, but she had said:

'No, dear; It's lovely for holidays but I couldn't settle away from London. Don't worry about me, I shall go into a residential home when I'm ready, along with Bea and Maggie!'

Lamorna, in spite of the occasional vagueness she had always cultivated, was very independent and showed no overt sign of missing her husband's presence. Her great grandson Harry was her favourite. Stephie now realized her mother had always wished her daughter had had a son.

'Well, we can only wait and see how Helena will turn out,' said Stephie philosophically. 'You never know, *she* might be a painter too like her Lorrian ancestors.'

'She is such a lovely little girl,' said Jo again.

Stephie was going from strength to strength, publishing novel after novel, so that by the time Lara was married she had published over a dozen. By the time little Helena was seven years old there were six more, the last set all belonging to a chronicle of mid-nineteenth-century Russia. Stephie had always wanted to write of her father's ancestors in Tsarist Russia and much enjoyed researching the lives of Turgenev and Tolstoy and Chekhov as intellectual and literary background to the trials and tribulations of a Jewish family.

Her own family had made some money over the years of the previous century, until about 1880, when the first of the Tsar's pogroms made them think about taking flight to Prussia or to France. They almost thought about it for a little too long; their skills as doctors, musicians and journalists were much in demand, but it was the next generation, that of Stephie's great grandparents, who eventually made the move. When at last they reached Paris and from there made the decisive Channel crossing to England they found a trickle of Jewish *émigrés* from the Ukraine who had never been rich and who had left their homes just before the last pogrom in 1905. The trickle became a flow, then a river, then a torrent, and London, Manchester, Birmingham, Leeds, and the north east of England took thousands of the dispossessed. Many went instead to America, land of the free, some even to Ireland.

'The joke was that they thought Dublin was New York and stayed on land when their ship left to cross the Atlantic,' Stephie told Jo.

Stephie found she identified as much now with her father's ancestors as with her mother's Cornish and artistic ones. The family were not Orthodox Jews, scarcely even Liberal ones now, but her grandparents had kept the Sabbath and celebrated barmitzvahs, and paid attention to the Day of Atonement. She knew that as her mother was not Jewish she could not lay claim to being Jewish herself but Judaism was half her own history, and she put her heart into her chronicle.

Jo had not seen Adam Angelwine during the first seven years of her marriage. He had stayed in the United States until the end of the sixties but then a new correspondence had grown up between them. She had sent him a small book she had published of a collection of her articles, feeling he ought to know she was alive and flourishing. Strange to say, Adam, who informed her in his first letter that he had 'taken seven years to get over her', approved of her marriage to Philip Ross.

She had known he would eventually move on from Rebecca Lawrence but had not realized how this would affect Rebecca, who had apparently believed he would marry her, once he was 'divorced' from Hermione. Rebecca had been overtaken by a nervous breakdown and never fully recovered.

In 1965, in California, Adam had fallen in love with Megan, a young, American, mature student of his, even a little younger than Jo, and only thirty-two at the time. Eventually he divorced from his first wife, and married not Hermione, but Megan. This marriage was to last five or six years. Megan left him in the end, and in great distress Adam returned for a time to England, where Jo saw him. Adam's willpower still prevailed, for he conscripted Jo to write a letter to plead with Megan, to ask her to return to him. Jo did not refuse him this, but had little hope of persuading a woman of her own age to change her mind. All she could say was what Adam had asked her to write: that she was sure he loved her and could not live without her, and, after all, they were married.

Megan however, whose marriage to Adam had not been her first, had evidently someone else waiting for her. She replied to Adam, who reported her words in a letter to Jo – for now Jo appeared to be his *confidante* – that she wanted a child, before it was too late. Jo suspected that she too had previously had an abortion.

The odd thing was that in this letter to Adam, Megan suggested that Jo was the person he had really loved: why not get back together with her? Jo absolved Adam from making this up, for he was too distressed, and he knew that Jo would never go back to him, never mind his no longer being in love with her. Adam had met Philip, who treated him with a mingling of slightly amused respect and cynicism. Respect for his academic work and cynicism for his love life. Adam even stayed once or twice with Jo and Philip in their house in Richmond.

Did Megan not know that Jo was happily married?

Americans were usually crazy for marriage. Jo saw Adam's earlier flight from her as a lucky escape. Her marriage had been a new thing, quite a different matter, and with two children she had no desire for future entanglements. She was quite aware that her youthful charms had faded, but she also knew that the fires that had burned in Adam for her, genuine as they had been, had flickered out in the cold winds of an impossible situation, and as a result of the passage of time. He might love her still, but he no longer desired her, and for him, that was the nub of the affair. Adam might have married again but it would never have been to herself or Rebecca. If he had married anyone it should have been Hermione, the mother of his children.

After this, from time to time, Adam went on writing to Jo, very different letters from those he had written to her years before. It seemed they were now friends. He imagined she understood him better than most people, 'because we are alike … like me, you always had plenty of nervous energy,' he wrote.

In most ways, we are not at all alike, thought Jo. But whose energy had been better channelled? A woman could not possibly live the way Adam did, unless perhaps the woman had no children and enjoyed a large private income.

Stephie and her Costas *had* been alike. How unlucky Stephie had been, and how unfairly lucky Adam was, to carry on with all his *amours*, moaning the while about the unfairness of life.

She said something like this to Stephie one day when they met for lunch. Stephie was in London doing some research at the London Library.

'You had similar interests, you and Lara's father. You were the same kind of people.'

But that wasn't why Stephie had loved Costas – that was something else, the sort of chemical affinity that Adam had thought he had with Jo, and she had not had with him.

Jo went on: 'I mean it would be one of the last things I could really be passionate about – wars and diplomacy and all that.'

Stephie smiled. Then she said: 'I still dream that he was not killed, that he came back, and that he found me with Lara, and loved her. We would certainly have married if he had lived.'

Jo was silent.

'But I would have had Lara in any case,' added Stephie.

She will never really get over it, thought Jo.

During the first seven years he was in the United States Adam had made Hermione's house his base whenever he was in England. Once he legally married Megan, Hermione had decided to take the plunge and marry another man. But this did not last, and by the time Adam's divorce was through, Hermione had also got herself divorced. Once free, she offered to marry Adam if he had truly got his American wife out of his system. They would go on as usual and share the home that had always been there for him.

Megan soon married her old flame and had her baby, and Adam decided to try to make a go of it with Hermione. He married her, which retrospectively legitimized their two daughters. But he was restless in England, found English academic life irritated him; he could earn more money in the States and continue in his post longer than he could in England. Hermione was content for him to work 'across the pond' so long as she could be there for him when he was at home in England. She visited him occasionally over there.

Jo heard all this from Adam in further letters and at a few meetings in London. She was invited to Hermione's house and found she both liked and admired her even more than formerly. Yet how could Hermione not see that Adam would never settle, that he must be always 'in love'? *Because she truly loved him, that was why*. In spite of his affairs, and his latest ex-wife, and both their botched marriages, Hermione wanted him for keeps.

Not long after this, Adam started yet another liaison, this time with a certain Clarissa, an unmarried woman the same age as Jo. Hermione went on living in the house in the country, which was still there for Adam, but, angry about Clarissa, she now divorced him. She was upset; it was all so unnecessary. At least, however, Clarissa didn't want to *marry* him. Married to him or not, Hermione's house would go on being Adam's base whenever he was over in England, and for the rest of his colourful life. Where else could he keep all his books?

Jo was invited by Adam to meet Clarissa in London. Clarissa led a pleasant independent life doing work she enjoyed, though she appeared willing to fit Adam into it when he was there. Jo was surprised to realise that she would now much prefer Hermione's life in the country to Clarissa's 'woman about town'. She must have been a genuine bourgeoise housewife at last. It would be far better for Adam too, at his age, than gadding about London going to parties he didn't really enjoy. Why did he want to lead the life of a much younger man when he could relax and write in Hermione's lovely old house? The answer must be sex, thought Jo. Adam stayed with Clarissa whenever he was in London and she visited him often in America and went on wonderful holidays with him to Mexico and Japan. Jo had no longer any wish to go on such holidays. Was she becoming middle-aged? She had loved all her travelling and living in Europe but needed not only to know the language but to study the people and their history if she were to be a tourist in an exotic place.

Hermione opined that Clarissa would not last for ever. She was proved correct. For some reason never disclosed to Jo, Clarissa left Adam after about five years.

Adam's saga was still very far from over. He was still to have one or two adventures with postgraduate students before this too palled and he 'fell in love' again. This time it was with Ellen, a much younger but already divorced woman about whom he was quite crazy.

How could such an intelligent man as Adam Angelwine be so lacking in self-knowledge? He had been a lucky man so far, continued to have his cake and eat it with gusto. Jo had come to recognise all his good qualities as time went on, but could not make up her mind whether self-pity now clouded his attitude to himself.

Once, long ago, he had given Jo self-esteem, made her feel valued, so that in future whatever happened she would know she had been loved. His later emotional career ought perhaps to have taken away this certainty from her. It did, a little, but not entirely.

'Perhaps only unstable or unhappy people go on falling in love,' she said to Stephie.

Whilst all these things were happening to Adam Angelwine's life, the years were speeding by. When he fell ill at the age of seventy-four he was still 'in love' with Ellen, the latest young woman. Jo went to see him and he told her how long it had taken him to get over her, and how he now thought the situation was what had defeated them. She did not say that he had caught her whilst she was too young to know what she was doing, and that he had been such a strong character that she had been overborne by him.

'What chance did you have,' said Hermione. 'Nobody ever escaped him if he wanted them!'

Jo still felt close to Adam in a strange way and she respected his mind, but she had been free of his tutelage ever since her marriage.

Two years later, twenty-six years after he had left Jo, Adam, still infatuated with Ellen, and expecting a transatlantic telephone call at any minute, died in Hermione's arms.

ENVOI
1995–1998

…Thinking about her own and her friends' lives, she had begun to sketch out some ideas. How else could the past be recaptured, except through words? Maybe people's memories might one day be transferred from private mind to computer screen to be shared by others? She did not believe that, and she distrusted pointless electronic inventions when at least a third of the world was starving.

…You could understand people's lives only through examining individual cases.

You were still left with countless questions.

Both Stephie and Jo thought the world they lived in had changed for the worse in some respects.

'Is it just that we are getting old?' asked Jo.

'Some things were not all that different when we were young,' said Stephie.

Jo said, 'I find it extraordinarily difficult to remember exactly what was happening in the big world the year I married or when Francis was born. And in those days I was a devoted reader of newspapers.'

Stephanie said public events had always gone on as a backdrop to human lives: earthquakes, droughts, floods, starvation, dead babies, train crashes, wars…. In spite of television, thoughtful

263

people were sometimes obliged to try and forget them, to concentrate on their own personal patch. If they did not, they felt they would go mad. If pundits tried to speak or write about the big things like 'moral responsibility', hardly anyone listened.

Jo was thinking; the death of Costas, a totally absurd accident, had set her friend's life on a certain path. But she would still have written her books.

If she had never met Adam when she was seventeen her life might have been different.

'But, knowing you,' Stephie had said to her friend, many years later, 'you'd have found someone else who was unsuitable – for a time.'

When they started their working lives there were nearly four years to go before the débacle of Suez, and the Hungarian uprising. People appeared to have forgotten all about these events. When Susie Swift's baby was three months old, Jo remembered worrying about the possibility of a war off Cuba – the Bay of Pigs – but Susie was too busy worrying about her Nicholas to worry very much about the world, though she did belong to CND.

They had all continued to fear the cold war and the possibility of nuclear bombs and hydrogen bombs. Now that the cold war was over they feared instead the cold peace; the degradation of the environment, the chaos and anarchy of drug-ridden lives, the unstable miserable lives of the dispossessed, the marginalization and the violence of young criminals.

Women keep up with youthful acquaintances, even those to whom they were never especially close. Some of them come to mean more as time goes by: 'Because she knew me when I was young.'

Others who were once important died, or disappeared.

Jo and Stephie went on making new friends, but found the oldest were the best. Jo was more and more aware that if she did see friends only from time to time, she noted the beginnings of the ravages of age. She saw her own face every day in the mirror so could no longer be astounded by the reduced lustre in the eyes and the deeper lines from nose to mouth. She and Stephie sometimes looked at photographs of themselves when young, and marvelled. Stephie's granddaughter Helena was particularly interested in her mother's past.

The friends sometimes confessed to seeing each other as emblems of an irretrievable Long Ago, belonging to a soap opera entitled: *What Life was Like before the Sixties*. They met quite often, usually in the country. Stephie's place had always been open house for Jo and her family. At such times they were inclined to indulge in long conversations, and often talked about the past. If they had not seen each other for some time they wrote long letters to each other, both disliking the telephone.

Jo said, 'You know, I remember only the things that touched me personally, like helping motorists in the smog and the coming of the Clean Air Act. When I was first married we had a little fire you could only burn Coalite on, and I remember longing for the old coal-fires of my childhood. I believe they gave a concession to mining families to go on burning coal. I envied them!'

'Can you remember life with a baby, or a toddler?' Stephie asked.

'I can recall all the things I used when Francis was a baby; his little Viyella nighties and the Flatley drier that was so useful. But I mix it up now with Dorothea's babyhood; I must be incurably small-minded, because I'm hopeless at remembering current events. I mean, there were things I was agitated about, and I can remember a few dates, but it's only because I can remember what I was doing at the time. You were different – you always knew *why*. I can remember your explaining to me why we were furious with Moussadeq in Iraq because he nationalized the oil fields, and we weren't having that. I was awfully vague about such things.'

'Dad wanted me to have wider horizons – it was possibly on

account of his being Jewish,' said Stephie. 'I suppose it always mattered to his family that they knew what was going on.'

'Well, I can remember things like, oh, when I was sixteen and staying in Burgundy, with Marie, my French pen-friend. She took me to a hospital where she gave up an afternoon a week to talk to soldiers wounded in Indo-China. I was very hazy about Indo-China but I did sense there might be more going on than met the eye and that there was room for more than one opinion on the subject of this French colony. I remember the face of a young conscript – he was only about nineteen, and both his arms were bandaged and one leg was in traction. All the young men in the ward liked Marie, I could tell. But I didn't know what to say to them. And later – oh, more than ten years later, when I was in Paris the summer Adam went off with Rebecca, I marched at the tail-end of a procession demanding freedom for Algeria. Sartre and Simone de Beauvoir were at the head of the procession – the French adore street demonstrations – but some people in the crowd were hostile and chanted *"Algérie Française, Algérie Française"*.'

'Well at least you *did* something,' interposed Stephanie.

'Not really. I was just following left wing fashion – Adam's fashion.'

'But I do remember your telling me a lot about Germany, about the American Zone that didn't really exist any longer even when you first went there.'

'I've always been interested in Germany, I don't really know why. I suppose the whole of Europe fascinates me. I've never wanted to live anywhere else. But it's little incidents that stay in my head, like Frau Donitzer saying in a whisper as Elinor and I walked along by the lake, 'Don't look now but that man on the other side of the road – he's a Jew! *Da gibt's ein Jude!*'

'Mad,' agreed Stephie. 'Some of Dad's family were still in Germany, you know, in 1933. They'd already been forced to leave Russia sixteen years earlier.'

'It all meant something to you,' said Jo. 'I was such an ignoramus. But I do remember Korea.'

'Lots of men our age were called up on National Service and had to fight there,' said Stephie.

'Yes, unless they decided to go into the army after university. But what I remember best is a newsreel about the refugees. The old women and children staggering along in the snow. We saw it in Oxford – do you remember? I remember it because I wrote a poem on the subject – I'm such an egoist it was my own reactions I was concerned with. As for Germany, it's the pupils I recall, the ones I took there and was responsible for – all those Valeries and Carols, and a bit later the Debbies and Julies—'

'More recently,' interrupted Stephie, 'I was coaching some Traceys and Sharons.'

'Are you still doing some tutoring?'

'Only a little now as I don't really need the cash – but there are some nice intelligent children living around here – I suppose we have to call them young people now. They're clever, but they don't seem to know anything, so they come to me.'

'The Valeries and Carols will all be grandmothers by now, if not great-grandmothers. God knows how I coped,' said Jo.

They were companionably silent for a moment and then Jo said, 'I do remember the day George the Sixth died, but that's because Clare and I lit a candle in a semi-superstitious way in the Sancti Pauli church. I believe it's been a bookstore or something since the seventies. It was very high – we loved the candles.'

'There were ten days of national mourning,' remarked Stephie. 'I thought it a bit much.'

'I didn't go to the coronation,' pursued Jo. 'I believe I was a republican rebel at the time. I'm sure you were always more truly political than I was. Do you remember then "capitalist" hyenas of Wall Street – what the Soviets always called the Americans? After the war, it was so depressing.'

'I remember you waxing very indignant over apartheid and the bomb – and abortion and homosexuals and all those things that were changed after the sixties.'

'Changed because of people who thought as I did then,' said Jo. 'Homosexual reform, and suicide no longer to be a crime, and abortion made legal.'

'They're not really left-wing issues, they're more about personal freedom, aren't they?' observed Stephie.

'Right, as usual.'

'But then we were all presented with new gods, commercialism, and pop and football, which none of us had planned or marched for,' said Stephie.

'We can agree about all that,' said Jo. 'But, Stephie, *you* would never have considered an abortion, would you – even a legal one?'

'I don't know. Not *his* child, anyway.'

'At least you had understanding parents.'

'Well, Mother did prefer that I lived in the country – have you forgotten? Actually, it was nicer for Lara here anyway, but I don't think Mother would have truly relished explaining my pregnancy to the bridge club.'

'God, doesn't it all seem so long ago!' exclaimed Jo. 'Can you believe Lara's been a mother herself for over twenty years?'

'Time does go by at an alarming rate,' agreed Stephie.

They were sitting in the small front room of the cottage. Stephie did most of her writing in the other tiny room downstairs which faced the estuary. She poured them out more coffee.

Jo was still in reminiscent mood. 'It was Hungary in fifty-six I cared more about than anything, I think. They were all demonstrating in Trafalgar Square about Suez – were you there? It was in November, and the Hungarians were being crushed after their few days of freedom. They begged and begged the West to help but they were too busy over Suez to do anything.'

'Nearly a quarter of a million Hungarians fled to the West,' said Stephie. 'One of them was a second cousin of Dad's. You were right to be angry about it. I remember two years later you were wanting to march to Aldermaston – but you never went, did you? I was too busy with Lara then and with finishing my novel. So you're not the only one to put the personal first. You were quite a keen nuclear-disarmer at the time.'

'Not keen enough,' said Jo.

She thought, what a paradox that Stephie, who always knew everything that was going on, should be the victim of an accident, not a war. It was terrible. *She* had never been made to suffer in that way.

'I often wonder about some of the friends, you know, from years ago; I even make up stories about them,' Stephie said one afternoon.

Jo was on another visit to Essex and they were sitting in the garden for an hour or two. It was a warmish April day and great clouds were posing over the estuary for any artist who cared to be inspired by them.

'So do I – I mean, I think about them – I'll leave the stories to you. When I hear of something happening to one of them, I try to put myself in her place.' Jo sounded earnest. 'Would you like to *be* someone else? Or just be young again?'

'No, not be anyone else unless I could just do it for a week or two and use the experience for a book; that would be useful and interesting.'

'And become young again?'

'Not *very* young! I think I was born at about age thirty. It might be nice to stay at that age, I suppose.'

'Think about some of the terrible things that have happened to people we knew – suicides, lawsuits, cancer, alcoholism, failed marriages. Some people have completely disappeared from view. Maybe they're just happy.'

'Well, they haven't disappeared from their own lives, even if from our point of view they're lost.'

'Do you think we only know of the successes and the really

abysmal failures? I mean, is happiness the result of worldly success? Is it success and failure we're thinking about, not good things and bad things that have happened to people, things they couldn't possibly help? I know an awful man whose business is flourishing. He's living abroad off land-speculation, and he appears excessively happy!'

'Some women find a rich partner to keep them,' offered Stephie.

Jo thought of Maureen Higgins who was superlatively rich. Maureen, that acme of selfishness, had enjoyed a very happy second marriage and professional success.

'That can happen the other way round too.' Jo absent-mindedly took a chocolate biscuit. She was not of the generation who spent their lives thinking about their weight. She said, 'If we wrote about our own experiences in the mid to late twentieth century would we be writing history?'

'History, like fiction, contains a lot of what we may politely call imaginative reconstruction,' Stephie answered firmly. 'Writers write from their own vantage point, however much they may try to interpret other people's, or think they understand them.'

'Pulling people into shape through writing about them in stories – inventing them, creating them, not *re*-creating them – is different, though, isn't it? You've done both.'

'I *hope* novelists may occasionally stumble upon truth,' replied Stephie. 'And now let's walk down to the shore.'

Another time, Stephie and Jo were sitting after supper in the big old kitchen at The Keepsake, Helena's new name for her grand-mother's domain. Great-Pa had left the Big House to Stephie *and* her descendants. Stephanie still used the cottage for the storage of books and for some of her writing. At first, when Lara was married, she had even considered going back to London, wondered whether her daughter might find her living only a few miles away a bit stifling, fearing Dominic might conceive of her as an interfering mother-in-law, especially as she was alone in life.

Lara had been indignant: 'Have a little *pied-à-terre* in London, Ma, if you need one, but please don't go away.'

Later, she said, 'Helena and Harry would so miss you if you left Gateswick.'

Stephie had been only fifty when Harry was born so she could be quite useful at weekends if both Lara and her husband were occupied with business, which was fairly often. Granny wrote her books during the week but her weekends were always free for her grandchildren.

Stephie poured Jo another glass of red wine. 'They say it's good for us, an excuse anyway.' Stephanie had never drunk very much.

'I've been thinking about what you were saying when I was here last,' said Jo. 'About historians and novelists, and what I feel I'd like to, or ought to, put in my columns. Philip says they won't want such serious things from me. Who would read it? Not that he disagrees with my conclusions. It was what we were saying about how things had changed without our doing anything to make them change. Technological things – like when LP's came in and they were the last word in up-to-dateness, and then the cassettes arrived, and the CDs, and it led me to wonder if people had changed too.'

'Well, nowadays most people are socially mobile, if that's the right phrase,' said Stephie. 'But I'm not up to all these new concepts.'

'Living as you do at the back of beyond,' said Jo in her rural Essex voice.

'You could write about social mobility, I suppose; it's always gone on.'

'I'd rather like to write about moral responsibility; but who am I to write about that? It would mean I had become an old conservative,' said Jo gloomily. 'Which I am, I suppose. I've been a paragon since I met Phil.'

Stephie said, 'Women were never more or less "moral" than they are now. Men probably got away with more! Do you remember *Room at the Top*?'

'Yes, and *Look Back in Anger*.'

'I was busy folding nappies when that arrived,' said Stephie. 'And ironing – like the heroine.'

'I went to see that with Stephen Carnforth. He always took me to Beckett as well. I remember Adam yawning the whole way through Godot.'

Jo cleared her throat. 'My question, Dr Fischer, was, how do we come to the "truths" the historians and novelists both describe in their different ways?'

'And the philosophers. As I think I remember telling you, I *hope* we novelists can occasionally reveal something – but I always feel a bit guilty, you know, having been trained as a historian. Historians have to generalize whilst novelists need not, and now and then I'm tempted, like you, to do a bit of moralizing!'

'Well, you've earned it,' said Jo. 'But even in small things historians can get the wrong balance. Have you read history books that go on and on about how after the war women went back into domestic life even if they weren't keen? My mother didn't though. She kept her job teaching. There must have been lots of women who seized the opportunity to cut down on domesticity. But of course then they had to do both – the cleaning *and* the job outside – like they still do. Anyway, most women up north had always worked from necessity, not just in wartime. If they wanted a bit more time to themselves at home after six years of munitions you can't blame them for holding back the so-called feminist revolution. Not that they had much time though, what with making up coal fires and baking every week and mending stockings.'

'My mother never worked after she was married, except in the war when she drove ambulances,' said Stephie.

'How glamorous. But *we* thought we'd be able to have brilliant careers, didn't we,' said Jo.

'We were what they call an élite,' Stephie replied laughing.

'Did we realise we were? We knew we'd been given a good education, yet we didn't really seem to expect wonderful jobs, did we? There were no women high-fliers in the City then, were there? And not many women solicitors, never mind barristers. Solicitors always seem to be female nowadays.'

'There were women journalists, and novelists, and artists fifty years ago,' said Stephie, 'and librarians and quite a lot of academics – even some famous ones—'

'Of whom we all thought you would be one. But weren't most women graduates of our generation some sort of secretary, or teacher, or slaving in some remote government department if they were lucky, never seeing the whole picture? I suppose there were one or two top civil servants, but I'm sure – apart from the people who got married young – that over a quarter at least ended up teaching, and others were into it later. They don't now, do they.'

'Not very often,' Stephie agreed. 'Perhaps the schools aren't so tempting, except to the missionaries. But you know, there were several working for the Foreign Office and in the Home Civil Service, and the other day I met an archivist at the library and museum over the estuary, whom I recognized from college. She told me two of her friends – same year as us – were farmers! She ought to have retired but she's staying on working there for her own pleasure. She has a pension but they don't pay her for all the new discoveries she makes.'

'And we've got you writing your novels – and Angela Brown was a probation officer and Lily Baines a GP. I don't suppose we've done too badly,' said Jo.

'These new sorts of jobs didn't exist then for anybody, not even for me,' said Stephie. 'There were no data analysts or corporate fund raisers or systems analysts or management consultants, for us to be, and I doubt that more than a few men had those careers either.'

'I don't know even now what jobs like that involve,' lamented

273

Jo. 'I mean, I can understand marketing and I suppose accountancy, but the rest....'

'You've got to find out what women did later on, after their children grew up – I bet there are quite a lot in local government, or magistrates, or working for the Church or tutoring in the Open University—'

'None of those jobs *pays* very much, if anything!'

'I wonder when exactly women started going out into banking and economics and television?'

'You seem to have been thinking it over. Is it for a modern novel?'

'No, it's because of Helena.'

Stephie's granddaughter Helena was still at university but was soon about to launch herself into the world of work. Unlike her mother, Lara, she was determined to work. Would it be business, or banking – or even making money on the Internet? Stephie hoped not. Helena had said she wasn't sure what she wanted to be – or do. She knew only that she wasn't cut out to be a writer.

'As you know, she's just finishing her law degree, but she can't decide what to do afterwards. Lots of her friends are gong into the City, or taking MBAs, or planning to be accountants or engineers. Or joining solicitors' firms, as you pointed out.'

'It terrifies me to think of having to start all that again,' Jo said. 'Looking for work, never having enough money. I can remember how I felt a few months after coming down when I was just beginning to recover from leaving Oxford working at that first job that I found so very uncongenial. Do you think your Helena will feel like that?'

'I think she wants to work abroad. She said the other day she wished she'd read environmental science rather than law. I believe she wants to "do good".'

'Perhaps she'll be some sort of modern missionary then, but not taking Christianity to the heathen.'

'No, I think she might work for Oxfam or Save the Children.

That's the impression I've got.'

'She might use her knowledge of law there, mightn't she?'

'She's a determined kind of person – she's got a mission in life, I think. A bit like Costas.'

'She looks so like him, doesn't she. I saw the way you looked at her the last time we all came over.'

Stephanie smiled, but said, 'If she wanted to be a barrister she'd have the chance to join very good chambers, but I don't think Dominic and Lara were ever very keen on that idea.'

'They'll be even less keen about her going to Africa or wherever.'

'If it had been my grandson Harry, rather than my granddaughter, they'd have been delighted to have him as an ornament in the Bar. As it is, all *he* wants to do is sing in a band!'

The two women often discussed all the changes that had taken place since they were young; changes supposedly for the better, especially for women: contraception, freedom to have a sex life, more or less equal pay in some jobs. They agreed that not everything had improved. But progress always brought problems, didn't it.

Not only were there now far better careers open to the latest generation of young women, there were probably also more young women who didn't want children – even – or said they didn't, so they'd be able to pursue a career with impunity. Some wanted both a fulfilling job and a thriving home life. Some of their mothers had thought it would be a rich and rewarding mixture, but most of them had found they had just doubled their workload: babies *and* briefcases. It was impossible for them to do either job properly, unless they had the money to pay other women to look after their children, or had only one child, or were lucky enough to return to interesting careers when their children were older. It was ironic that progress depended on other women doing your domestic work, said Jo

Helena was soon to confess she rather wanted to do some good in the world; VSO perhaps at first, or work for UNICEF, or *Médecins sans Frontières*.

Jo thought of the UN and the child's' grandfather. Helena did not only look like him.

She prayed the child were not taken up by some older man, as she had been. But Helena was probably far too sensible.

The places where she had lived in London during her twenties seemed now as remote to Jo as Roman Britain. If she was driven sometimes in a taxi past Browncliffe Square or Lansdowne Gardens or through Pimlico, everywhere looked unfamiliar, different.

Had people changed as much – or even more?

What had become of all the people she had met or worked with all those years ago?

From time to time Jo gossiped with Stephie about such matters as they mulled over the past. Barnaby-at-the-Fair, to whom Jo had taken such a shine? Only for a day, and yet she still remembered him. A gypsy, he had said – but a clever gypsy, going off to university? ... she might have had a wonderful affair with Barney if she had not had her wings clipped by Adam. She could still remember what he looked like, after all these years. She had never seen him again after that day but for some mysterious reason had never forgotten him. She had the conviction he would have changed his name and become a writer. Probably of science fiction, though why she felt this she knew not.

Matthew; oh, she knew about him. He was long since an American citizen, and an enormous literary success, carrying away several literary prizes. Gaye and Julia – both writers. Magdalen was not a writer, though she had wanted to be one. She was dead.

Jo had experienced anxiety and unhappiness but had never been sunk in a depression so deep that anything was better than continuing to suffer. Neither, she imagined, had Stephie, in spite of the tragedy of her youth. Others of their old friends had not been so lucky.

Whenever she thought of all those she had used to know, and what had happened to them, there appeared to be no justice or reason for some lives being cut short. Suicide, the premature deaths of the happily married, mortal illnesses, cancer, heart attacks, accidents, beginning with Costas.

Four happy women had died young. Her best friend from school; a young woman met on holiday with whose daughter John Francis had played and said he would marry one day; gentle Catholic Marie, forever off to confession, had been killed in a car crash going out of Paris one Friday afternoon; a front passenger without a seat-belt. Her poor mother never got over it, though Marie's children survived.

Nor could Jo find a justification for several fairly unpleasant people flourishing, just as there was no reason for the happiness of some and the misery of others, from those who were enjoying the high life, living off clever investments, to those who were permanently depressed or bitter.

Remembering them all as they were so long ago, and projecting them forward through the years, Jo saw no reason for one person rather than another to become insane or have a breakdown, or kill herself. Desertion, fallings out of friendship, concealments, failures, straying spouses, wives in their forties left by husbands. She was glad Adam had never actually deserted Hermione or his children. Some women remained cheerful; others fell to pieces. Was it having money that helped? Were the happy families mostly 'Bohemian' as well as being rich? Marigold Cassman, Victoria Butler, Nicole Balladur, still, as far as she knew, enjoying life, with large families and several husbands. No, being rich was not enough. She had known plenty of the miserable rich, usually the sons or daughters of financiers or entrepreneurs who had been forced to live under the thumb of a patriarch, their marriages arranged for them and their lovers sacrificed to Father.

She had known several male tyrants: the father of a colleague who ruined her chances of marriage to the man she loved; the self-made, many-times-over millionaire father of another French friend with whom she had later stayed in Paris. Mr White, the husband of a neighbour who had killed herself. Men were supposed to succeed better than women at removing themselves from life, but practically all the suicides she had known were women.

Mrs White had lived a few doors away from them and had drowned herself in the bath after taking barbiturates. It was when John Francis was little. The woman had left four young children. What made a mother take her own life?

Other suicides were usually when women were in their forties or early fifties and they had almost all become depressed because they were spurned by their husbands or the men they loved, and were also overburdened at a certain stage of family life. Even Patricia, Jo's fair-copy typist in Chiswick, before Jo learned to touch-type. Pat was a young separated woman with two little girls, and she had thrown in the sponge only a few days after talking to Jo on the telephone. It had been her father who had written apologetically to Jo to tell her why her typing had not yet been sent back.

Infidelity, abandonment, divorce, death. But some had had faithful husbands: Beautiful Magdalen, who had gone back to America; the ever-dissatisfied and cross Elinor Knight, who had put her all into her career and married a widower when she was forty-five. Elinor and Magdalen appeared to have killed themselves from depression or misplaced feelings of guilt.

Why was *this* life more unbearable than *that* one? Had she had anything in common with the suicides? The ones who ended their own lives were not the nihilists, or even the atheists. Others had lived on the edge, taken risks, but they had survived. So many had

278

been guests years ago on that barge moored at Chelsea Reach where Jo had first met Julia. Julia had not killed herself; she loved life too much. Jo remembered how when they were young they drank too much; since wine was so much more expensive in those days, it was usually the strongest Merrydown cider which she had never liked. Some of the guests on that barge had died as alcoholics, but none of them had as far as she knew taken any drugs but nicotine and alcohol. They had known of rich people who sniffed cocaine, and there was reputed to be a famous woman novelist in South Kensington who had been a heroin addict for thirty years.

Could one just say that some were luckier than others in their experiences or their temperaments, now that most things were beginning to be ascribed to genes? Stephie said you must accept life as a mystery. There was nothing else you could do. If she hadn't had little Lara to bring up after Costas died she didn't know what she would have done. Jo said, 'You said you would have survived, Stephie.'

Jo switched to thinking of happier people when too much thought of these victims began to depress her or make her angry with the way things were.

A happy woman was Susie Swallow, now a well-known and successful landscape painter. She had been for many years married to a man who had an off-licence in a village shop. Susie had worked at the village post office, as well as bringing up their three children, and had stuck it out until, apparently to her great relief, the children being old enough to fend for themselves, her husband had finally left her. She sold some paintings, rented a cottage with a large garden where she grew her own vegetables, and went on painting.

Jo's widowed sister Annette had also sold some of the sculptures she had been doing for some years in the holidays from teaching. She lived in Italy in winter now. Her two daughters, Jo's nieces, were both success stories.

Had Adam's old family friend André Bernard been happy when he died in his early seventies? He would not have wanted to go on living on the Rue du Louvre once the old market and the ancient courtyard, and his equally ancient apartment, were pulled down.

Stephie's friend, the cheerful chauffeur 'Old Mr Gong', was now in a home, having given up his taxi service at eighty when he began to lose his memory. But *he* had enjoyed his life, he had told Stephie once. Between the wars he had emigrated to Winnipeg and stayed there twenty years before coming home just before the Battle of Britain. He had probably forgotten all that by now.

Happy spinsters, wives and widows, travelled all over the world, among them Clare Jackson with whom Jo was still very close and who lived contentedly in real country in Northumberland. Fierce Françoise, an erstwhile communist, had come to live in London, and become less dissatisfied. She had finally left the party, not that there was in truth much to leave. Later she had worked for the ephemeral GLC.

And then there was Noah, caught soliciting after his lover left him. Yet Justin and Robin lived happily ever after, and Theo, father of a large family was still farming in Devon. Beth Ackroyd, her library friend, had died at eighty-five, when she had boasted she would live longer than her mother, who had reached a hundred at her death. Evangeline Glossop had been found dead in her chair without ever having disclosed her diabetes to the son who visited her every evening. Jo's Great-Uncle Reginald left a Will saying 'Not a penny to a Catholic'. The son of another cousin was killed in a car crash. Middle-aged cousin Gwen died of drink. Her only first cousin was dead at little over fifty. A neighbour in Richmond, a mother, one of the most successful career-women they knew had died at forty-eight. Philip's nephew's wife at twenty-seven. Their local MP taken away in his early fifties. Jo's Canadian pen-friend, deceased after a correspondence of over ten years, had never breathed a word to Jo that her husband was an alcoholic.

But what had happened to little Sammy Solomons at the Municipal Halls, who had taken her walking in Burnham Beeches and to visit Milton's cottage at Chalfont St Giles where the poet stayed during the plague? What had finally happened to those women like Primrose and Flora who hadn't quite known what to do with their freedom, and had hastened to marry young, and had divorced after ten or fifteen years? Oh, they had probably remarried. Most had been content, unless they began to resent their too many babies. Later they might put all their efforts into these children, who did not always turn out well.

A neighbour Jo had befriended in Leyburn Court had gone off in the end with another neighbour and been lucky second time round. Another neighbour went abroad, leaving broken hearts, and had never been heard of since.

Some women could not seem to do without men, as husbands or lovers. The more self-sufficient ones had managed better. What life threw at them had not appeared to affect their self-confidence.

Even at Gateswick there had been dissatisfied wives and mothers, and quite gruesome misdemeanours. Stephie adapted in one of her 'historicals' the story of a local undertaker who was prosecuted for squeezing in babies into adult coffins and then charging the grieving parents the full price.

Jo began to believe that the six years of her youth she had spent with Adam had inoculated her against all the marital misery she could not help knowing about.

Perhaps she ought to be grateful to him.

Jo had seen amazing patterns of love and lust over the years, as in the fifties film *La Ronde* which at the time was regarded as 'over the top', 'highly unlikely'. She explained it all to Stephie in a letter, suggesting it might be an idea for a novel, rewritten for a modern readership.

Adam had carried on a long affair with Jo who had later slept with Matthew who had also apparently slept with Clarissa, with whom Adam had lived after he had fallen in love with Jo. This was not all: Matthew's first wife had had a love affair with another of Jo's flings. La Ronde had taken place though it had taken some years rather than a few weeks to accomplish, and the pattern had been slightly different. All that was needed now was for Matthew's second wife to fall in love with Adam....

Stephie laughed about it.

They did speak or write, occasionally, of Adam Angelwine. Jo wrote: I knew him for six years, and he told me so much about himself that I started to write a novel about his childhood and youth in an attempt to understand him. I believe I once read you some of that. But you and your Costas knew each other in Oxford for eighteen months, and then for a few months before he died – and you were sure he was the right man for you. Did he talk much to you about himself? You've never put him in a book?

The next time they met, which was in the self-service restaurant at the Royal Academy, Stephie said:

'I never wanted to write about Costas – but I think I may have unconsciously used his character for Ragenov.'

Jo was thinking that knowing someone well, even living with him or her, usually only made you more sceptical about your feelings. But she couldn't say that to Stephie, although she was certain that Stephie and her Costas would have been happy together. They had hit it off straight away with each other, were right for each other, as she and Adam had not been.

Aloud, she said: 'You see, I was never given the chance to know whether I really wanted to have a love-affair with Adam. He just swept me off my feet. He said I was the right woman for him. I wanted to use him, I admit it now, to introduce me to sex; I hadn't had much experience – I thought he'd be the right man to do that. It was probably wrong of me but it was more wrong of him, whatever moralists might say about it being better for a man to "love" you.'

'It depends on your age,' said Stephie. 'You were too young for him – or rather he was too old for you. It was an unbalanced relationship. He needed a woman of forty-five with the body of a twenty-two-year-old!'

'He took over my life, and I was too much of a coward to resist – at first anyway. If a man is crazy about you without really knowing you – not in the way you and Costas knew each other at Oxford – if a man tells you he has fallen in love with you and tells you all sorts of wonderful things about yourself, what must you do? Women are supposed to wait for this sort of avowal, aren't they?'

'I don't remember Costas ever quite saying he was mad about me, he just showed me he was. And he did say he loved me – and other things – the week before he was killed. I knew anyway without his saying so, and I'm sure he knew I loved him. Even if I hadn't said so. But I did tell him. We were so right for each other. We were lucky.'

'If only I could have had a fling with Adam, and then been freed. If he'd really loved me – apart from always wanting to make love to me – he'd have given me back my own life afterwards, wouldn't he?'

Jo was thinking, even now, after all these years since his death, Stephie knows she was lucky. People would say *I* had been lucky, I suppose.

'What does Phil think of Adam and all your past?' asked Stephie. 'I suppose that interests me as a novelist!'

'He's never been jealous. He thinks Adam was a difficult man and that I escaped just in time, and that the person who comes best out of it all is Hermione.'

'That's true,' agreed Stephie.

'Yes, he was her Costas – but he didn't die young,' said Jo.

She began to speak of some of the people she had once known who were now famous. Tilly with her fringe and her tragically sad 'little girl' poems; Noël who only wrote in his card index when he was supposed to be writing his last and best novel; clever colourful Katie Drines who went on fascinating Oxford until she died, only to be despised by later generations of scholars who preferred their poets unbiographized.

Tilly Smith had become famous; her verse was taught in schools.

Noël had died in his seventies but received some posthumous recognition.

Katie Drines would never be forgotten, but as a person rather than a scholar.

Because they had been successful, had they been happier than the ordinary people she had known?

'Even the seventies now are "the past",' said Jo another time, when they were looking at old diaries from the late sixties and early seventies. She and Philip and their son had stayed at Gateswick in an old lodge half-way to the farm when Lara had been about thirteen or fourteen and John Francis five or six. They had enjoyed playing together.

The elm trees had still stood then, and the children had paddled in the less polluted estuary. Since the discovery of the bones, nobody but the extremely foolhardy had swum in the estuary water. There were far more birds than twenty years later, when the autumn sowing of crops had upset the delicate balance. It had been pre decimalization, and Jo's second cat Koschka had still been alive. There had been no central heating, no thick carpets or new curtains in the lodge, and no telephone, but they had an old car, the old green banger. They had been busy, happy days; collecting leaves, J-F learning to recognize trees by their leaves and making a 'magazine' with Lara, who liked drawing and painting pictures for it. All gone now.

And here was Jo over twenty years later, with a commission to write a short book about an even earlier period of the century, her and Stephie's time of their lives; the nineteen fifties....

*

Jo began writing some notes for her book whilst she was on holiday at Stephie's in August. Philip was at a conference and John Francis, now usually called just Francis, was at home with his sister.

Jo was still asking herself the question: How have our lives changed in the last half century?

By the time feminism arrived, or rather re-emerged, some of her friends already had teenage daughters and were wondering how differently *their* lives might turn out. One day soon, like Stephie, they might have granddaughters the same age as they had been when they started work, and might be amazed by the changes in young women's lives.

Or would they have miserable unattached daughters, dieting and drinking Chardonnay? Had anything really changed about women? There was still a lot of thinking to do for this book.

Jo put her pen and notepad down. She always wrote her notes and first drafts by hand. But instead of thinking about improving her plans she found her thoughts returning to her friend.

Stephie had always appeared to steer on an even keel. A daughter, and the vocation of novelist, could never cancel out the death of her great love and Stephie would not have wanted anyone but Costas. Also, Jo once again concluded, if you don't go on falling in love you cause less misery to fewer people.

I still do not completely understand the nature of love, she thought....

She knew a lot about its failures. More strongly than she had admitted when she was young and rebellious she saw the need for marriage, for public commitments. Before she met Adam she had thought a public acknowledgement unnecessary or superfluous, but then she had had to confess that she wanted Adam to marry her, or leave her. It was all very well living with men if they were monogamous types. Many men, however, were not. Marriage did not seem to have made much difference to Adam's carryings on, and he had not been a believer in monogamy until he was an old man. At over seventy he had written to her about its importance! That was perhaps because he wanted young Ellen to marry him. Then he could lay claim to her.

As time passed Jo also had seen how much people needed to make the attempt at stability. It had been a few years after she and Stephie had left university that the first tiny rents in the social fabric were beginning to show. For the last forty years they had slowly and inexorably widened and torn great holes in the lives of the people, when more and more of them began to behave as Adam had done.

After she had written two or three thousand words Jo handed her notebook over to Stephie to read, and to suggest improvements to her plan.

'There is just too much to write about,' she explained.

Stephie took it away and pondered it. As usual, Jo's writing had turned into the nostalgia of remembrance. All she wrote was true, but she would have to make it less personal. It was not a novel. But maybe Jo did still hanker after the writing of fiction. Still, it was always salutary to set a few memories down first.

She was going to stay with Jo the following month in Richmond and she would tackle her then.

After her introduction Jo had written:

I've known difficult men and nice men, selfish women and saintly ones. I knew a prominent colonial freedom-fighter who seduced all the nice liberal women he came across. I saw a man dying from an injudicious drink after five years on the wagon....

At the time I married there was supposed to be a general moral consensus. Humanists were not even allowed on the wireless before 1956, though our circle of friends was predominantly atheistic or agnostic. We knew of a lesbian club in Chelsea; we had male friends who were 'queers' – homosexuals, who might be active in homosexual law reform, though some of them rather seemed to enjoy a life of risk. If they were caught they were sent to prison, until the Wolfenden Report eventually improved matters, and after poor Peter Wildeblood had suffered for his nature. There were 'straight' reformers too, and reformers of the abortion laws...

She had gone on in this vein for some time.

'I feel you should write a novel,' said Stephie at last, over lunch at Jo's. They were eating an omelette and salad.

'What?' Jo could not believe her ears. Stephie to say this!

'Yes, I really do. You write better about people. You've been writing for years about society and modern life. Why not change and write some old-fashioned fiction? When we've talked about the old days, the things you've said about Adam, and work, and love, and London, and the weather – *you* know – have brought back the past to me far more than your trying to remember all the big events.'

Before Jo could reply, she added; 'You could do a sort of feminine *Tom Jones* – call it *The Picaresque Life of Josephine*!'

She smiled, wickedly, but affectionately.

Jo said, 'I can't believe what you are saying. *You* are the novelist, Stephie.'

'I can invent the distant past,' replied Stephie. 'But you needn't mythologize – just write about what you know. It's worth a try, use all those quirky people you've known. I expect there were scores more. There's the material for lots of stories in your memory. I do truly advise you to do this.' She took up her glass and drained it.

'But what about my commission?'

'You can write that kind of journalism with your eyes shut,' said Stephie. 'As you said, you've heaps of material. You needn't come to any conclusions in a non-fiction piece – I don't suppose there are any. But write the novel first. Fiction before history!'

287

Jo had tears in her eyes. She respected Stephie's judgement. Yes, she would have a try!

'I will then.'

'Good.'

'It won't stop me worrying about the state of the world though – living as well as writing—'

'Why should it? Write it for Helena, and for Dorothea!'